Land of Promiscuity

Land of Promiscuity

Sherryle Kiser Jackson

www.urbanchristianonline.com

Urban Books, LLC
78 East Industry Court
Deer Park, NY 11729

Land of Promiscuity Copyright © 2012
Sherryle Kiser Jackson

ISBN 13: 978-1-60162-736-0
ISBN 10: 1-60162-736-X

First Printing November 2012
Printed in the United States of America

10 9 8 7 6 5 4 3 2 1

Distributed by Kensington Corp.
Submit Wholesale Orders to:
Kensington Publishing Corp.
C/O Penguin Group (USA) Inc.
Attention: Order Processing
405 Murray Hill Parkway
East Rutherford, NJ 07073-2316
Phone: 1-800-526-0275
Fax: 1-800-227-9604

Land of Promiscuity

A Novel

Sherryle Kiser Jackson

To Andrea Ross Phillips
Like the best friends in this novel, no one else
shares the context of my past. You've expanded my
village, whereas, I feel, your family is my family.
Best friends are forever.

Acknowledgments

I'd like to think I have matured as an author. In doing so, I understand the stories that get my blood pumping and am compelled to write. I write soul fiction of burgeoning love and burgeoning faith, redemption and revelations and chronicles of exodus. The Land of Promiscuity is all of that. Weary, Will and I go back like Cadillac seats which is not entirely true since I came up through the old school hip hop generation of Jettas and Jeeps. Nonetheless, I made a vow a long time ago to chronicle these scriptures come to life because aren't we all, at one time or another, walking verse?

I can't drive down Route 50 East toward Maryland's Eastern shore without thinking about cracked crabs and runaway slaves. It's refreshing sensory-wise down there, saltwater, seagull songs and stretches of farmland. I went one day looking for Harriet Tubman's birthplace and came back with an ideal setting for a novel.

To Valerie Jean who graciously took my manuscript with her as she cared for her parents, your eagle eye and purple pen was appreciated. To my Managing Editor at Urban, Joylynn, I sincerely hope I didn't grieve you too badly. My line sister and legal advisor, Crystal (Evans) Flournoy, thanks for your speedy response about paralegals. Charge any misinterpretations to my head. To Ella Curry, publicist, strategist, coach, friend, your new name might just be superwoman.

Acknowledgments

Thank God for family and friends who alter their lives to help me out in my time of need, you are all loved. I believe 2011 was the pressure cooker that made my family stronger and the precursor to something exceptional.

—*Sherryle Kiser Jackson*

Chapter 1

The Madame was dead. A massive heart attack had left her face down on the tile floor in the middle of Boscav's department store, clutching her chest with one hand and a thirty-eight double-D long line bra in the other. Rebecca Lucas was relieved that the last tidbit didn't make it into the full-page news report and tribute to the Madame in the *Easton Star Democrat* that she read from the Madame's four-poster bed. Her mother would have been horrified, Rebecca thought with a slow shake of her head.

Far from a salacious story, the article was so glowing in its commendation that it could have been written by the Madame herself. It highlighted her philanthropic endeavors, being a major contributor to the city's library system and Grace Apostle Methodist Church and school. She had made a name for herself by moving her money.

There was probably a write-up in the *Salisbury Daily Times*. Rebecca had forgotten to check before she left her apartment, left her life, to come back home to Easton. She had driven due west from Salisbury on Route 50 last evening past countless fields, peppered with an occasional farmer's market and strip malls. On the way, Rebecca had pondered the fact that her mother had been just around the corner from where she lived and worked when her heart arrested. Strange, Rebecca had thought, that no one had driven to or ridden with her on the more than an hour trek. Rebecca didn't bother wondering why her mother had never popped in for a visit, or at least phoned to say she was in town. "*A lady doesn't come calling,*" she could hear her mother say; apparently, not even on her only daughter. But Rebecca had gone calling since the drive in last night. After leaving the morgue and viewing the Madame's body, Rebecca had taken up with the local mortician.

The Hughes family, who had lived no more than ten miles from the Madame and Rebecca when she was growing up, was entrusted with the preparation of the Madame's body at their Bucktown funeral parlor. The eldest son, Randall, had been a classmate of Rebecca's, but not in her graduating class, which was known to everyone as the Chosen Twenty-Three. He was the star of their high school basketball team and the whole Christian school league that consisted of five other schools in the tri-county area. She had always thought he was attractive. He would have been considered out of her romantic league in high school because he was a sophomore when she was a senior, and by all accounts she had been considered a nerd back then; shy, self-conscious, and otherwise off-limits to guys and dating. She was, after all, Madame Ava's daughter.

Randall Hughes had greeted Rebecca last night as she entered the alcove of the funeral parlor minutes before closing. She had hoped to drastically cut her viewing time by running extremely late. Everyone else had gone and the dead bodies were set for a chilly night's rest. The thought of seeing her mother's lifeless body had left her numb. Rebecca didn't know how she would react to her mother's limitation—her silence.

She wore the same fitted jersey dress in black that she had worn to work, with sunglasses so big, round, and dark they could shade the eyes of someone off to drug rehab. That morning, she had given the appearance that she was in mourning, so much so that the associate attorney to whom she was assigned to help hadn't dared ask for an update on his proposal let alone when she would be returning. She had not shed one tear since finding out about her mother's death. Although sudden and unexpected, the "Oh my God" of it all still hadn't hit her.

Rebecca had been keenly aware of the gorgeous, six-foot Randall who had stood off to the side of her shoulder, poised with a box of tissues, after he'd opened the cherry-maple coffin for her approval. She had been aware that Randall had grown stockier since her graduating class had left Grace Apostle Methodist school fifteen years ago in pursuit of their futures. While the funeral parlor in general held the scent of well-worn paper and the poignant wisps of something sterile, Rebecca had been aware that Randall's cologne was spiced with pine bark and spearmint. She could also tell that he had noticed she had dropped over twenty pounds and toned up considerably since anyone in Easton had last seen her. His admiring glances told her as much.

"Take all the time you need. It's okay," Randall had instructed her. "I'm here if you need me."

Rebecca had taken him at his word. She was in need. Perched on a stool in front of her mother's satin-laced lounger, she had looked back at Randall as if in a museum asking a guide if it was okay to touch. She'd told herself the Madame was sleeping, to separate herself from reality. She toyed with her mother's favorite strand of pearls around the Madame's neck, which she had always thought would be hers but she saw that Gail, her cousin, had obviously gotten to them first and brought them as part of the Madame's final costuming. For that, she had wept, if only to bring Randall closer. Rebecca had orchestrated a chorus of fake sobs because she was in need of a hug. She feared that being the only daughter of Madame Ava Lucas at the occasion of her death was a liability. She thought she had escaped the rank and file and order and procession of her past life. She had gotten accustomed to living as an adult in anonymity—not by association. Even in death the Madame still cast a shadow. Now, Rebecca felt she was expected to ascend the throne as some kind of mini Madame.

Rebecca had wondered if Randall gave good hugs. *Is he the kind of guy who holds sincerity in his touch?* He draped one arm around her shoulder where she sat, maybe for support, or maybe to rush her along. She climbed up his torso to bury her face in his solid chest. He told her once more that it would be okay, and she prolonged their embrace as Randall hugged her straight on. Rebecca used the slightest of nuzzles into his collarbone to communicate how good his body felt up against hers.

"It's okay," Randall said again, trying to break their embrace for a more appropriate hold.

Rebecca held on and muttered, "I don't know what I should do. I'm just not ready to be alone in my mother's house yet. You know of any place I can hang out?"

She stared at him intently and waited.

Randall was first to pull away. He motioned to her with a finger that he needed a moment. She watched the wrestling match between Randall the bereavement specialist and Randall the man, as he went to the door of the viewing room and looked up and down the corridor. She watched him take his cell phone from his pants pocket, and with one hand apparently check his availability based on any incoming text messages. He paused, with phone still in hand, before returning to Rebecca's side. The man had won out. The look of sincerity had been replaced with opportunity. He told her he was going straight home, and that she could join him if she'd like.

From there, Randall had appeared in a rush to close up shop for the night. He had rolled a protective lining up over the Madame's head in preparation of shutting the cover on her casket. Rebecca had diverted her gaze. She couldn't bear to look at the finality of her mother's closed coffin. That would come soon enough. She had fallen into his frame for support as soon as he was finished. He melded into her as if it were his civic duty to comfort her at all cost.

Rebecca followed him to a nearby Hardee's to grab a bite to eat before proceeding to his small brick house off of Cynwood Drive. She knew not to bring him back to the Madame's house, for fear her mother would haunt her for the rest of her life, or at least for the extent of time she decided to hide out at the family estate. She had questioned herself, as always, on the drive over as to why she needed to hold on to him—to hold on to someone. She wouldn't have been completely alone at home. Her cousin Gail was there, but Gail couldn't give her what she needed.

"Never depend on a man. A man will never give you what you want." As she watched Randall abandon his tie upon entering his home, Rebecca thought about this lesson her mother had preached to her. He led her to the less-than-modest eating area off the living room and sat across from her. It had taken her less than two seconds to surmise he lived alone. She had watched Randall play with his straw before finally unwrapping the long stripped column and taking deep pulls from

his thirty-two-ounce soda. Wanting desperately to feel the scratch of his five o'clock shadow against her face, she forced herself to eat the burger he tossed her way. He had apparently completely devoured his food on the short ride from the strip mall to his house and held the balled-up fast food bag in the palm of his huge hand. He got up to dispose of his trash.

"Rebecca, right?" he had asked.

"Rebi." His question reminded her that they really didn't know one another. She knew of no other black woman named Rebecca. She hated her name. Then again, there was no other person whose mother was referred to as Madame. It was a self-proclaimed title, she was told, that her mother had given herself when she tried and failed to get her PhD in philosophy. Her mother desired a title. Rebecca felt her mother needed a title to explain her eccentric nature, and there were some in the community who felt she deserved explaining. The Madame resigned herself to being a community advocate, master fundraiser, and den mother of sorts for the Grace Apostle school, and everyone resigned themselves to calling her Madame.

"Do you want to watch TV or maybe listen to some music?" she remembered him asking. His mind seemed to be moving faster than his body as he fumbled with several remotes, dropping one or two after picking them up from the edge of an impressive entertainment center. She watched every lever and pulley in his upper arm and back muscles through his thin, starched white dress shirt as he bent and stretched in an attempt to tidy up. She was in the presence of modern-day Adonis. Rebecca smirked, thinking about her love of Greek mythology. So what did that make her? She decided that for that night she would play the siren, alluring to men but potentially dangerous. That made her smile.

He knew he was being watched. Angst took over his expression, as it would with anyone receiving a visitor who was not quite sure as to the nature of the visit, she thought. He snuck suspicious glances of her as he busied himself with trying to find a home for the gaming system controllers, attachments, and games that took up residence on the couch inches away from the wide television console. She felt empowered that he was not completely comfortable with her being there. Rebecca allowed him to squirm a little before deciding to help him out.

She had joined him in the living room. Her intention to stay was clear when she kicked off her two-and-a-half-inch heels before folding one leg beneath her on the couch. "Did they ever find a guard who could stop you on the court after I left Grace Apostle?"

One mention of Randall's former basketball career broke the ice. He was quite chatty. She learned that recruiting to a NCAA team was nearly impossible from their small town and nearly unknown Christian league, but he was quite talented. He played abroad in Italy right after high school for two years, trying to work his way up to their pro league after an acquaintance of his summer league coach invited a scout to their championship game. He was very dissatisfied overseas. Superstardom never came; Italy was expensive, and he missed his humongous family.

Randall also spoke of a woman he had been dating over there. His very intonation changed. It became slow and measured but no less passionate than when he spoke of basketball, as if every syllable reminded him of her. He and this woman parted ways when talks about returning home and taking over the family business with his siblings became a reality.

For a moment, Rebecca wondered what it would take to make a handsome and hardworking man like Randall fall in love with her. She listened to him drone on about himself, but none of what he had said mattered to her. She felt she had never met anyone so foolish. He had been somewhere, had actually gotten away, only to return to the eastern shore of Maryland. Rebecca didn't even try to keep her tone free from judgment. "You left Italy to come back here?"

"It's home—mines, and, if I am not mistaken, yours as well," he replied.

"Yeah, but you got to admit, it's wicked slow here. That's why I had to leave." *Among other things.*

"Outside of the vineyards of Tuscany and Rome, a city is a city, same dissatisfied people with the same struggles, just another shade and dialect. Where I stayed outside of Sicily is not that different than Easton if you ask me," he said after taking a loud slurp of his drink. "So, where do you live now?"

Rebecca felt ridiculous for revealing, "Salisbury." It was a jewel of a town to those on the eastern shore of Maryland, but it had nothing to boast except a fairly decent university and the Perdue Farms.

Randall smirked. "Oh yeah, that's the fast lane."

Rebecca smiled and shrugged her shoulders at the irony. Their banter had given way to silence. She was lapsing into the reality of her own very recent past and what lay before her in the days to come. She moved closer to him on the couch as if Randall could catch her from falling. "You are such a sweetheart for entertaining me and letting me hang out. How can I ever thank you?" Rebecca asked.

She peeked her eyes in his direction while sending her fingers through her own shoulder-length bob. She was waiting for them to talk about why they were there together and what they were going to do with the time they had. She knew men, and men always had a plan.

He expelled a puff of air before smiling sheepishly in reply.

"I mean, I know this can't be customary in your profession," Rebecca baited him. At least she hoped she was special in this regard and that he didn't take any other grieving daughters home with him.

Randall shrugged his broad shoulders. "Everyone grieves differently. It's about whatever you take *comfort* in."

"Is that what you call this?" Rebecca asked, tapping his thigh, then deciding to leave her hand there. "Taking comfort?"

Randall cleared his throat. "Some people need to see their loved one twenty times before the final service, or expect us to dress them over and over again. One woman even called to speak to her deceased father on the telephone." He shook his head and chuckled before getting suddenly serious again, as if his training had taught him never to make fun of those who mourn. "I can't presume to know what's going through your head right now. I could tell you wanted—I mean, were in need of—something. I'm just happy I can help out a fellow Grace Apostle Guardian."

Go team, she thought sarcastically. She didn't want lame loyalty. She had been the aggressor in their exchange, and now she craved to be pursued. She was dying to speed up their involvement into a relationship on steroids, bulked up and believable. She wanted someone to make her extended stay in Easton worthwhile.

With arms across his chest, he bumped her playfully. "Plus, it doesn't hurt that you are smoking hot now. I mean, it was real good seeing you again, but, I got to say, I don't remember you quite like this."

Smoking hot, I'll take that. She wanted to propose to him. She decided to oblige Randall with much more than a hug in that moment. She imagined him extending his hand with that compliment as if in a dance, and she curtsied. In one fluid movement, she straddled him and then hugged his neck like a long-lost friend.

Randall was reluctant to continue this sudden affectionate trail at first, letting his arms dangle to his sides like a young boy forced to hug his fat auntie. Maybe he was caught off guard or maybe he was thinking of his ex-girlfriend in Italy.

"Hug me back," she whispered into his ear, "like you mean it."

Rebecca nuzzled her face into Randall's neck and sniffed and kissed and nibbled until he brought his arms to the dull ache in the middle of her back before paving his own trail down her backside with his hands. Her conscience and common sense were silenced under his touch. He hugged her back and held on way into the night.

In their own postcoital confusion, partially clothed and lying side by side, Randall asked, " Why didn't we ever hook up before, huh? I guess, in high school, you were so big time that you didn't have time for an underclassman like me?"

Rebecca took that to mean that if she was passing out cookie back then like she was now, then why didn't he get a piece. "No, I think it was the other way around, Mr. Basketball Star."

He'd have been surprised to know she took her purity vows seriously in high school, unlike some of her classmates. Something had changed about her attitude and outlook after graduation though. While everyone was taking the summer off before college, she took advanced courses in anatomy and physiology by losing weight and sowing her wild oats in the process. She learned there was an art to attracting men by taking an interest in her own appearance and hanging around the local boom boom room. The more weight she lost the more she loved to show herself off.

They both shifted, she on her back and he on his side, to better share the space and the conversation.

"I mean evvverybody knows Madame Ava. The funny thing is that I didn't even know that you were Madame Ava's daughter back then. It's like I never made that connection," he admitted with a chuckle.

She didn't know whether to thank or curse him for that comment. With that, Rebecca began to feel the ridicule and scorn of her former days. The majority of her classmates didn't so much make fun of her, but, rather, of the Madame which seemed to further fuel her mother's idiosyncrasies. Then there were her mom's own ill-conceived notions of love and perfection that had driven Rebecca to her breaking point. She balled herself up on her end of the couch.

"I probably have to play low-key with my family handling your mother's funeral and all, but make sure we exchange numbers, all right? That way we can hook up again before you go back home." Randall yawned and absentmindedly turned toward the back of the couch.

"I may be staying for a while," Rebecca admitted. "Like you said, this is home, right?"

"Even better," Randall pushed through a yawn. "We'll definitely get it in before you go."

The reality of her mother's death was rushing to the surface, compounded by the fact that she had just had sex with her mother's mortician before they could even get the Madame in the ground. *Who does that?* She felt

Chapter 2

Rebecca had come traipsing in after midnight in a camouflaged mood. She had announced to the four walls and her slumbering cousin, Gail, that she would be taking over the Madame's nineteenth century–styled boudoir on the first floor. At least being with Randall had helped her, if only temporarily, release some of the anxiety she'd felt since hearing about her mother's passing over forty-eight hours ago—anxiety about returning home close to fifteen years later with no family of her own and barely a job to speak of. Sex always trumped her anxiety, took the edge off, diverted her attention. She had failed the Madame in so many ways, and now, it no longer mattered if she lived up to her mother's expectations.

I am no longer a siren, she thought, *I am a beast*. She had bedded one of the town's most eligible and physically gorgeous men. That was a piece of gossip she wouldn't mind being shared from under the helmet dryers at the local beauty parlor.

Rebecca now strained her eyes to see the newspaper's 9.4 serif font as she read, because she had not been ready to part the heavy brocade draperies when her cousin peeked in that morning to drop off a copy of it for her to read. Ms. Ava Lucas. She reread the name and then the article as if it were some random article about some random person, like a war veteran or county librarian, in the obituary section.

Gail interrupted her thoughts with a short rap on the door with her delicate knuckles. "How long do you plan to sleep, Rebi?"

"Until after the processional, funeral, fanfare, and tributes are over," Rebecca said through a lazy yawn.

Gail stood in the doorway as if it wasn't proper to enter. "I know it's a lot to deal with, but it's for the Madame."

Rebecca noticed that her cousin was visibly affected by the whole ordeal. Her blush couldn't hide the puffiness, and Visine couldn't clear the veiny red streaks across the iris of both eyes. Although grieving, Gail was functioning. Every arrangement made to this point for the funeral that was less than twenty-four hours away had been made by Gail. Her voice seemed pinched, but Gail proceeded to run down a laundry list of the day's events, including a visit from the Bucktown Women's Association carrying personal condolences, and a reception with the other members of the Chosen Twenty-Three, many of whom had traveled back to town and were expected to do their own tribute at the funeral.

Rebecca was coming to recognize her role. Gail did the grunt work behind the scenes as she had always done for the Madame, but Rebecca was the new figurehead of the family.

Before Rebecca could protest, Gail gave herself permission to enter the room, walk the hardwood flooring, and snatch open the curtains that had kept the shadows at bay. "I am afraid to ask, but, where, pray tell, were you most of the night that you couldn't come home first?"

Rebecca didn't have to answer. Her cousin was secretly shaming her with her disdainful expression. She should have come straight home—for Gail.

"You're inappropriate, you know that," Gail said from the foot of the bed.

"I ran into an old friend."

"Uh huh." Gail rolled her eyes. "Anyway, I called Honeywell caterers. I hope you like them, but it is too late if you don't. The Madame adored their spiced apples and creamed spinach, so that's what we're having."

Rebecca watched Gail plop on the edge of the bed as if her work was done. Her head dropped into her chest temporarily, and she shook her head as if trying to rid herself of inner demons.

Gail covered her face and sobbed. "I'm so sorry, Rebi."

This is indeed a sad occasion, Rebecca thought. Gail was usually the rock. She actually felt sorry for her cousin, who had lost her only confidant and friend, or at least that was what Gail had always been to her mother. Gail had kept longtime boyfriend Milo Green at arm's length, never committing more than an arbitrary date, to care after the Madame. She wasn't sure the Madame was capable of the reciprocation that Gail's companionship deserved. Rebecca righted herself and slid down to give Gail a one-handed hug. She rested her head on her cousin's.

"I'll get through this, I will. We both will—for Madame Ava," Gail assured Rebecca when she pulled herself together with a heavy sigh. With a deep breath, she regained her full posture. "I will receive the caterers at one-thirty P.M. You should be prepared in forty-five minutes to receive our guests."

Before Rebecca could get mad at the lack of personal time or space, she realized Gail was only doing what she had always done, which was keep the schedule for the lady of the house. Being a personal assistant was not what Gail was paid to do, but rather an unwritten payment for being taken in at twelve after her own mother, Cynthia Lucas, whom everyone called Cinnamon, and the Madame's only sister, passed on. Gail was somewhere between the Madame's age and Rebecca's. They would have felt more like sisters if not for the sixteen-year age difference.

That was why Rebecca elected to call her Auntie, to Gail's chagrin. Gail kept a few of Rebecca's secrets, and had kept her out of a lot of trouble when she broke curfew between her senior year and the time she left home for good. She was a thin, refined woman with a sharp fashion sense, who didn't mind shifting into her younger cousin's vernacular for good girl chat.

There were no men in their lineage, no patriarch, for at least four generations back. When she was much younger the Madame was said to have been widowed by a Vietnam solider missing in action. A war hero seemed so cliché. That fact could neither be confirmed nor denied when it came to writing the obituary because the Madame retained her maiden name, and their bloodline was limited to the women in the room. Whether that was the case or not, Rebecca knew the unknown soldier was not her dad.

In high school, when Rebecca thought she was grown enough to do so, she confronted the Madame about the identity of her dad. At that time, the Madame, maddened by an occasional drunken spell, replied, "A man who would leave us took a one-way ticket to nowhere. Once there, he probably bought another ticket to hell. You don't need to know where you came from, young lady, as long as you know where you are going."

That was why Rebecca didn't mind the rumors, because they gave her something to go on. There were rumors about how their family had come to get the house, and the wealth that the acres of land that supported the only working well in a twenty-mile radius afforded them. According to classmate Nina Pritchett, whose mom was a librarian and the only token black on the Historical Society until the Madame was inducted, there was a woman in the Lucas ancestry who came to rent forty acres in the back of an old abandoned horse farm during the Reconstruction era. This woman was said to have been a field hand as well as a cook to the fraternal order of Freemasons who were housed in the guest chambers. They were working on what was now Grace Apostle Methodist Church. Concubine was the word used to explain this woman's relationship with the plantation owner.

Rebecca didn't know what was legacy or lore, but it had been the Madame's mission to abolish the ugly rumors about their family and cast them in a more respectable and charitable light. It was secrets like these that drove Rebecca away from this land directly after high school. Ironically, it was her own secrets that were driving her home to stay.

"Why do I have to be here?" Rebecca whined. "I ain't got it in me to suck up to these women today, Auntie."

"Girl, did you just say 'ain't'? Your momma isn't even cold yet. Forgive her, Madame," Gail said, casting her eyes toward the roof. "I could give you twenty-eight . . . Wait, how old are you now?"

"Thirty-one, Auntie," Rebi replied.

"I could give you thirty-one years' worth of reasons why you can and will entertain these ladies this afternoon. Madame Ava was slated to get an award of some kind from this association. She always wanted to be a part of this group that just saw fit to drop their, uh, stringent standards, so don't worry me, Rebi. The day is not our own. We've got things to do."

Rebecca was coming to understand that there was not a day, evening, or night that would be theirs until the Madame was six feet underground. *Once again I have to get with the program,* she thought.

Gail looked at Rebecca and gave another heavy sigh before standing up, as if she was going to offer her a reprieve. "I guess I could greet the Women's Association if you'll go back down to the funeral parlor to check to see if Mrs. Hughes has fixed the mess that was your mother's hairstyle. As if I'm going to send my auntie to her eternal rest with a beehive on her head. I told that woman a chignon, a simple chignon."

Rebecca noticed Gail's voice get shrill again. She was near tears. They both had tasks they'd rather avoid. They both had bargaining tools. She wondered if it would be more painful for Gail to see the Madame's lifeless body again as it would be for her to see Randall. She couldn't face the shame she felt that she now associated with his adorable face, frame, and physique; not this soon, and not if he would be ignoring her. She had used him, and she reasoned that he had used her in return. At this point he looked better going than coming. *Sorry, Gail.*

"No, Auntie, you're right. I will stay and talk with the ladies of the association about how great my mother was to this family and community. I know the drill," Rebecca said, springing from the bed to the window overlooking the grounds. She could see in the distance the steeple of Grace Apostle and the annex of her alma mater—the school that was expanded courtesy of the Madame's generosity. "I'll have the caterers set up the great room." Rebecca felt Gail staring at her.

"Good," Gail said, resigned. "Afterward, I think I'll join you at the church for the reception. I think it is fabulous that your entire class has gotten together to pay tribute to her."

As if they had any choice, Rebecca thought. Even in death, the Madame stripped away a person's options. Rebecca's stomach knotted with dread and indecision as she looked again across the clearing of the grounds, through the woods to Grace Apostle. She felt shackled to this place. Being in the company of pretentious women who couldn't care less about her dead mother would be a walk in the park compared to coming face to face with her classmates again. She had been trained by the Madame to be modest and discreet. Those characteristics would not prove to be her strong suit as she remembered that she had been less than discriminating with every male in her senior class.

Chapter 3

Rebecca was off with her body count. There were actually a few of her male classmates with whom she hadn't played her own version of the "make me blush" game. The class delinquent had gotten himself killed six weeks after graduation. The class do-gooder, who had gotten caught stuffing the ballot box with his own name for Most Likely to Succeed in high school, ironically was now the town's mayor, who had tried to take her for a ride in the backseat of his car and met with the firm handle of the Madame's broom. The only other guy was the man who stood smiling at her now from across the church rectory, the pastor's son, who was the only perfect gentleman in the lot.

"Will?" Rebi questioned, recalling that William Donovan had been her only friend from high school. She had forgotten that Gail had met up with her until she sidestepped across Gail's path to get to Will. She crossed through a row of pews, to the aisle, and then went through another row, with Gail following. She was still squinting although it was clearly him up close now.

"Weary! Hey, friend," he said, referring to one of the many nicknames he had for her that spoke to her tendency to complain about everything.

She recalled that only he'd been the one she'd done that to. He was the only one who would listen.

"Oh, but, I guess you have got cause to be weary now. I am so sorry, Rebi." Will stared at her until she began to shiver. He nudged her in the arm, and instinctively she nudged him back. "I'm glad to see you."

"It's good to see you too," Rebecca replied.

"You cold dumped me when you left for college after graduation—didn't even come to the reunion or anything. What's up with that?"

"I . . . I . . . I . . ." she started. Once again, he stared. She never remembered his eye contact being that intense. *Why haven't I kept in contact with him?*

"Every holiday and even that *one* summer you came home I'd remind Gail to tell you we should get together. Nothing," he said.

"I told her," Gail added, exonerating herself.

Without waiting for an explanation this time, he pulled her into a half hug. He bent down to kiss her forehead and the room got brighter. He extended the hug with his other arm to include Gail, who was standing by.

"Pastor," Gail said.

"How's my man Milo? I know he will be joining us." Will raised a bushy eyebrow as he sized up Gail's petite frame.

"He had to work today so that he can be off for the funeral." Gail ran her right hand up and down her left arm as if she was chilly.

"You know I'm saving a date on the calendar for the two of you. Just let me know."

Rebecca watched Gail wave off their apparent inside joke. Rebecca then looked around for a familiar face obviously missing from this picture, and when she didn't see him she asked, "Didn't Gail say she saw the Pastor? Where is your dad? We are supposed to go over the program and discuss the service. I can't wait to see him."

Pastor Donovan lived and breathed Grace Apostle. He was the pastor, teacher, and chancellor of the K-12 program at the school. He was a caring man who had supported Rebecca through the toughest period in her life. He was the closest thing she had to a father. Rebecca remembered her mother had formed a friendship with Pastor Donovan and the late First Lady Donovan while working on some of the same causes they had succeeded in, causes that affected the African American working class in their community, like getting a commuter bus to add stops throughout Easton so its residents could get to higher-paying jobs outside the city limits. That was the same bus that had taken Rebecca and Will to Chesapeake Community College to take advanced calculus and trigonometry when they had reached the mathematical ceiling at Grace Apostle by their senior year.

"He, um, doesn't feel well," Will shared. "You know he's seventy-five now. Frankly, he's been a little overcome lately. We've had three deaths in three weeks at the church, and then news about your mother hit him hard. Since I am the pastoral assistant now, I hope it's okay with you if I eulogize your mom tomorrow. It feels only right since you and Madame Ava were there for me and Pops when my mom died."

Rebecca remembered First Lady Donovan falling ill and living with terminal lung cancer for many years before she passed away in their junior year. She remembered Will taking a few weeks off before returning to school, and how she had brought him up to speed on his assignments. They had come full circle. Now he was set to lay the Madame to rest.

My best friend is a minister, a pastor? She noticed the cross over the covered baptismal pool on the back wall just over Will's shoulder and felt as if she needed to take a dip. Will didn't seem to notice her scarlet letter. He was talking as fast as Rebecca had remembered. It was as if he was always excited about telling her something. She couldn't help being drawn into a dialogue with him.

Will had stepped between her and Gail and began guiding them into a different direction, then to the back offices. "Don't worry. I don't do sad funerals. This will be a Homegoing. The Madame had a servant's heart, so I'll be coming out of the book of James. Faith without works is surely dead faith, right? I think your mom understood that," Will added. "I got a copy of the order of service from Gail before it went to print. So, if there is nothing the two of you have added, I don't want to keep you from the luncheon that has been prepared."

"I think that's it," Gail said.

"Good, I am hungry," Will said, then turned to Rebecca. "You'll be glad to know the class of '95 is in da house."

"I can't get over the fact that you're a minster, a pastor," Rebecca said in an effort to stop and prolong the inevitable.

"I know, right? I did a lot of growing up. I became the assistant pastor about a year ago after my ordination. My dad still rules the roost though. He still puts in work. I just want to preach from time to time. What can I say? It's in my blood," Will said. "We have got to catch up before you leave."

Will's mouth was steadily moving as his feet led them across the vestibule to the closed multipurpose room doors. Once again, Rebecca halted abruptly just shy of the doors. "Wait! Slow down. I should freshen up before I go in there. Does my hair look okay?" she asked Will and Gail.

Will let out a heavy sigh. "Tell me you are not taking
me through the whole smell-my-pits-does-my-breath-
smell-fresh routine. You're fine. Matter of fact, you
look amazing. You must have left a quarter of yourself
at home. Here, let me mess your hair up a bit and rum-
ple your clothes. It's a sin to be in mourning and look
this good—the both of you."

Will used the hand that was around her shoulder
to shift the collar on her black-and-white shirt dress.
Then he pulled the arm of her coordinating sweater off
her shoulder.

"Stop, dork." Rebi slapped his hand away. Immediately she heard the voice of her mother admonishing
her for playing in church. It dawned on her that maybe
she shouldn't have hit him. He was, after all, a minister,
even if he didn't act like one. "Oh, Will, I'm so . . ." she
started as she turned to face him. There was no need
for apologies as his tongue stuck out between his teeth
in a wide and devilish grin. This was Will. She didn't
know how it was possible, but he hadn't changed.

Will was surprisingly casual cool in dark jeans with
a black mandarin-collar shirt. He always reminded
Rebecca of a stockier Dwayne Wayne from *The Cosby
Show* spinoff, *A Different World*, with his now sporty
horn-rimmed glasses replacing his split bifocals. But he
was way more adorable than Kadeem Hardison could
ever portray. He was a brainiac, quirky and quick wit-
ted, with one dimple on his right side that demanded
attention. He had become quite handsome.

"Where's my security?" he asked, looking around in
jest.

They both laughed.

"Seriously, I'm glad you're okay," he whispered into
her ear while giving her another half hug. Then, turning to Gail, he said, "If you all need anything in the
weeks to come don't hesitate to let us know."

Members of her senior class and their families stood on the other side of the auditorium doors, mingling as if waiting to yell "surprise" at a birthday celebration. Will ushered them inside the door. Rebecca felt eighteen again with every bit of the twenty-five odd pounds she had lost still on her stomach, waist, and hips. She told herself to look them all in the eyes even if it wasn't her eyes they all seemed to be staring at. Rebecca looked around. Many were staring at her right hand, which she had unconsciously intertwined with Will's left hand before entering the room. As if on cue, they both abruptly let the other's hand fall.

There was a hesitation. Then her classmates were upon her, hugging her and Gail while whispering condolences. First the women, they were the majority—thirteen of the twenty-three. Rebecca couldn't keep count of the barely recognizable faces. Their well wishes were supposed to show that they shared her grief. Rebecca noticed that Tiffany Redfern and Nicole Paige, both former cheerleaders, had both gained a considerable amount of weight, and they commented about her weight loss as if they couldn't believe it could be done.

There were just ten guys in her graduating class. A few of them brought up the rear to greet the girl who, many had commented, only looked good from the neck up. Jerome Curtis, her first real boyfriend, got to first base and lied that he stole second and third. Quite a few in the crowd didn't have to lie. Rebi remembered them all: like Alford Edwards, who quickly diverted his hazel eyes from hers; and Steve Kirkland, whose eyes were pleading with her now not to divulge their secret of drinking and dancing at the local boom boom room and doing things they were hastened against in their Christianity classes. Those two hadn't wanted to as-

sociate with her while at Grace Apostle, but they sang
quite a different tune after her graduation grand makeover. Nothing stuck. There had been no relationships,
just regrets. Now they were back to ignoring her.

The receiving line died down and finally Rebecca and
Gail were allowed to sit at a head table across from a
generous buffet. She set her purse on the sturdy alumi-
num folding chair to the right of her to save a space for
Will as he faced the crowd. Will quieted the assembly.
Valedictorian to her salutatorian, now minister, he had
to be used to speaking to a crowd by now, she thought.

"Let's give an honor to God, the Father; our Savior, Jesus Christ; and the Holy Spirit that comforts
us in our time of need. Friends, I'm glad to have you
all back at Grace Apostle. It feels like an impromptu
class reunion. Praise God for His favor and for keeping
us fifteen years. For those who don't know, I am Will
Donovan, the assistant pastor of Grace Apostle Methodist Church. The tradition continues. Right now, as I
speak, one hundred and forty-five students are in class
in our school. We became a part of the county's charter
school program, and this year's graduating class almost doubles ours."

The crowd seemed to be delighted by those details.
Will led them in a hearty hand clap of praise. Even
Rebecca shook her head out of fascination. She hadn't
thought much about her alma mater since leaving. She
was more interested now in Will and his seeming de-
votion to the place, and the eloquence with which he
spoke. "A petite powerhouse of a woman came into our
lives here, in this place. I'm sure I don't have to remind
you that she sacrificed and blessed each of us—Grace
Apostle's first graduating class—with a two thousand
dollar scholarship. That ain't nothing to sneeze at,
y'all, even today, and definitely not in that time." Will's

gesturing arms were wide and sweeping. "It was only befitting that we would gather today to show one of our own, Rebi Lucas, and family, that we love them as much as we did the Madame."

The applause was loud and unexpected. Gail dabbed her eyes and handed Rebecca an extra handkerchief, as if Rebecca would surely need it before the afternoon was done. Rebi looked to her next of kin and followed suit in her gracious head nods to show her appreciation to the onlookers.

"We want you to know, Gail and Rebi, that many of us texted and e-mailed as soon as we found out. We all had fond memories to share. Some recalled the Madame as a substitute in math and social studies, and a supporter of all our fundraisers. A few of the ladies clued us fellas in on how the Madame added to their home economics experience as well when she taught here for a semester."

Rebecca could hear amusement as she shaded her embarrassment with a smile. She recalled those mortifying months when her mother convinced Pastor Donovan that she was qualified to take over home economics for Ms. Miller who went on maternity leave. She took liberties with the lessons, adding one part sex education and one part advice columnist to the primarily cooking and sewing curriculum. A simple pattern cutting lesson turned into a discussion on remaining chaste. *"The fatal flaw of the chastity belt is that it could be removed by its owner,"* Rebecca remembered her mom lecturing, while holding several panels of muslin-colored canvas used for a tote bag dangerously close to her own genitals. *"But the idea remains a good one. Keep it clamped, ladies, for the one who holds the key. Remember, your mind is your metaphorical chastity belt."*

It was bad enough that her mom worked at her school, but after that, it became impossible for anyone to take her mom seriously. She was the driving force behind the Young Ladies' Cotillion that she insisted upon sponsoring after school. Once again she preached purity (and fundraising) as part of the preparation. For a meticulously bred and groomed woman, the Madame's shirttails were always out. Where Rebecca tried her best to blend in, the Madame did not. Rebecca became known as the one with the strict weirdo mom who had a sick fascination with their burgeoning sexuality. God must have heard Rebecca's prayers. Shortly thereafter a group of parents complained about the inappropriateness of a religious layman speaking to the students about such personal matters. The Madame was relieved of her duties at Grace Apostle. Rebecca remembered her taking her release particularly hard. The Madame never again returned to the church in any capacity.

"Everyone agreed, though, the Chosen Twenty-Three would gather in Easton to pay tribute, which we will do tomorrow," Will continued, bringing Rebecca back to the present. "Some took trains and buses to be here today. Some arrived as late as this morning. We want to help this family anyway we can." He clapped his hands together as if to tell himself to wrap it up. "You all know I can talk. I'm going to sit now and let this committee take over from here with the food service. Please remember to keep this family in your prayers."

Will was hardly in his seat before Rebecca asked, "This can't be our entire class. Who are these people? They are so—"

"Pleasant," Gail offered.

"Well, yeah," Rebecca agreed. She stopped her explaining while volunteers served her and the rest of the head table.

"You don't see my graduating class gathering," Gail responded, raking through her piping hot macaroni and cheese with a fork to check its consistency.

"You didn't graduate from Grace Apostle, Auntie," Rebecca reminded her. At that time Grace Apostle only went through junior high school. "Plus, the Madame didn't pass out cash to your senior class." *Trying to guarantee herself sainthood in the eyes of the community.*

Her classmates began to form lines to serve themselves at the buffet table. Rebecca turned to Will, who wasted no time digging into his luncheon meal. "Don't act like you and I both weren't ridiculed and treated terribly by these very same *pleasant* classmates," Rebecca said.

Will pacified her by patting her hand as he continued to eat, obviously unfazed by the trip down memory lane. Gail just "tsked" at her pettiness.

"Ridiculed because we didn't fit into any of their cliques, because we were in AP classes at the college, basically because of who we were." Rebecca searched the crowd for a particular tormentor.

Gail took a napkin to the corners of her mouth. "I can see that. You both were directly related to two of the most influential black people in this area. They were just jealous. It was high school, after all."

Maybe she is right, Rebecca thought. It was hard to come to that conclusion as a teenager though.

"Thank God people change," Will finally said between bites. He tapped Rebecca's wrist. "You gonna eat your cornbread?"

Rebecca passed him a lick to the arm. "You're the assistant pastor. Surely you can get another piece of cornbread for yourself."

Her last comment was hysterical to him. "See how you do me? Reminds me of the same line the thief hit Jesus with on the cross. 'If you're all of that, save thyself.'"

She watched him stand while laughing to himself. His laugh sounded like a series of hiccups. It was contagious.

"Biblical humor," he tossed over his shoulder as he walked off to the front of the buffet line, where he signaled for and got not one, but two additional pieces of cornbread.

He's such a dork, Rebecca thought as she watched him joke with a few classmates standing guard over the pans of fried fish, macaroni, and garlic greens. Rebecca looked down at her own untouched plate.

"Is that wrong that those are my only memories from high school?" Rebecca asked him with all sincerity upon his return.

"You're just being Weary," he said, placing a piece of fish between his cornbread to form a sandwich. "Sure I remember that stuff, but I am man enough to let that go. When I think about it, we were major haters as well. We probably sat around talking about folks in our class as much as they talked about us. All is forgiven, I pray. There will always be some who still smile in your face and talk about you behind your back, some in this very congregation. I don't try to figure what I've done to them. I look at it like this: if anyone is sitting there with malice in their heart toward you or me after all this time, then just do like it says in the Bible and 'fret not yourself with evil doers.'"

She listened to how God's Word glided off his tongue. It made perfect sense in that context: freedom from judgment. Wasn't that what she was trying to exercise right out of school? She thought about how she tried so hard to prove she was just as normal as her classmates, although her mother was slightly eccentric. She had the same hopes and desires as everyone else. She was someone people should get to know. Will had his methods of coping and she had hers. Once again she felt she had to censor what she did or said around *Pastor* Will until she remembered his comments from earlier. "Hey, I didn't appreciate that comment about my mom and home ec class. Were you trying to embarrass me?"

Will put down his sandwich and held his stomach as if it ached. "Please, I thought that was hilarious when I heard some of the things that she was telling y'all. Better the girls than the boys. We were way too immature to handle the real talk she was throwing down." He laughed out loud, despite the solemn nature of the occasion, drawing attention once again to the head table.

Rebecca couldn't help but smile at seeing him so amused. *This is the man bringing the eulogy?* Gail cleared her throat as if ringing a decorum bell and they sobered up.

Two women and a man came through the doorway with smiles of their own, passing out select greetings as they scanned the room for available seats. One of the women was pregnant and almost unrecognizable by the apparent havoc the pregnancy was doing to her body. Rebecca soon realized she was the missing link—Nina Pritchett.

Rebecca didn't feel like fixing on the phony face she wore for Nina back in those days, and was relieved when her party located seats with her fellow retired cheerleaders. To be cool with Nina was to be accepted by almost everyone else. She was the queen bee and the Madame's biggest critic, along with her mother. No one was supposed to know more than Mrs. Pritchett, local librarian, who published a scandal rag known as *The Society Pages* in the nineties and distributed it through the library's community kiosk. The mother and daughter both derived sick pleasure from dismantling her mom's pedestal anyway they could. It was their mothers' feud, which they had inherited and kept inflamed.

"There's Veronica with Nina and her husband," Gail said.

Rebecca watched Nina stabilize the chair with her hand before resting her girth down gingerly and kicking her legs out in front of her. The man with them went off to inquire about the buffet as they looked around. Rebecca turned to Gail this time. "I thought she ended up with Jerry West."

"That's Mayor West," Gail replied. Their eyes met briefly over that revelation. "Apparently when he was ready to start his political career he found a newer model, and I do mean model. Now, I know you can't stand him, but it's only right that he say a few words at the funeral as the mayor."

Rebecca wasn't worried about Jerry West. She watched Nina's husband out of the side of her eye. He was not at all the accomplished businessman, attorney, or congressman she imagined Nina would end up with. His disposition had "trucker" written all over him from his work boots up to the baseball cap that he obviously wasn't raised to remove when entering a building.

Back then it was all about who a person hooked up with or intended to marry. Women in general in Easton were ready with pickaxes, mountain crampons, and harnesses to drop their rural beginnings, rappel into the dating pool, and get a foothold on someone deemed better or more upwardly mobile. They were supposed to be different. Grace Apostle graduates produced smart women who shouldn't need a man so desperately. Every girl in her class knew to hide coming down with bad-boy syndrome or actually broker a broken home with an un-wedded pregnancy after their parents scraped together couch change to send them to a private school. There was still that lingering air that remained that said if a person stayed close to home, a woman needed a man by her side.

Rebecca could not make out the other woman. "Who is Veronica?"

"My lady friend," Will admitted, not taking his eyes off the latecomers.

"Lady friend? What are you, sixty? Just say girl-friend, Will," she said, just a little agitated. Rebecca ignored his questioning gaze. This time it was her eyes that became fixated on the pair of ladies. Veronica was perfect, slender where she needed to be, and curvy at all the right spots. Her energy read eager, perky, almost presidential in appearance with her staunch gray business suit softened with butterscotch-yellow accessories. Rebecca noticed Veronica wasn't a hugger, but rather the type who expressed herself with either a single- or double-handed wave. She was working the room now with smiles and winks. She was obviously familiar with many members in their senior class. Re-becca tried to rack her brain to see if she remembered Veronica from this area as well.

"I want you to meet her," Will said, standing and beckoning to Veronica with the wave of his hand.

They watched as Veronica leaned over Nina's shoul-der to whisper something and point in their direction.

When Will sat down again, Rebecca asked him this from the side of her mouth, as if to disguise to onlook-ers that she was talking about his girlfriend."Where'd you meet her?"

"She's from Wye Mills. We met at Morgan. Oddly enough, she and Nina have become close friends since Veronica relocated here last summer," he replied, using the same ventriloquist technique.

"You don't say," Rebecca replied dryly. "Your girlfriend is pals with your high school crush."

Will titled his head and scrunched his face as if trying to remember something. "Only you would remember that, but then again, what guy didn't like Nina back then?"

Nina looked in their direction just then as if she was surprised to see them there. *She is so phony.* She waved from where she sat, rubbing her bulging tummy as her husband set a generous plate in front of her before going back for his own. She had an excuse to be rude and not come greet them.

Many of their classmates lined up to greet Nina as they had done to her and Gail over an hour ago. Rebecca felt it was the high school cafeteria all over again with them looking on at the popular kids' table. Rebecca lost sight of Veronica until she was on the opposite side of the table, extending her hand to Gail, and then to Rebecca.

"Hello." She cradled Rebecca's palm in a double-handed pump handshake. "I am so sorry for your loss."

"Thank you," Rebecca replied.

Will took over the introductions. "Veronica Deeds, this is Rebi, uh Rebecca Lucas, the Madame's daughter and my very good friend from high school."

Veronica nodded her head at Will, then Rebecca, as if his point was duly noted. Her smile was bright and appeared genuine. "Nice to meet you. "

"Of course you know Gail from church," he continued.

"I'm told your mom was an exceptional woman. I wanted so much to talk to her about her association with various organizations around town. She will be missed in this community," Veronica added, talking directly to Rebecca.

She is definitely courting votes for something. Rebecca had no more words, so she nodded graciously. She could find no flaws in this woman upon first inspection, except that she was friends with Nina and she wore the type of perfume Rebecca hated with a high concentration of alcohol to support its heavy floral scent. She busied herself in her purse as Veronica rounded the back of the table to get closer to Will.

Rebecca couldn't help but study the pair of them. Veronica was quite tall, topping off at Will's earlobe. She wondered how the two of them dated in such a small town without being a public spectacle. She remembered Will was also deemed undatable in high school. *But look at him now,* she thought. She suddenly wished she had brought her own date to this luncheon, one of the gorgeous, jaw-dropping variety. Thoughts of Randall made her briefly turn her attention downward where she blushed into her half-eaten plate.

Will pulled Veronica into the same half hug that he had given Rebecca earlier. Then he pulled out a chair to his right for her to join them, before leaving for the buffet to serve his lady friend.

Rebecca gave Veronica another smile and waited to go home while Veronica waited for her plate. For the first time since reuniting with Will, Rebecca remembered the occasion. She went back to her purse for the handkerchief her cousin had given her before. She felt as if she might need it. She was, after all, in mourning.

Chapter 4

Rebecca walked every inch of her childhood home the day of her mom's funeral to see if she could stay there, if this could be her new home, her refuge. She felt the Madame all around: in the hallways where there were framed portraits of the three of them; in the library study where the Madame kept classic novels Rebecca never remembered her mother reading; and even on the wrap-around porch that had a clear view across Holly Oaks in the front. Around the sides and back, they could view the rear campus of Grace Apostle. The Madame was in the air, and for that reason, Rebecca decided to abandon the selection of reserved and tasteful black suits Gail had set aside for her, and donned the Madame's sky-blue Calvin Klein dress to bid her mother farewell.

Cinched at the waist, the feminine silhouette fell a couple centimeters short of Rebecca's knees. It wasn't because of their weight difference anymore, but rather their slight difference in height. It placed the modest slit at an interesting angle in the back. *Shame on them if they should look,* she thought. She was excited to say that now she could fit in to all her mother's designer and tailor-made wardrobe pieces. To her surprise Gail smiled at her wardrobe choice as she made her way down the stairs. No doubt, she had been by the Madame's side when she purchased the dress.

Gail was draped in black from head to toe, but broke up the monotony smartly with silver accessories and Mr. Milo on her arm. He appeared to be helping Gail stand upright as Rebecca met her only living relative in the foyer to walk to the awaiting family car.

Rebecca felt for her clutch bag, then for her pearl earrings that she remembered selecting but not actually putting on. *I am missing a major accessory,* she thought as she watched Milo help Gail into the car. Who was going to stop her from falling when today got to be too much?

Grace Apostle was literally behind their house. They would drive down Zion Hill Road on a path that resembled a horseshoe shape, to Hubbard Square, then on to Church Road to the front of Grace Apostle—a five-minute ride. She opened her window slightly to be welcomed with the crisp remnants of cedar, orange, and the charred remains of a distant neighbor's burnt trash. The streets were already lined with cars just around the bend. Some stood just outside their vehicles to watch their arrival, showing enough respect to let Rebecca and Gail settle inside the church sanctuary before coming inside themselves. A funeral was a public occasion in Easton whether the person was someone you knew or not. The Madame was enough of a local celebrity that her newspaper obituary practically read, "come one, come all." The lure of the wake, the hour of viewing before the actual funeral, brought many out in this community, young and old, who believed in the old tradition of watching, guarding the body, or waiting in case the deceased should wake up.

If Rebecca had her way she would have said goodbye at the family viewing, she thought as she saw people congregated on the church steps. She was surprised to see the striking yet stoic face of Randall through the crowd, descending the stairs. Flashes of his seductive and then satiated facial expressions filled her mind. The thought of him and her together made Rebecca want to repent on the church altar, which was cloaked now in floral sprays to offset her mother's coffin. Being with him two nights ago had been so careless.

Ironically, Randall was there with her now, but not as she had imagined. He met the car and assisted her up the stairs, no more, no less. He was in pure professional mode. She could not get his eye. He had to feel her pain and confusion through his hold, she thought. Where was her hug now? Gail had her own manservant. Mr. Milo held on to her arm as she steadied her foot on the pavement at the base of the church steps while she adjusted her clothes. Just when Rebecca thought she may have Randall to rely on as a personal comforter, he was gone. His leg of the race was apparently over when they were safely inside.

The Hughes sisters, Randall's siblings, attended to the Lucas girls after that, collecting cards and passing out Kleenex. They guarded the family row and fanned away irritating guests and hangers-on as much as they fanned away the stuffiness inside the sanctuary with sturdy cardboard fans. Rebecca was told that a few dignitaries and auxiliaries had asked for reserved seating. Those on the program were seated to the right and extended the length of the sanctuary. No one who really knew the Madame was slated to speak, other than Will—no immediate family, no real partners or friends. Either a person loved the Madame or hated her, but it was socially unacceptable to show any disdain for the woman. There would be no end to the accolades because there was no end to her affiliations, almost ensuring a long service.

The Chosen Twenty-three slowly trickled in and were placed up front in the reserved section. In the interest of time, Will told Rebecca to expect a fill-in-the-blanks recital from each of her classmates as to how they spent their $2,000 scholarship money from the Madame.

Rebecca felt they might as well have thanked her for the scholarship at the previous evening's reception. She remembered her mom cornering her in her room as she was doing homework to ask about her classmates, specifically the girls, as they neared their senior year.

"You know nowadays girls can be so common and sassy, talking back to adults and coming on to their male teachers. I didn't tolerate that nonsense when I was teaching at Grace. How are your classmates, really, Rebi? Are they still nice, respectable girls?" the Madame queried.

Rebecca remembered she'd say anything to keep her mother off the school premises, anything to keep her from instituting another etiquette and social graces program. She never gave her mother insight to the ridicule or isolation she felt being her daughter. The Madame had already been fired; she didn't want to hurt her further.

"Yes, Mother, we are all really good friends," Rebecca shared under her mother's close inspection.

"Well, you never invite anyone over to the house," the Madame said from her perch in the doorframe.

"We are all so busy studying. There is so much pressure. We just all want to get into a good college." Rebecca pressed her nose further into her biology textbook to prove her point.

"Well, I'm glad to hear that. Donovan must be doing a great job then. I was thinking about doing some-

*thing big for the first graduating class, the ones I had
a hand in educating. I want to do something memora-
ble."* The Madame studied the sky as if the exact thing
had not quite occurred to her.

Rebecca snapped to full attention, insistent on getting the inside scoop. *"What, Mother?"*

*"I just as soon keep it to myself until I've discussed
it with Pastor Donovan. Yep, I think I'll pay one more
visit to Grace Apostle. You have to give if you expect
to receive, Rebi. It's just money. You can't take it with
you. They can't fault me for being charitable, can
they?"*

Rebecca thought nothing of that conversation until
now. Her scholarship of close to $40,000 was a pay
off, Rebecca thought. Mother and daughter couldn't
agree on anything as she neared graduation, but it was
understood that she was to make something of herself.
It was also understood at the end of her reckless summer, when small-town rumors had come home to roost
on her doorstep, that she would make do with what she
was given and not return home, bringing shame to the
family.

"Obviously you are ready to make a name for yourself, but Easton is my town. I've worked hard for what
I've built, so maybe you want to start anew and make
your statement elsewhere," the Madame had said to
her only child.

Rebecca looked around at all the people assembled
as if they were whispering about her even now. Many of
whom she didn't desire to share her grief with. Rebecca
kept her eye on the flow of traffic rather than the stand-
still in front of her mother's coffin. She took in only
glimpses of her mother through slits in the passing
crowd. Rebecca felt Gail tap her leg. When she looked
up, Nina and Will's girlfriend, Veronica, were mak-

ing their way around to view the body. Rebecca was slightly resentful at how beautiful they both appeared, made up in their Sunday best. They moved with an assurance that Rebecca did not herself feel at this time. Rebecca thought about what the Madame would do when faced with an adversary. She stood and tried to shake off her defensive posture as they came down the family row.

Rebecca hadn't quite figured out Veronica. She was, after all, Will's girlfriend and someone she would inevitably have to get to know. Veronica extended an arm to Rebecca's shoulder while telling Rebecca that she would be praying for her, before moving on. Nina was the one who had always put her on the defensive. Not that she expected a hug, but Nina initiated an air kiss with about a foot of space between them.

"How've you been, Nina?" Rebecca felt obligated to ask after the awkward gesture.

Nina smoothed the matte jersey fabric of her dress over and around the underside of her belly. "Good."

"Thank you so much for coming," Rebecca said, preparing to sit. Something in Nina's hand grabbed her attention.

"If you all decide to sell the house, I am a part-time real estate agent now," Nina said, extending the business card to her. She couldn't drop her smugness to do a decent sales pitch. "Some of us in this community are dedicated to keeping our choice properties on this side. My husband knows a lot of contractors who can help get it ready for potential buyers."

"On this side" referred to within the black community, which was only 30 percent of the total population of Easton, who held less than 7 percent of the wealth of the town. "Their side," the struggling middle class of black folks, prided themselves in giving a leg-up to one another, even while some were steadily stabbing one another in the back in the process. Her audacity almost made Rebecca want to assert that they would never sell, but the implication that they would sell out made her keep Nina's offer in mind.

One of Randall's sisters practically raked the business card from Rebecca's hand to place with the sympathy cards brought by others. Apparently she needed her hands free to mourn. This prompted Nina to move on as well. Rebecca didn't sit immediately. She scanned the church. Apparently Nina wasn't the only one making an appearance and striking deals. Ralph Tremaine, the Madame's longtime friend and lawyer, along with Clayton Green, the Madame's accountant, were posing for pictures with the town's new mayor and fellow Chosen Twenty-Three Grace Apostle graduate, Jerry West.

Photo ops at a funeral, she thought. *They should title the photo, "The Snake and Two Respectable White Men."* She couldn't miss the brief but concentrated effort of both Nina and Jerry to hold each other in their line of sight, yet promptly ignore one another. It was all like a scene in a movie to Rebecca. She wondered what that was about.

As the viewing hour drew to a close, the aisles were cleared and the Madame was in full view to Rebecca now. High profile, fully adorned, and ashen skin; Rebecca was at least thankful they redid the Madame's hair as Gail had demanded. *This was all for you, Momma,* Rebecca thought. The organist changed from a background hymn to something more official. Rebecca sucked in a deep breath as if she'd be able to preserve the air for later. She heard Will's voice from the back of the rectory.

"'How are the dead raised? The body that is sown is perishable, it is raised imperishable. It is sown in dishonor, it is raised in glory, it is sown in weakness, it is raised in power, it is sown a natural body, it is raised a spiritual body,'" Will recited, taking few glances at his open Bible that he carried with him up the aisle.

This is it, Rebecca thought. *This is really happening.* She inhaled deeply as she told her internal voices to be silent so she could hear the voice of her friend. He had always listened as well as comforted her in the past. She hoped he still had that effect.

"'I declare that flesh and blood cannot inherit the Kingdom of God, nor does the perishable inherit the imperishable. Listen, I tell a mystery: We will not all sleep, but we will be changed—in a flash, in a twinkling of an eye, at the last trumpet.'"

Rebecca looked over her shoulder to watch Will, halfway up the aisle now. He wore a black robe that reminded Rebecca of their graduation cloaks. He had delight in his voice as if he were reciting poetry in their senior literature and composition course. She couldn't tell if his steps gave meter to the Biblical verse or vice versa. It was as if he led the line of local clergy, including his father and the other elders of the church, not on a march toward death, but ascension to something higher. At the end of the line was hope.

At the top of the aisle, Will turned the corner in front of the family row but kept on with his declarations. "Then the saying that is written will come true, 'Death has been swallowed up in victory. Oh death, where is thy sting? O grave, where is thy victory?'"

Rebecca wondered if this was the Bible or some Shakespearean irony. *Is there really victory in death?*

Will grabbed Rebecca's hands in his huge, outstretched one and held on while he spoke. "This is the good part, saints."

To which most in the congregation replied with him in a shout. "They are all good parts. But thanks be to God, which giveth us the victory!"

Will's dimple came out of hiding with his irreverent smile. "Therefore, be ye steadfast, unmovable, always abounding in the work of the Lord, forasmuch as ye know that your labor is not in vain." Will released her hands and moved quickly on down the row, greeting Gail and Milo while he spoke about the works of Madame Ava Lucas.

Pastor Donovan, Will's father, leaned forward and kissed Rebecca and Gail both on the cheek. Then he stood and paused a moment at the coffin as if he wanted to salute a fallen comrade at a public memorial.

This time, two of Randall's sisters came for her and Gail, and Rebecca wanted to swing her arm out in defense. It was time to close the casket. It was time to take one last look. *Oh my God, she's gone.* Her heart cried out in a wail for her momma like she did when she was a little girl and had skinned her knee dancing on the concrete deck right outside their back door. Her body wracked as if suffering from violent dry heaves. This was not proper decorum, she heard the Madame say. She had to get herself together. She silently repented to God in her heart before her momma, and condemned what she now considered her past behavior, when she regained her breath.

She had always felt inferior, so small next to her mother. Now she felt flimsy, as if she had no backbone. Although being steadied by her attendant, she reached out for Gail, who was dabbing her eyes and shaking her head repeatedly. Together they spent what felt like eternity at the foot of the Madame. Now their time had come to an end.

When Rebecca looked up she saw Will from the pulpit platform, nodding his head, telling her in that gesture that it would be okay. *Is it okay to feel cheated?* She felt she needed more time with the Madame to fully understand her mother and, in doing so, hopefully understand herself.

Rebecca suspected those revelations would come much later, as she took her seat. As they sealed the casket, she told herself the sting of death would be swallowed up in victory—her victory. She would be victorious once she redesigned her life.

Chapter 5

Will didn't know how his father did it. How did he make himself so available to others? Will was mentally and physically exhausted. He was relieved that his duty day was officially done. With only a few left in the multipurpose room, he was ready to decompress. He had done it, been charge minister for his first funeral, the mother of all funerals. Earlier, he had taken a text from the Bible, evoked the Spirit, and preached a eulogy befitting royalty. Then, he and his father had driven behind the family car along the Madame's final ride, or tour of important places in her life, before serving the last rites over the casket at the cemetery. They arrived back to the church multipurpose room to a hearty repast meal and a line that seemed to go on for miles, where he was served alongside the bereaved family and other clergy. He felt proud almost to the point of celebration, but then he remembered the occasion, remembered the family.

So many faces were in and out all day. He had to have talked to every single one like his father did when he was in charge. Out of all the people he had seen that day he only saw one face. He felt only one heart so keenly. He had played the tailor trying to mend the broken pieces for her, but now that he had hung up his minister hat with his black robe, he went looking for his friend to whom he had spoken in front of an audience, but not specifically one on one. He could have sworn Rebecca had taken off in the direction of the rear bathrooms possibly to avoid another good-bye kiss, another hug, another "I'm sorry." He excused himself also when he could break away. He walked the back hallway headed in what he hoped was her direction.

He leaned on the wall between the male and female restrooms for a while, hoping to catch her on the way out. He wanted to call out her name but didn't want to startle her. Then he heard a faint voice, and then a second one, a couple of doors down. He righted himself and walked in that direction. Will wasn't prepared to find Rebecca in the window frame of a small classroom with a man. Their backs were to him. She was staring straight ahead at a view that had to be the extended grounds of her own backyard. The man was behind her, whispering something in her ear. Will wondered if he should just turn away because clearly they were having a moment, but he stood there, trying to decipher the scene.

The man whispered, and Rebecca nodded. She didn't appear to be in distress. It didn't occur to Will that maybe she had a boyfriend who would naturally come and be with her in her time of need. *But where was he during the service?* Only when the man removed his hand from its comfortable resting place on her waist and turned to leave did Will recognize the man as Randall Hughes. Will couldn't believe it. *This joker is on the clock and still trying to put the mack down.* Not that a fairly decent-looking jock like him had to rely on charm or sensitivity, but, at this time, in this church, with his friend? Really? On second thought, Will considered from their cozy stance, Randall and Rebi may have had a previous relationship. Maybe she had kept in touch with Randall after she left Easton.

Will did not immediately yield the way for Randall's curt exit when the pair noticed him gawking in the doorway. Will just nodded his acknowledgment of the town's funeral director once eye contact was made.

"Pastor Will." Randall extended his hand as a greeting and closing. "Great job today."

"Thanks, man, I guess I should say the same for you. Please carry my appreciation to your family for handling everything *professionally*." Will's eyes were on Rebi, who appeared to be feeling for another inch of fabric at the end of her dress. Returning his attention to Randall, he added, "I guess I'll take over from here. I'm sure you'll keep this family in your prayers."

There was nothing left to be said among any of them at that moment. A strange silence remained after Randall left. Rebecca turned to face him with a slight smile and her arms folded across her chest.

"I was . . ." they both said almost simultaneously.

The silence returned. She signaled with her clutch bag for him to go first.

He took a temporary seat on one of the rectangular tables. "I was heading out soon and hadn't gotten a chance to talk to you. My dad is ready to go home and get some rest, and a long nap could do me some good too. We got Deacon Contee locking up."

"Yeah, I'm sure Gail's ready to go too, but she's got Milo," Rebecca said, shrugging her shoulders.

There was that pause again. This was so unlike them. Their chattiness was usually incessant, but he attributed it to the occasion. At least for him, he was trying to avoid what he had witnessed—what he really wanted to say.

"How about you, you cool?" Will asked.

"Yeah, yep, I'll be fine," Rebecca replied a little too quickly. She let her head rest back on her neck and expelled a breath of air. "This has just been the longest day of my life."

"Unfortunately, you'll feel the gravity of it for a while. You know that I know firsthand. Each day gets easier." He let that settle in. He didn't want to regurgitate his sermon from earlier. "You need to get out though. Don't stay cooped up in that house. We've got to get together, get caught up; that is, if you can spare some time for an old friend."

"Definitely, just tell me when and where," Rebecca said, rocking back and forth on her heels before crossing one foot over the other and then back. She was one constant motion.

"That would depend on when you're heading home." He threw it back in her court. He didn't know why, but he desperately wanted to get on her calendar before Randall Hughes did.

She ran her hand through her mane. Her eyes were everywhere but on him. "I'm here for a while, at least until the estate hearing, I don't know, maybe longer."

He didn't know what to make of her ambiguity, but he was delighted nonetheless. *Could she really be thinking of relocating back to the area?* "I'll call you next week."

"Cool," she said, slowly making her way to the door.

He knew he should bring the conversation to a close. They both had people waiting for them, but there was something still bugging him.

"So, Randall Hughes, huh? Let me find out you're quite the cougar," Will chided.

"Excuse me?" Rebecca stopped, frowning as if she had just been insulted.

"It's a term people use now, meaning you're dating someone younger," he explained.

"I know what it means, Will. He's a former class-mate of ours, remember—a fellow Guardian? He was the first familiar face I saw when I came home. I went straight to the funeral parlor. He helped me . . . cope," she defended herself.

"No, I totally get that," Will said, putting a hand up as a white flag. "I was kidding. We're just talking right?"

She nodded her head. They both paused to examine each other's unspoken language. He reached out his hand awkwardly but let it rest on his knee, where his fingertips tapped out time.

After a minute passed she asked, "Do you have something against Randall?"

Will thought about that question and had to check his own intentions. He just wanted to make sure no one took advantage of her. "Naw, Randall and I are cool. Death is a part of life, so I see him around here quite often. I can't say it's ever in the pews on Sunday morning though." This time he shrugged. "And when I'm out and about, I rarely see him alone. He's usually with a woman named Shelia, the espresso girl down at Starbucks."

"This is just weird, 'cause I don't know if you're coming at me like my buddy Will, who obviously can't fathom that a guy like Randall would be really inter-ested in me, or moral advisor Will, who is this minister now."

Will thought about what she said. They weren't six-teen anymore when she ran every teenaged crush by him. Once again, he couldn't understand the strain in their conversation, but attributed it to the lateness of the hour. He decided to lighten the mood real quick. "My bad. I guess this wouldn't be a good time to invite you back to hear me preach. Let's start over," he said, extending his hand to her for a handshake. "Hi, I'm

Will Donovan, assistant pastor at Grace Apostle Methodist Church. Come join us every Sunday morning at eleven A.M. where I guarantee you won't have to worry about judgment. Just join the rest of our congregation in jubilant praise for Jesus," he said in his best commercial announcer voice. Will was pleased when Rebecca dropped her head and chuckled.

"I will certainly have to do that, maybe not this Sunday—you know, the day after tomorrow—but soon. I want to tell you, though, you did an amazing job earlier. I was so nervous for you in the beginning. I was like, why won't Pastor Donovan get up and save you? Oh my goodness, Will, I was shocked. You can preach. A couple of times I wanted to shout, 'You go, boy!'"

"Is this from my buddy Rebi, who obviously only views me as an awkward geek, and would therefore be shocked and amazed when I spoke and didn't sound like a bumbling idiot or . . ." He paused.

"My bad, okay, I guess we're even now." She swatted at him. "Can we go?"

He reached out for her arm and held it to halt her exit. "I am your buddy just looking out for you as always. I just need to say, though, that there are some guys around here who may view you as this attractive and available heiress now, and go on the hunt."

"Heiress? C'mon now, Will. We own a well, not an oil well. That's the misconception in this town: the Lucas women must be stuck up because we have so much." She backed up slightly, forcing him to release his hold. "Would it be so bad to get a couple of dates? I think I can take care of myself."

"I know, and I'm not saying that. People around here can be a trip. Sometimes"—he paused—"we don't know we've been used until we have given too much of ourselves away. Just be careful."

There, I've said my piece, he thought. Will knew what he saw in Randall's eye when he turned to leave Rebecca's side. Randall's hungry eyes had spawned from pure lust. The fact that Randall was hired by her family to do a job but was all over her was still eating at him. He'd feel like a fake as a friend and a minister if he didn't call it like he saw it. Will watched her sigh heavily while biting repeatedly on her bottom lip. He was as ready to go now as she had been earlier in the conversation. All he wanted to do was steal away with her for a moment and make sure she was okay. In some strange way he felt as if he had done just that.

Chapter 6

Rebecca awoke past noon to the sound of a ringing telephone. It had been so peaceful the first few days after the funeral. It had taken a moment for Rebecca to re-adjust to the symphony of insects outside her door and the virtual blackout without streetlamps. She stayed up until ungodly hours. In the dark, she thought about her mother. When she did drift off, she got her sleep on the back end of the morning where she could hear evidence of human existence in the distance, and it was light enough to make out a path to the bathroom. She was re-lieved that the phone had stopped ringing. For a minute she felt a rush of panic in thinking that maybe it was her job wanting to know when she would be returning, but she didn't have an answer for them.

She had spent the last six years at Sanz, Mitchum,& Clarke where she was a paralegal. She reported directly to Anthony Jacobs, a junior associate attorney at the firm. She loved working with him although she had been nothing more than a glorified secretary at first. He was young, overzealous; he did a lot of his own leg work. Rebecca had noticed that a lot of the other at-torneys didn't take him seriously. He was brilliant, but lacked self-confidence to be a real impact player for the firm. She began to dole out advice for everything from skincare to presentation skills. He'd come to value her opinion so much so that he loosened his reins and delegated the kind of substantive legal work for which she was trained.

Recently she had been pulled from Mr. Jacobs, summoned personally by Kenny Burke further up on the totem pole, at least in Burke's mind. He had his own team. He seemed to also have his own agenda that went beyond the docketing, calendaring, and other trial prep assignments he threw her way. It was a blessing for her to get away from there. *Maybe I could leave the Eastern shore permanently if I had the money to do it.* Living at the Madame's home awhile made perfect sense to her; and maybe after the Madame's estate was settled she would see the world.

This time when the phone rang again both Rebecca and Gail met in the kitchen and huddled around the offensive cordless device off its base.

"Go ahead, Auntie, answer it, but if it's my job tell them I'm busy, grieving, or have gone out to handle some of Momma's business," Rebecca instructed while making an about-face toward the kitchen cupboard. She knew the contents of the refrigerator were the same leftovers ordered or dropped off before the funeral. Nothing remotely resembled breakfast food.

"Sounds like there is a story behind that big fat lie," Gail said, following her. "Spill it."

"There is no story," Rebecca answered coyly.

"Well then you can answer the phone." Although Gail was nearing the end of her leave from the local ophthalmologist office where she was the receptionist, she was fully clothed as if she were off to work. "I got my own line, and I'm not screening your calls. Between here and the office I don't have time to get caught up in your drama. As much as I love having you here, I know that you are most certainly running from something."

"Like you're running from Milo?" was the first thing that traveled the pipeline from Rebecca's mind to her mouth.

"If I'm running, he's running right alongside me." She smirked. She returned to her already marked place at the buffet counter with her coffee mug and newspaper.

"Exactly." Rebecca sighed in relief when the phone stopped ringing.

"The man has been married before," Gail offered as a reasonable explanation.

"Yeah," Rebecca said, circling her hand at the wrist as if to ask, "and?" "But now he's not, Auntie."

"First off, I'm not your auntie, and secondly, I'm not fast to be any man's second anything. He and I both have an understanding."

Rebecca thought about Gail's logic. "Are you sure you both have an understanding, or is it just your conclusion?"

"Girl, close your mouth and mind your business," Gail demanded. "You've always been a smug little thing. I keep telling people he and I are friends, just like you and your friend, um, you and, um, Will, like you and Pastor Will."

Some friend, Rebecca thought. He hadn't called, and neither had Randall for that matter. She couldn't stop thinking about what Will had said to her shortly after the funeral. *"Sometimes we don't know we are being used until we've given too much of ourselves away."* Did Will know she had already given herself to Randall? She realized that she could hope and pray that Randall would come around, that he would want something more with her than just sex, but there would be no more trysts.

Rebecca knew if she spent another week in the house when her cousin returned to work she would go crazy. Hadn't she preferred to be alone in Salisbury, perpetually playing the part of the new girl around town? In Easton, she was a true local. She was supposed to know everyone and have friends in place. To be friendless was to be lonesome. There wasn't much else to do. *No wonder the Madame busied herself with club meetings, and Gail consumes her free time with her "friend" Milo,* she thought.

The phone rang. Once again she was led to the phone by curiosity and maybe even hope that it was either Will or Randall. She viewed the caller ID. True to her word, Gail didn't even respond. The number was marked from Talbot County. Once again she chose to ignore it.

Rebecca saw promise in a jar of peanut butter amid random canned goods and a miniature bottle of Chivas Regal Scotch. She wondered if the alcohol was meant to be hidden or just misplaced in the cupboard, but there it would stay. She grabbed the jar and a spoon from the drawer to carve out a wad of the peanut butter, and began licking it as if it were ice cream.

"I miss Anya," Rebecca said, faintly remembering the small, polite nanny-cook-maid they used to employ for a good five or six years when Rebecca was growing up. "Why did she leave us?"

"She was let go."

"I remembered Mrs. Pritchett stirring up a fuss about a black family hiring black help, or at least that was what Nina taunted me about, as if we were modern-day slave owners." *She didn't even get into what she insinuated about the then four women who lived together under the roof of a woman named Madame,* Rebecca thought. "Maybe that had something to do with it."

"I always wondered why, myself, but I doubt your mother was swayed by anything Nancy Pritchett said or wrote in that newspaper of hers. Anya was a perfect fit for this family. After she left, it was either peanut butter or the Madame's culinary treats." Gail chuckled.

"We ordered out a lot, didn't we?" Rebecca said, catching Gail's facetiousness. *The Madame's cooking was a shame.*

"Yes, we most certainly did," Gail agreed, "until I took to the kitchen and answering phones, but that day is done for a while."

Rebecca wondered at that moment about their futures. What was going to happen to them? She also thought about her mother's house and how much it would go for on the open market. *Surely, the Madame left me the house,* Rebecca thought, *but what about Gail?* She vowed she wouldn't sham her in the deal. She had to continue to provide a home for her cousin even if it meant renting out the rest of the house for a monthly income. If only she could get her cousin to see Milo as marriage material. The man had been courting her since the early nineties. Either way, she figured, Gail would be okay.

Rebecca stared at her ornery cousin in disbelief. Gail didn't even look her way until Rebecca asked, "What are we going to eat?"

Gail just stared at Rebecca with an arched brow of indignation before dropping her head back down to her paper. She didn't feel persuaded to dignify the question with an answer.

"What about the other workers with the grounds crew? Am I supposed to tend to the yard now as well?"

"We did retain one guy who mows," Gail said.

Rebecca remembered the excitement she felt when Mr. Leon and the grounds crew would come to work.

He had a massive riding mower that glided across the yard like a prehistoric hovercraft. She had fleeting memories of being a silly teenage girl, fantasizing that any one of the often shirtless crewmen left to trim and hedge would find her staring from the window above, and volunteer to escort her to one of her school dances or, better yet, fall in love and carry her far, far away. She'd fantasize so much at that window that the collective aroma of fresh-cut grass would assault her nostrils and spur an allergic reaction.

It occurred to Rebecca that maybe the Madame's money was dwindling. The thought of her mother cooking, cleaning for herself, and answering her own calls gave credence to her fears.

"Remember when the Madame wanted to answer the phone especially when she thought it was too late or too early for a call?" Rebecca laughed to keep her mind from the possibility of returning to her own life, where she managed to scrape by as if she were living on skid row.

"Did you realize you have called my residence on a Sunday?" Gail imitated in the Madame's brash tone. "Now I don't know your day of worship or the reverence you pay to your Lord and Savior, but do not call my house again."

"And they wouldn't," Rebecca said amid her amusement. "Ooh, I got one."

The phone rang before Rebecca could proceed with her impersonation. On the way to the phone she dropped her spoon, licked clean, into the sink with the other dishes piled high and awaiting cleansing. It was the same official county number.

Rebecca and Gail looked at one another. Rebecca gestured that she would handle it. *Madame style.* She figured they wouldn't stop calling until she started answering the phone. With her greeting, she knew that she didn't have enough moxie to dismiss the caller straight away.

"May I speak to Ava Lucas?" the caller asked.

"I'm sorry to inform you, but Ms. Lucas is now deceased." Rebecca was curt and it actually hurt a little to put it so plainly. "May I ask who is calling?"

"Mr. Earl Clip. Maybe there is a next of kin I can speak to, someone who would have interest in the land marked at 5920 Zion Hill Road, like a child or spouse?"

Who is this guy? He had enough moxie for the both of them.

"I am her daughter, but before you continue, you must agree the timing of your call is mighty insensitive. She hasn't been dead over a week yet. Let me get back to you at my earliest convenience. Then we can discuss any business you may have had with Mother," Rebecca added. She wondered if she wanted to deal with the brusque man at all. First order of business was to call Madame's lawyer. Could this be about an outstanding debt? On second thought, Rebecca needed to know what was going on. She detested surprises. She considered for the moment that she may need backup, so she placed the phone on speaker so Gail could listen in.

"Can you tell me if her estate has gone into probate?" Mr. Clip asked.

"Oh no, he didn't," Gail said, forgetting she could be heard.

"Sir, what is this in regard to?" Rebecca pressed.

"An access road has been proposed to run parallel between Zion Hill Road and Church Road."

"An access road?" Rebecca stalled to get her bearings. She tried to visualize just where this strip of land ran along their property line. In her estimation that would place this proposed road somewhere between

her backyard and the back of Grace Apostle. She wondered if Will or his father entertained a similar call.

"Yes, ma'am, a road will affect part of Ms. Lucas's
property. The county, as well as a few neighbors representing a third party, are interested in preserving a
graveyard that sits southwest of the rear egress of Ms.
Lucas's property."

"In the past people would just cut through the Wiggins plot without any problem to get to that old graveyard," Gail shared.

Rebecca sliced her hand through the air to indicate
to Gail to cut further comments, feeling that they had
already given Mr. Clip enough free unsolicited infor-
mation. All this sounded vaguely familiar to her. The
graveyard via Wiggins Way was a popular make-out
spot.

Mr. Clip cleared his throat as a reminder he was still
on the line. "No agreement was made with the present owners farther south. This road will eliminate that
type of arrangement. The county wants an official and
permanent route to this graveyard. Several documents
sent certified mail have been sent to your residence in
this regard requiring immediate action."

"Papers?" Rebecca asked, trying to digest what had
been said.

"That might be what the Madame had left lying
around. I think I moved them to the den or her office to prepare for guests," Gail chimed in. "But, she
was always adamant about her land. The Madame
always said they couldn't stand a black woman to have
anything in this county, and now this. People came
snooping out back from the county a few years back.
Next thing you know it's legal to put a water meter on a
private well we've operated for years. They surely don't
help to maintain it, but they get their share of the rev-

enue. She nearly had a fit. You can't tell me the stress of fighting that one didn't take her out of here."

It was futile to ask Gail to calm down. Rebecca could tell all the sentiments held by her mother were shared by her only niece. With a few charades-like motions, Rebecca sent Gail on her way to go find the papers. "Could you give me a minute, Mr. Clip?" She didn't wait for an answer before taking the phone off the speaker function.

Rebecca was thinking like a lawyer. Probate law went hand in hand with real estate law. Her present job made her more familiar with the codes of the latter. It could take at least thirty days to open the estate publically for any debts and creditors to present themselves against the value. This was different. She couldn't see how this road could be an asset or a liability. She tried to figure out how it would fit into her plans though. She wondered if the government was willing to fund this project, which might include compensation for their contribution of land. *Who are these third parties now concerned with my space?* Maybe it was someone wealthy enough to make the pot sweeter if they gained access to their relatives' remains.

Gail came back with her arms extended to indicate that her brief search proved futile. Again, Rebecca felt she needed to talk to her mother's lawyer. There would be no more hiding out. She had business to take care of.

Rebecca picked the receiver back up. "Mr. Clip, I'm afraid I'm unprepared to speak to you about this matter at this time. Like I said, I'll have to get back to you at a more convenient time."

There was a pause that made Rebecca think for a second that Mr. Clip had simply hung up in frustration. Then he spoke, "There is a means to get the land. I don't know if you've heard of eminent domain? We've surveyed the land at the rear of your property, and I'd say you have a couple of unsafe structures you need us to take care of for you."

This time it was not his moxie, but sarcasm that spoke loudest to her. She had indeed heard of eminent domain. Now, she had to worry about the county condemning parts of the land deemed unsafe. Somehow she knew they would carve a bigger piece of the pie when servicing themselves.

Their home was an old abandoned horse farm. There were a number of structures on the three-acre spread that still remained on the perimeter of the property line for that purpose. All of the stables had been brought down long ago, and the Madame had warned them repeatedly to stay away from the old carriage house. Rebecca always imagined herself buried in a heap of lumber like the piles of wood left around from the old stables when she was adventurous enough to travel that far from the back porch. Why hadn't the Madame taken care of this? She really did have to be the groundskeeper now if she wanted to keep her land as a resource. She had to find someone to take care of that for her.

Either way she wasn't going to let Mr. Clip rile her. "I guess you'll be waiting like the rest of us until the estate hearing. Do me a favor though, don't call us, the family lawyer will call you." Then she hung up.

Chapter 7

Will picked up two recently delivered newspapers as he ascended the stairs in front of his childhood home. Situated at the edge of Easton, near Queen Anne's County, the house represented the first ministry lesson his father, William Henry Donovan Sr., had taught him: separate your church life from your home life. Will's dad often joked about living on the outskirts of town. In case the saints wanted to run him out of town he'd be closer to the Bay Bridge.

The church was the second home of the family anyway. There were nights Will remembered him and his dad camping out in one of the classrooms for fun. Then other nights his father would work so late on church or school projects that his mom would come get Will, leaving his father to work and eventually sleep on the couch in his pastor's study.

Lately, it seemed as if his father didn't have the same zeal for ministry, delegating certain tasks or turning over complete responsibility for other tasks to Will or other church members. Will was supposed to oversee everything after just a year of becoming pastoral assistant. After fifty years of ministry, Will wondered if his father could be ready to retire. The thought sobered Will. He didn't think the years growing up in church, the sixteen years since giving his life to Christ, or the four and a half years since he accepted his call to ministry and studied for his ordination was enough time to fill W.H. Donovan's shoes. As far as Will was concerned, his dad had to shake off this funk he was in and give Will more time to be a student. That was part of what he wanted to talk to his father about today. As he approached the door he felt that familiar anxiety he felt ever since his mom died. He knocked hard on the front door before using his key.

"Hello," Will bellowed to make sure his voice carried throughout the rambler. He idled at the door, waiting for a reply from his dad. He looked around the beige and blue interior of the living room, which had been untouched since his childhood. He looked at his watch, which read a quarter until eleven A.M. He called again when he didn't get an immediate response. "Dad?" Any other child would have ambled through the door, especially with their own key to gain access, but not Will. Every time, he had to mentally prepare himself to move from the foyer. Make himself push past closed doors—make himself stop looking for clues that something was gravely wrong. He had to stop imagining finding another parent dead. This time he wouldn't have his dad, hospice care workers, or members from the church around to shield his discovery.

Why hadn't he called first? Will walked across the front room. He'd have much preferred his dad's welcoming greeting than to deal with this anxiety of not knowing how he would find him. He thought about consulting someone for his unusual fear. Maybe seek out his therapist from adolescence the hospice social worker had suggested for him shortly after his mother's death. Pride had been a factor, but not his own. When his dad turned down that offer, stating, "He's a man; he's all right," he knew he had to be. The truth was that today he wanted to catch his father off guard and really see what he was doing on his little sabbatical away

from the church. He heard a sound from the direction
of his dad's bedroom. He didn't know whether it was
a grunt, snore, or moan, but it was a sign of the living.

"Why didn't you answer me, old man?" Will said,
barging into his father's stark white and airy bedroom
that was stripped and painted by volunteers at church.
His father chose white. It was hard for any of them to
imagine color after his mom passed, Will thought. His
father was still in bed, covered to the neck with a sheet
and a thin blanket.

"You'll be old one day. I hope you remember how
you've mocked me," his father muttered, registering
more amusement than disagreement.

"Why are you still asleep, Pop?" Will asked, taking a
seat at the foot of his dad's sleigh bed.

Pastor Donovan shed the layers by tossing the covers
in Will's direction. He took his time sitting up on the
opposite side of where his son was sitting.

To Will's surprise, his father was clothed in a tank
top and trousers held up by suspenders, as if he'd been
lying in wait for the alarm to sound so he could slide
down the pole and start his day.

"I've been up to take my medicines." His father
shuffled around to the side of the bed Will sat on. He
swatted at Will's knees to tell him to get up before he
bent down to get his slippers.

Will couldn't help but think his dad reminded him
of Redd Foxx's portrayal of Fred Sanford. It appeared
that his dad had lost bone density overnight. Will compared his dad's height to his own five foot nine frame.
His dad seemed shorter, more bent over. In the pulpit,
his dad was the tallest man on earth. He watched more
intently as his dad found his plaid robe on the chair and
tied it in front of him after putting it on. If Senior was
Fred Sanford then that made him Lamont, he thought,

following his incredible shrinking dad into the front room, the spot where he entertained company. Will became more concerned.

"Do you know what time it is?" Will asked.

"No, why don't you tell me, son," his dad said, not bothering to look back as he made his way.

"It's past morning prayer and well into the first session," Will said, referring to Grace Apostle's school schedule.

"You're missing it then, if you are here bothering me," his dad said.

They both had a way of taking the bite out of sarcasm. Their banter was always peppered with harmless stabs at one another.

Will's patience with his father's indifference boiled over. He raised his voice to the octave of amazement. "You're missing it, Dad. That's just it. You're the chancellor. In the past missing any kind of time with those kids would have killed you."

They reached the front room and his dad plopped down in his favorite recliner for emphasis. "This is what time off looks like—freedom. That includes freedom to sleep in when you feel like it."

Will couldn't help but notice his dad didn't look free. His eyes held a vacancy. Will's eyes bounced between his dad's chair and the television set that he would automatically turn on when they entered the room. He tried to follow his father's gaze across the room. First, he thought his dad was looking at where Will's eyes always rested when he entered this room. Will loved the Olan Mills portrait of their family of three. His mom's hair was full of curls, his dad's lip was loaded with a thick moustache that tapered around his mouth into a full beard, and Will had a mouth full of missing teeth.

His dad wasn't staring at their likenesses, but rather he was fixed on a focal point Will could not see.

"Dad, you know I'm not ready. Barely a week's notice, I can't hold up a pillar or a plank of wood let alone your mantle," Will said, stroking the back of his ear between his fingers for comfort. Will saw his dad's eyes come to life as he pressed forward in his chair.

"Lift the bloodstained banner, son. Don't try to emulate me. What do the kids say nowadays? Do you. I know you think you're not ready. You have always had the annoying habit of downplaying your abilities. You're more than capable."

Will sighed at his dad's vow of confidence. His dad had always been an amazing encourager, but Will didn't want to be encouraged to take over. Ministry was not yet his entire life. He had a job. He had things he wanted to do before being tied to the church. Once again, he thought of his dad's departure from ministry. He had seen others who left their passion behind only to go broke, go crazy, or go meet their Maker shortly after retirement. He needed his dad. "My capabilities didn't stop Bible Study from running amok," Will said.

"Bible Study?"

"It wasn't my finest hour." Will sat on the couch and grabbed the remote from the coffee table, but didn't turn the television on. "I mean no one listens, at least not to me. Are they there to extrapolate on their own ideas or learn what the Word of God says?"

"They don't listen to you 'cause you use words like extrapolate." His dad smirked.

"The truth gets lost, Father," Will said, aiming the remote at his father as if to turn off his last comment. "Mrs. Sylvester and her clique were out last night. I hate to say it, but that is exactly what they are. They didn't come for Bible Study. They came to gossip and talk all over everybody else."

His dad shook his head. "I hope you called them out."

With both hands up and out for guidance, Will asked, "How do you do that exactly? She was my Sunday School teacher. I assumed she knew the Word a little bit better than she does, and she is old enough to be my mother."

"God doesn't need your assumptions. He needs your discernment," his dad remarked. "Meet people where they are and He'll meet you. Where were the brothers?"

"I don't know. Contee is overwhelmed with the responsibility of supervising the school, and the majority of them are apparently taking a break from the Word until you come back."

"Wow," his dad said, pushing himself up in his chair.

"The ladies were on one last night, just plain rude, Pop. I welcomed a new member who made it out for the first time. I brought her over to meet them. I thought she might be a good fit for the Pastor Aide committee. They just told her to leave them her name and number and they'd get back to her." Will shook his head in disbelief. "And Veronica is becoming one of them."

His dad chuckled at the reference. "One of them?"

"A church lady, you know . . ." Will said, failing to put into words exactly what he meant.

"Now Veronica, I'll bet, they'll let in their little club," his dad added.

Will nodded his head in agreement. *Veronica has her own club.* She palled around with a few women their age including Nina Pritchett, who apparently had had a volatile situation at her house with her husband that same night. He failed to share that with his dad because he sent Deacon Contee in his stead. Veronica didn't want Will to go because, as she put it, "the situation doesn't call for rhetoric and reasoning, but rather brawn in case that Negro gets out of hand with my girl."

He took a blow to his ego, but he stayed in prayer at church after Bible Study was over. When Will had asked Deacon Contee whether it was a domestic dispute, the deacon had replied, "Yeah, but I think it was her going upside his head rather than the other way around."

Will reflected on his own girlfriend, Veronica. She was much like the other church ladies in leadership at Grace Apostle. She had a bossy assertiveness hidden under her docile and friendly manner. He found this was her way of winning allies and aligning herself with where she wanted to be. She didn't know the difference between the church house and the boardroom sometimes.

He remembered when he'd met her in his second year of graduate school at Morgan State University. They were both interested in getting a jump on the job market and spent a considerable amount of time at the career counseling center. They were introduced by one of the advisors who sought to find them employment in their fields back home upon graduation.

After going to college "Big Willie" style, the pastor's kid was in culture shock and tried to shake his nerdy past and partied his way into barely passable grades. His father informed him that if he lost his scholarships, he'd be the one footing the bill for his education. Will took the threat seriously and recovered enough to get his grades up to par by his undergraduate graduation.

Veronica had been to two different universities before settling on Morgan. She'd transferred in the last two years of her undergraduate program then stayed in Baltimore to finish the MBA program. She was intent on leaving with the duality of a degree and a similar sign of commitment and dedication from a potential husband. To him, she was attractive and single. That's all he needed to know. Not for shallow reasons, but for a man who spent the last three and a half years shut off from the rest of the campus party life, in the library, and on the dean's list, he was furiously lonely. So many girls at school were willing to be temporary loans, but he was overdue for a girlfriend. She was a shining option. She in turn latched on to him after putting him through a twelve-point inspection and finding out that they were both shorebirds, driven and headed to the same side of bridge after graduation. It made sense for them to be together.

Studying for the MCAT medical school entrance exam, which he never took, and his eventual call to ministry, which led him into another round of studies, helped him to evade marriage. Each time he had a change in career plans, Veronica shook the Etch A Sketch of life and designed a new vision of their lives together. He had not proposed to her, although her move to Easton last year implied they were at the threshold, at least in her mind. He knew it would be the topic of their relationship review she seemed to orchestrate every New Year's Day shortly after Watch Night service. He had three months. Quite frankly, he didn't think getting married would be a bad idea now, especially if he was expected to go into ministry full time. A pastor needed someone to take care of him.

"You have the heart, but not the stomach for ministry, son. There is nothing new under the sun. Sin is ugly and flaws are magnified in our eyes so we can help God's people, but we got to lead," his dad said, reaching down to stroke his legs with his hand as an indication his legs were getting stiff on him. "And as far as Sister Sylvester and her clique, as you call it, you should have

just gotten Veronica on them for you. She's the assertive one. She would have set them straight."

"Veronica doesn't have to handle a thing for me,"
Will snapped.

"Must have snagged a nerve," his father said, turning as far as he could in Will's direction that his chair
would allow. "Why are you getting so upset, son?"

"I didn't come over to talk about her or even Bible
Study anyway. I came to find out what is really going
on with you, Pop. When are you coming back to the
church, the pulpit, the school? And, I am not accepting
'never' as a reply. How's that for assertive?"

His dad's eyes were back on the invisible focal point.
Will wasn't allowing his father to zone out. Will got up
from his spot on the couch and crouched in front of his
dad to block his dad's stare.

His dad shook his head several times before sighing
heavily. "I haven't been feeling well lately."

Will struggled to keep his balance. If anything could
have arrested him it was those exact words. He'd rather
hear that his dad had grown tired of ornery saints and
was ready to give it all up. Hadn't his mother offered
the same explanation to explain her sudden coughing
spells that turned out to be the lung cancer that killed
her?

"How so?" Will asked in a low voice.

"Sometimes I get these dizzy spells. My equilibrium
is all messed up. I think it's called vertigo."

Will stood to take the strain off his legs. "You think?
If you're dizzy all the time, I can't imagine how you're
getting around or driving to the store for your favorite
ice cream. Have you gone to the doctor?"

Why am I just hearing about this? Talking about
flaws, he knew his dad was prideful. The thing about
pride is that it blinds a person from seeing it as a sin.

His dad didn't allow too many people in his circle, and he allowed even fewer to actually help him. He definitely showed a particular disdain for doctors since his wife's illness. This worried Will. He could just imagine his father suffering in silence, hoping to pray it away.

"Beginning of fall, Dr. Tompkins usually goes on vacation, and I refuse to see anyone else."

"C'mon, Pop, do you hear yourself? How do you know for sure Dr. Tompkins is out if you don't call?" Will looked down on his father as if to reprimand him. "You're telling me you're dizzy, but don't want to get immediate help? What if you collapse somewhere?"

"I think I'm coming down with the gout or something. Maybe that's why my balance is off, particularly in the mornings. It will eventually go away."

Will was no doctor, but he knew that the gout wasn't something you come down with. It had a rapid onslaught and rarely was diagnosed beforehand. It became all too clear that either his father was a hypochondriac or his illness was not a physical one. He didn't dare accuse his dad of lying though.

"Which one is it, Pop? 'Cause I'm thinking I need to take you to the hospital right now." Will served up his ultimatum from the armrest of the couch facing his dad's chair. "I want to go with you the next time you go to the doctors. I can't help you if I don't know what is going on."

"It's a combination of the two. I'm just tired." His dad rubbed his face from apparent exasperation with Will's badgering. "I just need a break."

"How long?" Will asked. He felt like he did last night with Sister Sylvester. How long did he ignore the behavior and hope it would correct itself? "It's only right to tell your congregation, to tell the people you put in place to serve in the interim."

"A month," his dad said in a pseudo-confident tone meant to pacify him.

His mother always told him his greatest asset was his namesake—his will. He was told he had the power to make good decisions, go after his dreams, and choose right over wrong. He and his father shared the same name. Will hoped his father had the will to choose his old life of service to the ministry over his new indifference.

Chapter 8

Rebecca pushed send on a reply to what could only be considered a sext, or text heavily laden with sexual innuendos, from Randall. She never thought she'd be in a position to turn him down. He was so carelessly available and dangerously good-looking. Apparently death had taken the day off, and he wanted her to come over right away. She suggested they go out later, but he wanted to stay in. He wanted her, and that was exciting to her. Like Monica Lewinsky's infamous dress, she wanted to keep the text as proof. *It has been a week and two days.* She wasn't sure with each passing day that she didn't want him to make good on his promises of pleasure. Therefore, she did nothing to persuade or dissuade him. She just told him that she had made previous lunch plans with her best friend. It came down to him or Will.

She pulled her sunglasses away from her eyes and up on her forehead. For the first time in weeks she didn't want to shade her eyes when she went out. She wanted to feel the stark contrast of the sun on her face as opposed to the warm dim lighting at home. She felt as if she had been indoors forever.

Will had let her pick the meeting spot, suggesting everything from their favorite burger joint from back in the day, Juicy's, which was no more than a drive-in, to the very quaint and expensive restaurants in and around Saint Michaels island. Rebecca wanted to be in the center of town with the local scene. She had been away too long.

She had put a modern interpretation on the Madame's belted color-block dress, paired with a denim jacket and knee-high black boots, and was out the door just twenty minutes after receiving Will's call. She spotted Will sitting at a window booth as she pulled into the Applebee's lot. She parked quickly and told the hostess that she would be joining her party already seated. A chubby waitress who trailed Rebecca up the narrow aisle assured Rebecca that she'd be with them in a minute. Will stood when he saw Rebecca approaching.

"Have you been waiting long?" Rebecca asked.

"No, I just got here, actually," Will said.

They fell into an easy hug at his invitation. She immediately noticed his delicious earthy scent. He broke the embrace quickly and held her away from him as if to examine her. He mouthed the word "wow," and she surprised herself by giggling while waving off his obvious compliment. She smoothed the wisps of hair up toward her ponytail. She had been excavating the Madame's closet when he called, but suddenly wished she had let her hair hang loose. He extended his hand for her to sit opposite him before taking his seat.

"I guess you're no longer Bush Ball Becky," Will said.

"Forget you, Will." She remembered he had at least thirty nicknames for her. "So how've you been?"

"Well, and you?" Will replied.

"I'm all right," Rebecca said, squeezing the lemon wedge into the glass of water that was waiting for her.

"So, what have you been doing?" he asked.

She knew he was a great listener, and she needed a sounding board about what had been occupying her mind lately. "We've officially delved into my mother's estate."

"Wow, okay." He took his water glass and gulped half of it without the straw. His hand remained on the glass.

"We figured we might as well get all this legal stuff out the way." She didn't know how much she wanted to share with him about Mr. Clip and his call about the access road that was the catalyst for examining the estate. "The hardest part is going to be packing up the Madame's stuff. Although, I must admit, I'm finding great pleasure in playing dress-up in my mother's closet, something she would have never allowed me to do growing up."

"I'm glad you're at least enjoying parts of the process," Will said.

"It's the only part I am enjoying. We went down to the county courthouse to file the petition. Gail doesn't realize it, but it's a good thing I'm here to help her." Rebecca took a sip of water to wash down her growing resentment. She felt herself morphing into her alter ego, Weary. *Maybe it's just being around Will.* "Ironically, Gail was named the family representative who is responsible for the administration of everything. So this whole thing is going to move to her timetable. She's back at work now, but there are steps she has to handle."

Rebecca thought surely Gail had seen the Madame's will. The fact that she was keeping it a secret was suspicious. It left a strain on the house.

"She won't let me do things for her. I'm the one who works in the legal arena. I can explain things, but I hear her calling Mr. Tremaine, my mother's lawyer, for advice. I don't know what's up with that. She did mention something about the church. I don't know if Grace was mentioned in the will itself. Have you heard anything?"

Will wrinkled his forehead and did his signature tug on his earlobe. "No, I haven't heard a thing. Barely know a thing. I got sermons and lesson plans to write while I'm taking over for my dad."

"Where is your dad going?" Rebecca wondered.

"He said he wanted a month off. Can you believe that? A month, I shouldn't have agreed with that." Will shook his head in retrospect. "I let Deacon Contee deal with the administrative stuff, so he might know something. I found out early I need a tag team partner."

Rebecca wasn't used to him complaining and felt the need to encourage him. "It's good you get the experience of running the church, right?"

"Yeah, I guess." One more shot and Will's water was depleted. "So, it's probably good that you and Gail divide the tasks with your mother's estate. Gail will eventually see that. Madame Ava loved Gail like a daughter. They were a diehard team after you left. "

That's right, Gail was the one who stayed and obeyed, Rebecca was reminded.

"Well, if she would let me see the notice of administration, at least, I'll have a better idea of what I'm . . . I mean, what we are working with."

They both looked around as if to summon their waitress. Each candy-striped worker was busy with another table. She didn't fear running out of things to say with Will, but she at least thought they would be on appetizers before they started another topic.

"How's Veronica?" she inquired with an arched brow that suggested she wanted all the details. "I think it is so cute that you have a girlfriend."

This time his brow went north. "Cute? C'mon now, fix that up."

"I mean I'm happy for you." Rebecca swatted at him. "So, tell me, does she have your heart?"

Rebecca was desperate to know what that looked and felt like.

He looked as if he was giving her comment great consideration. "God has my heart."

Rebecca pursed her lips together and sighed heavily. "That goes without saying, Will. I get that you're a pastor now. You were also our valedictorian and probably a summa cum laude graduate. Pre med, right? You know full well what I mean when I ask does the woman have your heart."

"All right, to answer your question, she's getting there." He laughed. "I sort of got diverted on my career path through medical school though when God put the call on my life."

"You're not the only one who got diverted," she shared.

"Really? Miss Pre Law?" Will sat back and placed one arm on the backrest. "You said you worked in the legal field, right?"

"I do. I'm a paralegal. I took the easy way out, Will. I got a BS in liberal studies. I figured I needed an undergraduate degree. If anything, I knew if I studied I would ace the LSAT. Then it was supposed to be on to law school." She shrugged. "My money ran out. Really, it was more like my momentum ran low, I guess. I saved myself time and money and went through a certificate program."

She watched him for any signs of judgment, but didn't see or feel any. This was not where she was supposed to be. Law school had been the Madame's dream for her, and she tried her hardest to fulfill it. *Or did I?* She at least had a career that she had come to enjoy, and made a decent living for herself. All of that had rapidly started to change before she got the call that her mother had died.

"So instead of cutting cadavers right about now, you're doing what?" Rebecca asked to keep her thoughts away from her present woes.

"I work for Perdue Farms, been with them for eight years now. Not such a stretch for my biology degree. I'm a production specialist at the soybean plant." He paused to pull at his ear. "Impressive title, right? I collect and file soybean samples mostly."

"For what?" Rebecca asked.

"For chicken feed," Will replied.

Rebecca checked with him for permission to laugh. She saw his smirk and knew he suspected she was ready to blow. *Could there be anything more nerdy, more Will Donovan?*

"I always knew you would use your supersized brain for the good of the world." She laughed.

"You're just jealous, I know. I also got me a supersized terrarium at the crib," he said, bopping his head. He started using his fingers to list its benefits. "It's for decoration, observation, and propagation. You should come see it. I've been seriously considering dibbling with horticulture."

Rebecca found her friend both cocky and cute when he spoke the language of dork. "A terrarium does not give you street credibility, Will. I am almost certain in some neighborhoods you could be shot for using 'terrarium' and 'crib' in the same sentence."

He chuckled, but had an immediate comeback. "When you respect the birdfeed, you respect the bird. My people love to eat chicken. I get mad street cred when I am hooking the church community up with oven roasters for the holidays and fryers in the summer for their barbeques. Since you think what I do is so funny, remind me to tell the server that you are not allowed to order chicken of any kind." He said, pointing at their menus, which they had failed to preview yet, "That's right, I am the chicken police."

Rebecca threw up her right hand as she surrendered the notion of making up a chicken joke at his expense. "No, it sounds like the perfect job for you, really."

She watched as he sat with his arms crossed and supported on the table like a wounded child. His face told a different story, and she almost got lost in that dimple of his. She never remembered it being that pronounced.

"We were supposed to be a regular Clair and Heathcliff Huxtable," he said under hooded eyes after her lingering chuckles subsided.

The word "we" sounded odd, different, like a new word to her. Maybe she was thrown off guard because she hadn't realized she had been a part of a pair. Two was stronger than one—substantial. *Why did we go our separate ways?*

Their waitress came with a half-hearted apology before Rebecca could further contemplate his statement. The waitress got away with their drink orders after leaving them a peace offering of a bread basket for taking so long.

Rebecca smoothed her hair from behind. "Why are we having two conversations in one? *We* were talking about you and Veronica."

The dimple made a reappearance. "Isn't it funny that we never have a problem following each other's train of thought whether it is spastic, sporadic, or schizophrenic?"

Either it was just her or Will didn't want to talk about his girlfriend, but she did. She tried again. "Veronica moved here, I assume, to be closer to you."

"That was purely her choice," Will said quickly. He was the first to grab for a roll and a butter packet.

Rebecca kept silent. She knew women usually didn't make that leap without encouragement. She was a little disappointed in Will. Maybe it was a man thing, but he was downplaying his relationship like many men she had known. But, why?

She assumed after the other day that he would have asked her about Randall, or some other guy in her life, but how would she explain their relationship, or lack thereof? She wished she had something to tell him, someone to brag about. Randall had been a mistake, and if they hooked up again later she knew she would be nothing more than a booty call to him. What were her alternatives?

Suddenly starving, Rebecca pulled apart half a roll. "So you used to commute to Salisbury?"

"Every day in the beginning, but just two or three times a week now," he said. "I told you I have my own controlled environment at home so I am testing stuff all the time. They wanted me to be plant manager, which would have been cool, but I couldn't work that out with my schedule at church."

"It's a shame you didn't have my address in Salisbury. We could have hung out," she said.

Will wiped his mouth very dramatically with his hand several times before running his hands together to rid them of bread crumbs. His eyes were intense, his expression suddenly serious. "1515 Prairieville Lane, apartment 2C."

She tilted her head to stop her mouth from gaping open. "Huh?" *Did he just recite my address?*

"Yeah," he said in his way of expressing "my sentiments exactly." "You live among college students."

Both hands met her hips. "What's up with that, *friend*?" Rebecca inquired.

"I knew your location, just like you knew mine. Now, why we never bothered to hook up is another story, *friend*."

Just then their waitress returned with a colossal fudge brownie dessert for the couple directly in front of them, who apparently came in for just a sweet treat. It must have been one of their birthdays because the dessert was lit with sparklers, causing quite the stir in their corner.

"Will." She started and stopped as she tried to figure out just what drove her out of town, never to look back until now. She couldn't blame this one solely on her mother.

"I'm not mad," Will suggested, then pointed at their neighbors' dessert. "And just to prove I'm over your utter and total abandonment, let's be reckless and share one of those babies."

However tempting, she shook her head repeatedly. "Been there done that. You've seen me heavy, and you see me now. I'd like to stay this way."

His eyes were on her in a new way. She shuddered slightly under his inspection. "Don't forget, I've known you for a long time. I've seen you flagpole thin, then fuller in high school. You were never heavy to me though."

She had always known Will as the preacher's kid, who she literally felt lived next door. They didn't grow close until adolescence. The Madame swore he didn't start coming over to visit until Rebecca started sprouting breasts. *"You're not fooling anyone, Will Donovan,"* she remembered the Madame saying to him. *"If you got a home, get there, and stop darkening my doorstep. Don't you have any male friends?"* They never brought that up or the changes in their bodies, and took to meeting outside or in the library. Rebecca wondered if he remembered that.

"The point is I won't be the one getting sucked into the gluttony of milk chocolate with you. Then we'll both be begging God to take off the weight we've heaped on ourselves."

Will did a combination cough-laugh. "The doors of the church are open. Weary has just preached her first sermon, y'all. A heaping helping of sin and shame; you mind if I borrow that one for Sunday?"

The waitress turned toward them after headlining the "Happy Birthday" song with the help of some of her other servers. Rebecca ordered a Caesar salad before the server could run off, leaving Will to do a quick skim of the menu. He looked at his watch before ordering a simple bacon cheeseburger with fries.

"Please, I've been . . . I have not been . . ." Rebecca started. "Let me put it to you this way: I cannot describe the interior of any church in Salisbury to you, and I have been there for fifteen years. I'll leave the preaching to you." She lowered her head toward her lap. "I know you're thinking, 'she grew up in church and went to Grace Apostle school.' But my life has been full of contradictions."

She wondered if he knew about her sordid past from the men she had been with, or from the ladies who knew her then who were now a part of his congregation, like the conductor of the Underground Railroad herself, Nina Pritchett. If Will had known, she wanted to set the record straight to prove she wasn't wholly heathen. "You know, sometimes I try to search the scriptures for some sort of explanation, some sort of direction in life. I have not always made the best choices."

"None of us have," he assured her with another hand tap. "Don't feel that because I am a minister now you have to confess to me. I'm not even going to sit here and try to preach to you."

"Why not, huh? That's what you're called to do, right? You have a word for everyone else. Maybe you'll have one for me." She was coming to realize that his spiritual side was as much a part of him as the plants and chicken feed. It was all intriguing to her. He was intriguing and wise in a born-in-another-time kind of way. She needed for him to tell her what she already knew: that there was more to life than the Madame, men, and milk chocolate.

He was reflective. He leaned in as if to share an intimate secret, and she leaned in as well. "You are God's choice, Weary. That's my word for you. You may be feeling all alone now, but He adopts orphans. Maybe, He's trying to use this difficult time to bring you back to Him."

It sounded so simple and plain, yet complex and profound. She bit her lip and sighed because all at once she was ready to cry. "I feel like I did in high school, really. I want to be in your study group. Maybe I'd better understand it all."

"You gotta come to church though. Reconnect. Studying God's Word is not like us studying for a test. Study, yes, but you can't cram for it. You got to live it to get its full meaning."

All she could do was nod her head. Their meal was served with less pomp and circumstance than the table in front of them. Will had given her enough to chew on, so for the next twenty minutes they condensed their twenty-year friendship to small talk. The "little" lunch they were supposed to be grabbing turned into a three-and-a-half hour visit. Neither one was fast to leave when their platters were wiped clean and their bill was paid.

"So are you going to stay with us this time?" Will said, standing after peeling off additional bills for the tip.

Rebecca let out a slight moan as he helped her up. "I don't know. It's like I'm still waiting for my life to start all these years later. I feel like I'm being pulled back here. I used to enjoy Salisbury, enjoy my little apartment among the college students and my job, at least, but now it's a mess. With all that is happening there, I feel like I could leave it all behind."

Will and Rebecca walked to the entrance, where they paused in the threshold. She noticed that he gave her a quizzical look. Now was not the time to fill him in on her work drama—they would be there for another three hours—plus, it would be a moot point if she decided to walk away.

Everything she thought was tangible now felt temporal. She leaned on the door in the entryway. She glanced briefly at his same maroon Toyota Camry that he had owned and driven for fifteen years. It was parked directly in front. She then looked back at him. She was looking at dependability.

"I, for one, would be glad to have you back home, especially if that is what God has purposed in your heart. Sounds as if you need to tie up a few loose ends though. I'm sure you'll be leaving Salisbury better than you found it." His eyebrows arched to show his sincerity.

She wasn't so sure about that. Tying up her loose ends would require more of herself then she was willing to extend right now. If she received enough money from the Madame she planned to buy a big hatchet to sever the monster of a loose end at work, and start clean.

She thanked God that someone was happy to have her back in Easton though. At least she had Will, she thought, when his cell phone started ringing. He squeezed her arm as if to say good-bye. He raised the

Chapter 9

"What are you doing, honey?" Will heard his girl-friend say through his cell phone.

"Nothing." He was slightly annoyed by her inquiry, by her timing. He folded himself quickly into the driver's seat while cradling the phone with his cheek and shoulder. He tried to catch a glimpse through his rearview mirror of Rebecca walking across the Applebee's parking lot. The sight of her carefree gait made him smile temporarily. "I just finished having lunch with Rebecca Lucas, you know, Madame Ava's daughter."

She expelled a breath of air into the phone. "Well at least you didn't lie to me."

This time he brought his eyes up to view himself in the mirror. He couldn't believe what he was hearing. "Lie? Why would I need to lie?"

She was silent for a moment as if contemplating what it was she wanted to say. "Will, do you love me? Are we ever getting married?"

This was not anything he wanted to get into with Veronica again over the phone. He had told her before that a forced or coerced proposal was not a real proposal. They had a few examples of that with couples in their own congregation. The woman led the groom down the aisle with one arm bent behind his back. Now the couple sat miserably together in church, or she sat alone and no one had seen hide or hair of the husband again. A man had to feel secure in his plan to start and support a family. He often wondered himself what his hold-up was. Veronica had all but stenciled a concrete plan for them.

"What is this about? Help me out. I'm lost. We talked this morning and everything was fine. Now you're in doubt about our relationship?" Will said.

There was a pause. "Nina's Aunt Patsy said she saw the two of you having lunch."

Will wondered if he even knew Nina's aunt, as he turned on the speaker control so he would be hands-free to start his car. Apparently Nina's aunt was as nosy as Nina had come to be in recent years. He couldn't remember a recent conversation with Veronica that wasn't peppered with some thought, comment, or suggestion from Nina. He could only imagine their grapevine and how news about his lunch spread so quickly. He had just left the restaurant. He had been spotted with another woman. He guessed he should be flattered if Veronica was actually jealous, but he had a feeling that was not the case. Veronica knew him enough to know he was faithful to her. Whatever the case may be he knew he should probably pacify her before the drama began, but he was more than a little peeved.

"I also saw Maxine and Brian Ealey from church. They had come from taking Joshua to the doctor's," Will chided. "Why didn't Nina's aunt come over and say hey to us like they did?"

"I don't know, Will," Veronica said. Her words were grating. "Maybe she thought she would be disturbing the two of you. I was told you all looked mighty cozy."

"Don't, all right," Will cut her off. "If Nina's aunt knew me or had gone to high school with me and Rebi, like Nina did, she would know how close we were in high school. She was my best friend. I told you that."

"Yes, and now, I am your best friend." It sounded like an order rather than a question or statement.

Theoretically, he thought. "Yes, we have a very different relationship. That means you know what you mean to me, or don't you? I would hate to think that there is a jealousy or insecurity thing growing," Will said, knowing she would never admit to that. She prided herself in having it all together.

"No, not at all," she stated.

Will finally pulled off in his car after backing out of the space. He could see Rebecca in a teal-green Honda Sonata about to make a U-turn about a hundred feet ahead of him at the light. He wondered where she was going. His thoughts temporarily trailed after her.

Veronica's voice brought his thoughts back to their conversation. "I don't like it when you keep secrets. That's all."

"It wasn't a secret. We were in a public place. Besides I've never had to tell you who I had lunch with in the past. I hope that's not where we are headed."

"We're headed there if you are purposely trying to conceal things from me," Veronica threatened.

"My lunch with Rebecca was just that—a lunch. It was a spur-of-the-minute idea. I got hungry and decided to call her up to join me," Will said, immediately wishing he could reel his words back in.

"Her, and not me," she said, actually sounding hurt.

"We go out all the time. We can go out tonight if you want. I haven't seen her in fifteen years. That should tell you something."

There was silence. He hoped what he was saying was making sense and helping to wash away the seeds Aunt Patsy and Nina had planted in his girlfriend's mind. They were a very analytical couple, which suited his scientific and her business sensibilities. The rational worked for them. Her assumptions and roundabout accusations were irrational, he thought. "You've told me what you don't like. Let me tell you what I don't like. I don't like it when you come to me with other people's judgments. How can we succeed by other people's standards? If anything you should have cut off the gossip from Nina and her aunt and defended me," Will added.

"How can I defend you, and I didn't even know you were going?" she said incredulously. "You are a minister, sweetheart, preaching the gospel to these people about what's right and wrong. The reality is you are on display whether you like it or not."

"So does that mean I can't eat lunch with a friend?" he asked, ironically taking the path back to the church where his own members were spying on him, he thought.

"It means you should know what kind of scene your little outing could have caused. You have to flee the appearance of evil or anything that would cause someone else to fall in their walk." Her tone took on that of one talking to an imbecile. " We're together, practically married, and then people see you out in public with another woman and they start to wonder if you are any different than any other man scamming on his wife or girlfriend."

"Scamming, huh?" This was almost laughable to him. It was awkward times like these that let him know, ironically, that she would make a great mother. That's what originally warmed him to her: her ability to know and desire to do what was right. If she were his mother and he were her child, this would be the think-about-what-you-have-done portion of her chastisement.

"What if things were reversed and it was me seen out with another man?" Veronica asked.

That was left out in the air for him to contemplate. He had to admit he would be insulted, maybe even feel a bit insecure. She sought after a fairytale, not a scandal, so he wouldn't expect her to be out there with another man—friend or otherwise.

"Do you think your dad, the Pastor William H. Donovan, would have done that when your mom, the first lady, was living?" she asked.

Will thought she had some pretty convincing arguments, especially about his parents. His dad always held his mom in high esteem. That made him slow his roll, made him reconsider the position he had left her in. Veronica was probably more embarrassed than anything. She was, after all, slated to be his wife. He couldn't help but feel time was closing in on him.

"Are we really arguing about this? I get it. I see your point," Will surrendered.

"Good." She sighed. "I just think that I should have been invited to your little lunch date."

"It wasn't a date." *It was a refreshing change of pace.* "Plus, you're working. Aren't you working?" he asked, looking once again through the rearview mirror. He didn't put it past her to be hiding out at Applebee's herself, spying on him.

"Sure, but it wouldn't be the first time I met you in the middle of the day. I even came to your friend's reception and her mom's funeral," she said. "Did I tell you, Marigold Reynolds Lark from the Bucktown Women's Society told me at the funeral that she would recommend me to fill the Madame's spot?"

Will squirmed. That didn't sit well with him, that she was making power moves at a funeral. Never joined a club or organization in college, but suddenly she had all these aspirations to belong to something in Easton. He hoped his silence would communicate his disapproval.

"Look, I moved down here to be with you because I love you. I could have stayed in Wye Mills. I left my friends and family behind. I consider your friends my friends because we've built something here. I don't want to fight. I just want my feelings to be considered," Veronica added.

Will pulled into the lot of the church and let the car idle while he listened. He didn't want to bring the weight of the conversation into the church with him. He was jet-lagged. They both had frequent flyer miles from the continual guilt trips about her moving to Easton without a ring.

Will dropped his head on the steering wheel. "Well, tell me your feelings then. I don't want to hear about what this one and that one has to say when we are talking about us. Agreed?"

"Agreed, and you and Rebecca won't have any more breakfast, lunch, or dinner *reunions* without me, agreed?"

He could no more tell Veronica no, that her plan was not going to work, than he could have said "don't move to Easton." How does a man tell his girlfriend that he and his best friend, who happens to be a female, would not want her to go out with them? Veronica wouldn't understand their humor. She didn't have the context of their past and would misconstrue every reference. She'd only cramp their style. Veronica would give it the old college try, but she and Rebi were too different to be friends.

He lifted his head and gave his earlobe a good pull. At this point, he was ready to agree to anything. "Agreed."

Chapter 10

Rebecca felt like a modern-day leper walking down the aisle of Grace Apostle church for Sunday service. She hadn't been there in two weeks, since her mother's funeral, and everyone and everything seemed to be in its place. Will sat in the exalted throne-like chair on the altar reserved for the pastor. Trustees were on the left side, deacons in the middle, and even Veronica sat in the front on the right-hand side with a row of women who looked to have been seated in ascending order according to age. The stares Rebecca encountered let her know it was she who was out of place.

Gail insisted upon walking her down the aisle to the front like a two-year-old who might wander off. With one arm around Rebecca in a gesture that lately was repeatedly followed up with the comment "we'll get through this," the pair strolled in like they were joined at the hip.

Her previous predictions about the Madame going broke were confirmed when she confronted Gail about her weird behavior. Her cousin was never the touchy-feely type, none of the Lucas women were, so Rebecca had asked about her constant reassuring hugs.

"Mr. Green informed me that the Madame has little to no liquid assets, just the house and land."

"What about an insurance policy?"Rebecca queried, grateful for Gail's steadying hand.

"We'll find out about that soon enough," she said with pursed lips. "We both know she hadn't worked outside the home in years. Green and Tremaine apparently kept her out of trouble with the IRS by making sure she got paid a onetime stipend from the few nonprofits that hired her to fundraise for their events, instead of dipping off the net proceeds. She didn't want to be anyone's employee, and a cause was a cause to her. Sometimes she bartered and lobbied for compensation but got little pay. I don't know," Gail said, resigned.

"So what does that mean? We don't have a pot to piss in?" Rebecca asked when the realization hit her.

"Oh, girl, watch your crass mouth." Gail had grimaced. "That means we could build an outhouse, but we'd be hard-pressed to maintain the house we've got if we don't plan on working full time ourselves, smarty."

Gail hadn't said it, but Rebecca figured the water well to the side of the house had generated enough revenue to keep them afloat even with the meter tax. This was going to alter Rebecca's plans. She would have to look for a job in town, no extended breaks, no trips abroad. But, she had a job and a major dilemma in Salisbury. Considering there were only a few close-knit law firms throughout the Delmarva Peninsula area, wiggling out of one would affect her ability to slink, slither, or saunter into another. They truly needed all that Jesus had to offer them today. That made going to church a no-brainer. Rebecca pulled her red ruffled shawl up around the shoulder of the Madame's royal-blue dress. *Let them stare,* she thought. She added an extra bounce to her hips as they made their way to their seats in the fourth row.

This was Grace Apostle, a place that the Madame had called the haughtiest place on earth. That said something to Rebecca, if haughtiness was beyond the Madame's reach or tolerance. Rebecca left the church when the Madame stopped going, although she didn't find the ship run by the usually laidback Pastor Donovan intolerable. Gail had stayed.

It was well known that Grace Apostle was established by Quakers and it was the only mixed congregation on the peninsula. Would-be historians like the Madame recounted the scene of scores of black families flocking to the church on foot if it was feasible. Instead of the church being a major uniting factor, it spurred a type of reverse racism. Apparently worshipping with white folks made some think they were better than other blacks who couldn't make the pilgrimage or preferred an all-black church.

They were all products of the talented-tenth mentality of the blacks on the west side of town, especially when the school was added and saving for the meager tuition became an option to the public schools for those who wanted to keep that brand. That's the way the Madame claimed it to be in her day. They had lost the Caucasian leverage and added the Methodist title. Although all but a few of the white parishioners had moved on, it didn't seem to Rebecca like much else had changed with her own kind.

Rebecca was at least thankful for a few new and otherwise nonjudgmental faces. She waved at Veronica, who had her neck craned in Rebecca's direction. She didn't get a return wave. Maybe Veronica hadn't seen her, she thought. This time Rebecca didn't feel the warmth of an impending friendship. Veronica's good friend was not beside her, but could it be that Nina was rubbing off on her?

This was religion looking her in the face, she thought. This was all wrong. She would have to push past the people. She didn't want her return to church to be like a visit of an old friend who only calls or visits when they need something. She had to remind herself she didn't come for the crowd or the recognition. She was desperate at this point for some hope, and church was supposed to be the storehouse.

A pitiful few rose from the choir loft with hymnals in hand, prepared to sing. The chorale was surprisingly clear and strong once they began, sounding like the combined voices of a choir much larger. Rebecca began to relax with each verse as she swayed in her seat. She had missed the deeply personal and poignant connection she experienced from God's inspirational message in any form. Many of the rituals had been ingrained in her from the daily devotional time at the beginning of each school day at Grace Apostle's school. She was comforted with the fresh and familiar feeling that resonated within her as the Old and New Testament scriptures were read and the doxology or congregational prayer in song was sung. She looked forward to Will's message.

Will stood at the podium and joined in on the tail end of the hymn. His rich tenor was amplified by the microphone, displaying his perfect pitch.

"Give an honor to God, my Heavenly Father, and to my earthly father, who has so faithfully and skillfully led this church for forty-nine years and is still on a well-deserved vacation. I am humbled that you are here with me this day as I journey toward my ultimate destination, which is Heaven. You came hopefully to hear a word from God, and I am the mouthpiece." He smiled as if hearing a joke, then tugged at his right ear. "I know some of you are thinking, yeah, Will, you're a mouthpiece, all right. Pray for me that I might decrease in front of you and the Christ in me increases. Pardon me while I transform in front of you. Let us pray."

She took in the whole of him. He was never athletic, but he went from a string bean in high school to a solid adult man. She reckoned he carried a good 200 pounds on his rack. His wide stance showed he had found a suave balance over the years to his general nervous energy and awkwardness. He had a meticulously groomed and smooth cocoa-colored face. He had never had a problem with acne like she did. They had ruled out physiology and equated her frequent breakouts to the fact that, out of the both of them, she had all the hang-ups. Her forehead still bore the marks of her anxieties. That was why she wore blunt Chinese-styled bangs to this day.

She turned her focus back to Veronica, as if to try taking in the prayer from her point of view. Rebecca reckoned Veronica must swell with pride each Sunday she was able to see and hear her man preach. She thought it just a bit strange to see Veronica whispering and giggling with the woman beside her. Rebecca continued to stare to see if the two had shared a passing joke, but they continued their banter, thoroughly engrossed, through Will's introductory prayer. Before she could tally another point against her best friend's girlfriend, a small voice told her that she should be praying as well.

"'Transformers, robots in disguise.'" Will sang the hook from the old television series' theme song. The show was recently updated to a multi-million dollar special effects movie spectacular. Everyone, including Rebi, who had previously bowed their heads with him in prayer, brought Will back into view with his outburst of song.

In just his eight count of song, Rebecca remembered how she had talked him out of joining the boys' choir. As far as she had been concerned if popularity was his aim, harmonizing and bebopping with other guys wouldn't get him there. What did she know? His voice proved good enough to be a solid backup singer if not a lead.

Will began to beckon someone to the podium, and Rebecca's heart began to race, fearing he was summoning her. He was a preacher and she now had to wonder if anything they discussed as friends could, just like in a court of law, be used against her. A few looked over their shoulders and she chose to do the same. A small boy with a toy who was sitting on his father's knee a few rows back was now being hoisted up into the air to garner the recognition.

"Come here, Isaac. Bring Bumblebee," Will coaxed. "I told you I would need you to help me teach."

The boy willingly hopped down off his daddy's lap and with a carefree gait made his way to the aisle. Oblivious to the spotlight and time constraints, the boy floated his fairly large-sized figurine in the air as if it were flying.

Will gestured toward him as his dad called out to edge him on while the crowd orally delighted in unabashed innocence of youth. Finally, the boy arrived at the pulpit with the help of an usher who acted as a guide. Will bent in his robe and lifted the lightweight boy, toy and all, up to viewing level.

"Where is the other one?" Will said, continuing their one-on-one conversation. "Where's Optimus?"

"I couldn't find it," the boy said matter-of-factly.

Will struggled to hold the boy, who was determined to get his figurine to walk on the podium top and talk into the microphone. "You couldn't find it? It was just last week when I saw you with them and asked to borrow them."

The boy shook his head. "I think his head came off, but, but, but I got Buzz Lightyear for my birthday. He's a robot. I'll bring him next week."

"Amen." Will chuckled at the boy's generosity. "Tell the folks what kind of doll this is."

This temporarily halted the boy and his toy. "It's not a doll. It's a Transformer."

"That's right. I stand corrected." Will took this as an opportunity to put the boy down and detach the microphone to bring down to the boy's level. "Say that again."

"It's a Transformer." The boy's eyes went in flight as the sound of his amplified voice fascinated him.

"Do you mind if I keep Bumblebee up here with me?" Will asked, bending before his little helper and reaching for the toy.

The boy nodded his head hesitantly while maintaining a grip on his toy. Will also grabbed the toy on the other side. Rebecca found their exchange adorable. Will had a way with children. She instantly thought of Will as a dad. The thought made her turn again to the woman likely to make that happen for him. Rebecca was relieved that Veronica was at least listening now.

"I'm going to use it for a demonstration. Look, why don't you make it into a car for me," Will said, now trying to gain the boy's trust.

The boy was intent on compacting the robot toy at its hinges and folding it over and over until it resembled a large Matchbox car. He handed it to Will, who wiped his forehead as if the whole of his sermon depended on it.

"Thank you," Will said as everyone clapped. "Now Pastor Will is gonna use it for a while. It will be right here and you'll be able to see it from your seat. I promise I won't break it. I think we collected enough offering to replace this, right?" He looked out into the audience to the boy's parents, as if asking them for permission.

The boy's parents stood, and his father called out Isaac's name once more. The same friendly usher reached out her hand to help Isaac off the platform. Before she could pick him up, the boy leaped off the stage and galloped down the aisle to everyone's concern at first and then amusement.

"I thank you for indulging me and Isaac. I remember these toys as a child, saw the comic books, saw the cartoon on television, even recently saw the movie, but not until I saw little Isaac playing with it last week did I begin to ponder the spiritual implication. Let me give you all a little history."

It didn't surprise Rebecca that Will was quite studied about these animated characters. He shared that Transformers were robots that had the ability to transform or to change their bodies at will, rearranging themselves into multiple forms: vehicle, weaponry, or the robotic humanoid form. Will took pride in introducing the crowd to each character including Optimus Prime, Bumblebee, Ratchet, and the evil Megatron, who was the leader of a clan of transformers called the Decepticons. A guy named Sam Witwicky seemed to be the only human of significance among these machines.

Rebecca could feel the crowd start to zone out the way people do when a longwinded friend took too long to get to the point. He hadn't even given them a scriptural reference. Even she knew that was a preaching precursor. Rebecca was actually nervous. *Draw the parallel, make it plain*, she found herself praying. She knew Will; she knew he was going somewhere. He was finding it hard to unhinge the compartments to demonstrate the transformation Isaac so skillfully did before. She wanted to help him. Finally, he just gave up. He looked down at his sermon notes and plodded ahead.

"To be in Christ is to be like a child totally dependent on our Heavenly Father, to see things with new eyes. The Bible instructs us in Romans 12:2 not to conform to this world, but to be transformed. It has to start with the renewal of your mind though. We see it all the time on those reality makeover shows." He used air quotes to highlight the word "reality" to show his distaste for that type of programming. "The makeovers never last. The old habits never die, unless a person prepares by changing their mindset. Rarely does true change start from the outside, like people would have us believe. Rather, change begins on the inside, then blossoms out. Renewing your mind is key, then the body. The flesh that has failed us all in the past will follow. We must take on the mind of Christ before the pieces of our lives can fall into place."

The tide began to turn and "amen's" flooded the sanctuary. Rebecca felt Gail tap her leg as if to say, "he's talking to you." It was like her we'll-get-through-this gestures. Rebecca tapped Gail back but harder, resistant to the now surrogate-mother role Gail had adopted. Rebecca knew her older cousin didn't think she had any common sense. Rebecca didn't have to be reminded that her life was fragmented. Will was spilling her beans, and she had to figure out how to clean them up.

"Sam Witwicky had Bumblebee as a guardian, but you have your own Autobot to protect you, guide you. Our Lord, like Optimus Prime if you will, watches over all, but He also gave us a personal Autobot, the Holy Spirit, to carry us through this life. What was so cool in the movie that Sam didn't even have to drive. When the Decepticons were after him, it was best that he didn't drive. He'd be so confused and debilitated with fear, not sure what direction he was moving in. It doesn't occur to us to stop the car and ask for help. Has that ever happened to you when navigating life? I know it happens to me. I just yell out like *American Idol* winner Carrie Underwood, 'Jesus, take the wheel,'" Will sang again.The congregational backing was fueling his fervor. He was preaching now. His voice took on an assured tone.

"It's one thing to come upon a spill or ride up unexpectedly on a pileup and crash, but some of us know we're headed for destruction and keep going. Heck, most of the time we shouldn't be driving at all. It's like driving under the influence. Stop driving under the influence of anxiety, under the influence of a cocky attitude, under the influence of depression, under the influence of others' law and not God's law. That is deception. There are deceivers out there. They are modern-day Decepticons, y'all."

Will's eyes shone brightly over the congregation. He muted his voice and let what he had just said sink in before continuing. "Let's see, there is Frenzy, Ravage, Overkill. The names say it all. Don't be accused of being a Decepticon, y'all," Will said. "They even have one called Wreckloose, oh, Lord."

At that moment Rebecca made eye contact with Veronica again. This time neither one of them bothered to wave.

"The first time Sam saw a 'bot transform, it was a Decepticon transformation. See, our problems can blow up on us and blow up fast. They can change on us, get more intense, more menacing. Before you know it we're cowering in a corner. But then Bumblebee transformed himself before Sam and woo!" At that Will extended his arms and many of the hinges on the figurine snapped open and into place, leaving traces of the full assembly. Fast as fingers on a Rubik's Cube, Will locked the remaining places as if he were in a timed race to reveal Bumblebee in all his glory. Everyone was cheering. None as loud as Isaac, who raced up to give Pastor Will a high five.

"Won't he give you power right when you need it?" Will said, handing the toy down to the boy before he went back to the podium. "Sam realized that he had been chosen, that he was favored when everyone else around him was perishing under the same attack. Sam had the protection of an indestructible Autobot all around him. He could almost get cocky and say, 'Yeah, my 'bot is as big as yours, if not bigger.' My God is bigger than my problems. Like Sam, we've got to grow in the knowledge of what we really have when we not only get saved, but truly begin to live for Him.

"Trust your Autobot and get out of the driver's seat. Forget TomTom and Garmin. Jesus is the best navigational system out there. He has you locked on to God's plan. If He is driving, you don't have to worry about your destination. Jeremiah 29 reminds us of that. Head toward the hope and the future God has set before us. I end today with an invitation to join the church."

Rebecca stood up and clapped out her encouragement with many in the congregation. Rebecca remembered what he said to her in the restaurant when he told her that she was God's choice. This was just a continuation of that truth. Will had killed the crowd. From the reaction of the crowd and the man himself, this was a particularly special occurrence. She couldn't help thinking that Will looked like a rock star with his arms outstretched, as if basking in the cries of an encore. A few people began to move toward the aisle to meet Will, who was now on the floor level at the base of the altar, opening the doors of the church with an invitation to join.

Rebecca watched as Will summoned those in need of a transformation. She was in need, but she was locked in place. *I have been a member, used to go to school here as a child; surely I don't need to rejoin.* She blinked, and then felt an internal prompting. She had been so focused on Will that she hadn't realized it wasn't Will, but God beckoning to her. It was familiar and friendly. The one that always prompted her to err on the side of caution, yet boldly and confidently stand up for herself. Like Will had said earlier, he was merely the mouthpiece. She had made a habit of not listening to that voice. Maybe that was why she felt so powerless to her circumstances.

"Whether you have never accepted Christ or have strayed away from His teachings, come to Him like little brother Isaac with all the innocence of a child, bearing all you have rather than the arrogance of adulthood."

Rebecca took to the aisle before she knew she was moving, leaving her shawl and reservations back on the pew. Will passed his microphone to his awaiting deacon. He gave the two ladies and one man ahead of her a hearty hug before they lined up in front of the congregation, and she was no exception.

"Hey, it's you! Hallelujah!" Will said once he had broken the embrace. "Look at what God had done. This was my first substantive harvest, and you're among it? Wow!"

"Well, you won me over," Rebecca said amid family members and well-wishers of those being reclaimed, rejoicing in the harvest.

"God certainly did," came a voice over her shoulder. Rebecca turned to look into the now smiling face of Veronica, who had her arms spread open to initiate her own hug. Rebecca hesitantly stepped into them. "Oh, Rebecca, you've made the best decision of your life. I wasn't aware you were even staying in town."

Rebecca added hers to the awkward expressions that was circling among the three of them. "I guess I am."

"Great," Veronica replied.

Rebecca was grateful to feel the sincere arms of Gail encircle her body. She wiped the tears from the eyes of her slightly shorter cousin, the sight of which had started her own rivers.

Will took the microphone but kept it close to his chest as he whispered a reminder to his girlfriend of her duty. "Aren't you going to take them to the back and officially welcome them in?"

"Sure, I'll take care of her," Veronica said a little too ominously for Rebecca's taste.

Veronica gestured with her palm in the general direction to where Rebecca and the others should follow, before she did an about-face. Once again, Rebecca and Gail were joined at the hip, but this time it was Rebecca who would not let go.

Chapter 11

"They agreed to give you more time, but you had to know that you were at the end of your paid leave, girly. Paralegals are not necessarily beating down our door, but I saved your tail the other day when your absences came up. You owe me. Did human resources contact you?" Anthony Jacobs said.

Rebecca missed the country twang of his voice. She had neglected to call her coworker, who had apparently championed her cause to continue to be off because of her bereavement. She knew she had been tracked down when her cell phone rang out the *Perry Mason* ringtone used to earmark his calls. What she had failed to tell him was that she didn't know if the job was worth saving. She now felt as if she had at least emotionally moved back home to Easton.

Sanz, Mitchum, and Clarke was such a large law firm she didn't imagine her absence would have been a concern to anyone. She worked directly with three associate attorneys, who included Jacobs, Leonard Minor, and Kenny Burke, one of only three African American attorneys at the firm. She was helping Anthony with a deposition when she learned about the Madame's death. Minor was on vacation. Burke, forever climbing the executive fire escape in hopes of advancement in the firm, was spending his time on the golf course wooing wealthy business owners to hire the firm in their interest of acquiring properties. For a junior associate, he was raking up quite a scorecard with the partners. In that vein, he and Rebecca had a closed-door meeting prior to her leaving Salisbury, where it was insinuated how her services were essential to his plan.

A few innocent dates with Burke must have made him comfortable enough to ask her to entertain one of his wealthy prospects, Walter Calhoun from Dover, Delaware. The old tycoon became enamored with her during a visit to meet the partners. Although she barely remembered the older gentleman, she got a strong feeling from the conversation with Burke that "a bit of her time" was the contingency of a very profitable working relationship between the firm and this man. An indecent proposal awaited her back home.

"What are they saying?" Rebecca asked, more concerned about Burke than human resources.

"You can request to extend your bereavement leave with sick leave, request leave without pay, or start taking your personal leave. What's your pleasure?"

"I meant about the caseload. I take it you finished the Watts deposition?" she asked.

"Oh yeah, no problem," he said. "I even credited you for preparing my motions, did 'em myself, piece of cake—keeps me sharp."

"Jacobs, Jacobs, Jacobs." Rebecca slapped her forehead. She was sick that he went into court alone on a case he could have easily settled. He was mocked at the firm, most notably by Burke, as the one who saw more court time than a criminal lawyer. No one understood why he relished the judicial process. No one understood why he bothered.

"I'm not that crazy or aggrieved that I wouldn't clock those hours for working in the field or teleworking," Rebecca said. "What about Burke?"

"Oh gosh, Burke was even more of a jerk than he normally is. He was mad that I acted as the manager in regard to your leave. He claims he's got so much going on. He has no trial prep. What is his problem?"

Rebecca contemplated telling Jacobs like she almost revealed her dilemma to Will the other day at lunch. Burke had a problem, all right. She had a feeling he had a handsome commission coming to him when all was said and done. What would she be getting in the deal? She wasn't a saint, but she wasn't a sleazebag either. This felt filthy.

"I'm surprised he hasn't called you. I didn't bother to tell him you had gotten a new cell phone and number. You let me know if he calls harassing you, and so help me God, I'm in human resources on his behind. I'm tired of his crap."

The thought of this country boy taking on the smooth-talking Kenny Burke, who was two times his body weight, was almost laughable until she considered what it was Kenny was doing—harassment. That was what left her fearful to check her messages at home even remotely or be seen in Salisbury right about now. She didn't all-out refuse because she'd hoped the whole thing would blow over. Apparently from this conversation the strong wind she needed hadn't come through. How long could she hold this man's interest and be a pawn in Kenny's game?

She didn't have many allies so she decided to let Jacobs in on the circumstances that led to Burke's suggestion. "I give a little, he gets a lot, all in the name of being a team player. And to think I thought Burke might actually like me, just to find out he wants to pass me around. Lord knows what this old goon has in mind for me. I just want to work. I didn't ask for this. That's the dilemma in a nutshell."

"That friggin' pig." He paused. "You know what we got here? He's gone a step too far this time. This is classic harassment. You've got to report him."

A booty swat is classic harassment, Rebecca thought; this she wasn't certain was so clean-cut. She didn't need the ink-and-paper trail of a complaint haunting her. She wanted to do her own ghost busting because she had a feeling Kenny Burke had a much darker aura once crossed than he previously presented.

"Wait, let's not get ahead of ourselves. It was an idea, a suggestion that I'm sure by now he's ready to renege or has forgotten altogether. If I come back—when, when I come back—I just want peace."

There was a pause as he contemplated what she said. She knew his momentum out of this pause would be that of a runaway train. "Admit it, he's got you spooked. I can tell. You're afraid to come back. That's harassment. Guys like Burke get away with stuff like this because we let them. He can't commission you out, or even suggest the sort, Rebecca. Giving him the benefit of the doubt just gives him a chance to dangle this bank roll, whoever he is, in front of the partners like a steak to salivating dogs. Let me find out that they are all in on this. Some things are bigger than you—the cause. You know I have friends at Princeton and Hope I can call."

She wondered, if he was so connected, why didn't he call in a favor to get them both a position at Princeton and Hope, which was a law firm a fraction of the size of their firm?

"I just need time. Promise me you won't say anything, especially to Burke. Time—use my leave. I don't care," Rebecca begged.

Reluctantly, Jacobs got off the phone with the promise to report back to her from the front lines. Rebecca was restless after that phone call. It felt as if everyone wanted a piece of her, wanted to control her. First Kenny Burke with his unorthodox request, and now Jacobs with his unbridled desire to stick it to his adversary. She hated feeling like she owed Jacobs for helping her out. She didn't want to be his cause.

Rebecca picked up her cell phone to look for Will's number as she trudged back to the Madame's suite there on the first floor. She wasn't sure if she was in need of his pastoral care or the advice of her best friend. She would have thought he would have called her after she restored her membership with Grace Apostle last Sunday. She didn't know how welcome the other new members felt, but Veronica had given her the distinct feeling that her return had cramped her comfortable existence.

Rebecca's fingers manipulated the touch screen of her phone. The menu on her phone led her to the saved messages instead of her contacts. There she saw her saved text from Randall. A slow smile spread across her face. She had successfully evaded him and his decadent overtures. Now she was thinking it was completely harmless to send him a thinking-of-you message. She left him with the option of going out if he was free, and added enough heat to the message to make him strongly consider altering any previous plans. Then, with a laugh, she tossed the phone in the center of the mattress she also climbed atop. She knew she was playing with fire, but it was all in good fun when she wasn't the one being burned. She lay down with the notion that she would start the day over when she awakened.

Chapter 12

Rebecca didn't know how long she had been asleep when she heard the knocks on the door. *Gail forgot her keys,* she thought as she made her way down the long hallway that led back through the kitchen to the front entrance. She didn't bother to look out the peephole or inquire about who it was before snatching the door open, revealing Randall standing in the doorway.

"Randall?" she questioned. "What—"

"Got your text," he explained, looking beyond her frame into the atrium of the house, like he was trying to gain entrance to an exclusive club but was being held behind a velvet rope. "You gonna let me in?"

Rebecca realized she blocked the entrance, but kept her position. Before she asked how or why he had chosen to come there, to her house, the Madame's house, he picked her up and swung her around, making the way clear for his entrance.

"Let me up in here, girl. Whatcha doing?" He was looking around now as if he were in a museum.

Rebecca had neglected to see if Gail's car was in front of the house, but hastened her pace to get in front of Randall, who was now in the great room. She had to tell herself, *he's inside now, the Madame is gone, and I am an adult.* She was still stunned at his audacity to just show up at her house. She didn't even have time to change out of her dress skin wrap, which was sheer and meant to be worn over a leotard, and old ballerina slippers she'd found among her abandoned things that she'd mulled over.

"I figured you'd call me first if you were available. I would have met you someplace," she hinted, lingering in the expanse of the open space while he peered into the darkened doorway of the library. Their house was a part of the family mystique, large and ornate looking from the road but quite cozy once inside. She gave him a minute to take it in. She cleared her throat as she nodded toward the kitchen at the back of the house. *Yeah, the kitchen is where you entertain guests,* she thought. Although he looked good enough to be served in a slim-fit gray suit and black shirt, she figured she'd stay out of trouble in there.

"You sent out an SOS and you know I can't leave a damsel in distress," he said, running up behind her and tickling her as they reached the threshold of the kitchen.

"I hope I didn't take you away from someone's dearly departed," she said breathlessly, spinning out of his grasp at the same time. She pointed at the refrigerator. "Can I get you something to drink?"

He bit his bottom lip seductively as if concealing a laugh or stopping himself from sharing a lewd joke. "I'm good. I was on my way back into town from a conference. This seemed like the perfect pit stop."

He said no more, and they stood silently for a moment.

"Why don't you sit?" she suggested.

"Why don't you come here?" he said, closing the space between them instead. Their bodies left a narrow passageway between the refrigerator and the center island. He began to tickle her midsection from behind.

Rebecca squirmed. He did not know she couldn't stand to be tickled nor did he know she couldn't resist being hugged like he initiated next. Hugs had gotten her into a lot of trouble in the past. Rebecca wondered if he'd settle for a strong hug because she was not about to get busy with him in the Madame's kitchen. *It would be wrong*, she repeated as a mantra to counter the craving for this man's affection. *Yes, this feels wrong.*

Randall swung her around as if she were his partner in a Latin tango. It was a sexy move that ended in a lift, but a not-so-graceful landing on the countertop. He took residence in her personal space, circling her waist with his hands after unbuttoning his suit jacket and quite possibly his pants. *Not the waist*, came her internal screams. She had to stop herself from automatically wrapping her legs around his torso. He moved as if he were on the clock: quick and concise. Anywhere else but here and she'd be down, Rebecca thought honestly as she feebly pushed against him. She couldn't blame him for being bold and pushing the envelope. For all he knew, she wasn't afraid to assume the seductress role. So what was stopping her now?

The fact was that Rebecca hated as much as she loved the fake sincerity of just hooking up with a guy for sex, the balancing acts both physically and emotionally and the locomotion. It all was great for the moment, but left a bitter aftertaste that she wasn't sure was worth it now. How could she get out of this?

As Randall bent to partake of her neck, Rebecca wondered if he smelled like basic earth in the crook of his neck the same way Will did when she hugged him. Why was she thinking of Will at this time? She told herself that Will was her pastor now and represented her newfound faith.

Rebecca could not escape the fact this time that it was wrong to be here with a man who had his hands all over her like he knew her—like he owned her. This man, who had her atop a kitchen counter, hadn't bothered to engage her in a kiss or even the basics of conversation. Her secret shame soaked her. She was a pit stop: fast, convenient, and cheap. She had invited him, and once again, she felt she owed someone something. She owed it to him to go through with what he'd come for. He had known her, like many men before him, and her walk to the altar last Sunday could not erase that fact, or could it?

"You are God's choice, Weary." When would He be hers? This time Rebecca put effort behind her shove. "Uh-uh, it's not going down like this tonight."

"What?" Randall barked, his passion quickly turning to anger. "You sent me a text, not the other way around, and I quote, 'the playground is open.' What the hell was that, huh? A freakin' tease? You think this is a game?"

Rebecca cowered under his harsh tone. Like a turtle retreating into its shell, she pulled her legs and feet, ballerina slippers and all, up into a ball and covered her head as if to block out his words. He backed up slightly, allowing just enough space to come back at her with another blow. Only he knew whether it would be physical rather than verbal this time. Rebecca prepared herself for the assault. Then they both heard a sound from the back stairwell, and it halted them. It was Gail. She appeared, dragging a Louisville Slugger baseball bat. The Madame had purchased each of them one for under their beds to ward off any possible invaders. It was the only home protection the Madame thought they needed out in the woods. Gail hoisted it on her shoulder to show Randall that it was authentic.

"You know what? I don't need all this drama from a crazy jump off," he spat at Rebecca.

"I reckon you don't," Gail agreed.

Randall collected himself, never taking his eyes off Gail or her bat. "I guess the rumors were right. You all are crazy."

"I reckon we are," she agreed before altering her bat to her swinging arm, grazing his suit jacket in the process.

Randall took a defensive posture. "Hit me and see if I don't sue the both of you."

Gail didn't flinch. "Act a fool in here and see if you don't end up broke down and out of business by the time I get through with you." She put the bat down and leaned on it while she posed. "Why are we still talking? Good night, Mr. Hughes."

Rebecca was shell-shocked by the whole encounter. She continued to hug her knees into her body until her bat-slinging surrogate mother escorted her guest out. Rebecca knew she would never hear the end of this. To be reminded of it would almost be as bad as the encounter itself, she thought.

Gail returned to Rebecca's perch. She caressed the side of Rebecca's tear-stained face without saying a word before extending her hand like a lead in a Russian ballet for Rebecca to step down from the counter. Rebecca stepped down gingerly, but gracefully. Gail picked her bat up and started for the hidden stairwell. Rebecca caught her and initiated the biggest and most fulfilling hug she had ever given in her life.

Chapter 13

Will wondered why he was dining on baby glazed carrots and arugula salad next to a sirloin so petite it wouldn't even be classified as a kiddie entrée at Outback Steakhouse. This was the third dinner date this week with Veronica, and they had gotten dressed up and traveled the twenty minutes to an inlet restaurant on Saint Michaels island for this emasculating meal. Remote locations, romantic atmosphere, and pricier meals were retribution for his one lunch with Rebecca, he reasoned.

"This is nice. Isn't this nice? I want you to propose to me in a place exactly like this," Veronica said in between bites.

Will didn't even react anymore to her not-so-subtle hints. She didn't understand that frequent references to the act caused him to passive-aggressively do nothing. She tried to narrow down the time and now the circumstances surrounding the event. There was nothing left for him to do but buy the ring. He wiped his mouth with the thick dinner napkin, as if his meal were hearty enough to have oozed down the side of his mouth. *The meal isn't the only thing emasculating,* he thought.

"I thought you wanted me to propose to you in front of your family," he reminded her.

"Good, you've been listening." She smiled. "Oh yeah, speaking of family, we should go stay with my parents this Christmas. Please?"

Her smile reminded him of how lucky he was to be involved with someone so stunning. The glow of the candlelight sculpted her cheekbones even further and deepened her amber hue. He wondered what she saw in him, and if it was enough to sustain her if she didn't get what she wanted by the end of the year.

"I don't know, we'll see," Will said to pacify. He didn't know why it was so hard for him to make a decision nowadays. It was as if there was some hidden variable to consider. He just didn't know what it was. The past couple of years they made the drive up to her home for a day visit. He didn't know why they needed to deviate from that game plan.

"Wye Mills is beautiful at Christmastime. You know, you've seen it, way better than Easton, especially if it snows," Veronica droned on.

Everything is better in Wye Mills, Will thought. Will knew if he didn't stop her that she would take his indecision as a yes. "What about Dad? I think he may be depressed. He's sticking pretty close to home—alone."

"We can bring Dad along, and anyone else who wants to go for that matter. The more the merrier. I'll be the host and guide." She was almost giddy at the thought.

Will cleared his throat. It all sounded like a setup to him. He thought of 1001 ways the holidays could end in complete disaster with only one solution. Part of him felt she deserved the "Winter Wonderland" engagement. Part of him wanted to catch her completely off guard and serve up a proposal with the stuffing and cranberry sauce on Thanksgiving. Then there was another part of him—a growing part—that was still unsure about any proposal.

He tried to shade the doubt in his eyes. "Like I said, it depends on my dad. He has an appointment this coming week that I plan on attending with him to see what is really wrong with him. Who knows how he will feel nearly two months from now."

Veronica dangled a carrot off the edge of her fork like a hunter to a pack of hounds in a dog race. "I think it's time. We might want to start considering—"

"I'm not going to consider anything but his return to the pulpit," he said, cutting her off.

"Gosh, Will, can you bring your voice down?" Veronica said, looking over her shoulder at other diners nearby. "C'mon, I just meant we should discuss alternatives."

Will stared at her as if she were an alien. "My dad is not some sheep you can just put out to pasture, Veronica."

"I wasn't suggesting that at all. Gosh, listen to me. Maybe we should take him out with us, visit him some more." Her tone took an abrupt about-face from condescending to caring.

"Maybe we should do just that." He thought, *you're in such a rush to be his daughter-in-law.*

His dad loved everybody in general, including Veronica, but Will didn't feel the bond of a special relationship between the man who raised him and the woman he loved. Veronica made grand gestures of affection toward his father when there was an audience around, like at church. On his last birthday she had a huge ice cream cake made and caused a big fuss about keeping it on ice until the end of Sunday service. She never initiated a call or visit otherwise, but seemed to have a spark in her eye at the prospect of him retiring.

He knew he couldn't judge her based on her relationship with his father. He wasn't exactly sterling silver to her parents either. He knew his value fell each year he dated their daughter but didn't do anything about legitimizing their relationship.

"Here," Veronica said, shoving something at him.
"What's this?" he said.
"A card from your friend, Rebecca. It's for your father—and, I guess, you—and the church for handling her mother's funeral. She gave it to me last Sunday when I welcomed the new members. I told her we'd get it to Dad."
Will did not bother to pick up the envelope until he had devoured the sirloin slice smothered with steak sauce. He didn't want to be accused of being too eager to grab or look at the card. He did not want to get into another conversation about Rebecca and be inclined to defend her. They dined in silence until Will assumed it sufficed his girlfriend that reminders of Rebecca were out of his system or out of her own.
"I remember when you told me you were going into the ministry, whatever that meant. I didn't even know what that entailed. Remember that?" she asked.
Will nodded his head.
"At that point you had a vision, a plan. You were no nonsense. I could be still waiting on you to become a doctor. I had no choice but come aboard or get out of the way," she said, her eyes locking on to his. "We decided that we were going to leave a lot of things behind, stuff we used to do in college, for instance. I was okay with that. We were gonna be faithful to the Lord and each other much like your mom and dad, be extraordinary. These were your words not mine. What happened to that?"
"Nothing happened to that plan." Will tugged his ear. He'd be a fool to say otherwise.
"It just seems that you take offense anytime I mention our future at the church. Your dad will retire one day, whether it be sooner or later. I'd just like to see us begin to build our legacy or at least talk about it like we

used to. Make me feel like I am not wasting my time," she said, resigned, snatching her eyes away from him.

Will thought about what she said as he pretended to check the dessert menu or something more substantive to order. He remembered the zeal of his fresh call. She was the mistress to his ministry education. They had a long-distance relationship at that time, and he didn't have the worries of sustaining a face-to-face relationship and full-time ministry like he did now. They were supposed to be extraordinary, escaping the many traps and pitfalls of a young couple because they had like vision and plans for a church. He wondered why his vision was failing him now. He wondered why it felt like nails on a chalkboard anytime she referred to him as the pastor and herself as the future first lady.

Will pushed the menu aside to look at her. He decided it was time to stop pacifying her and dish out some real validation. "I love you. Excuse me for being so selfish. I guess I forget you are the brains in this operation with enough vision for the both of us. I would like to know how you think I am doing as the interim pastor. You know more than anyone else how we can improve what we are doing at Grace Apostle."

"Yes." She rewarded him with her stunning smile again. "I feel Grace still has an old fogy feel. I like what you did this past Sunday. You were on fire, baby. I was telling Nina to get her butt back to church the other day, and how you used that teddy bear as an illustration."

"It was a Transformer," he said.

She laughed. "You're so funny. Now you're quoting a four-year-old. But if that's what it takes to wake people up, make church a little less boring, then I'm all for it."

This was what she felt about him and his dad's ministry. Did she really think church was boring? Was she even getting the lessons he was teaching or did she think it didn't apply to her because she was his girl-friend?

"I say, recruit new members, use some new scrip-tures, you know, mix it up," Veronica continued.

Are there new scriptures I am unaware of? "Um, I don't quite think it works that way. The Word is the Word, there's no adding or subtracting from that," Will said, wrinkling up his forehead.

"You know what I mean. Oh, I just thought of some-thing. My home church has a show choir. They've per-formed at the county fair every year. They hold audi-tions for that choir. Think of how many members we'd bring in with a decent choir that didn't dwindle down to a quartet by fourth Sunday. Then you wouldn't feel compelled to try to help them out like you do, blaring into the microphone each week." She shook her head with a smirk.

He had asked for her opinion, so he couldn't go get-ting his feelings hurt. He swallowed hard to stomach her insults as well as her suggestions. This was a very telling conversation. All their earlier planning and pro-jecting were predicated on a common vision. He put his heart and soul into helping people find Christ and see God in their everyday lives. Her input somehow didn't match his output and vice versa.

Now he knew what was off, what had been nagging him. That's why he had been feeling unsupported lately and unenthused. That was also why he was starving after a meal at this foo-foo restaurant instead of sati-ated at a steak buffet or burger joint. They were out of synch, and she didn't notice it, or worse, didn't care.

"You know another ministry I'd love to see at Grace that we had back home? A dance troupe," Veronica said excitedly.

Just when he was set to tune her out he thought about Rebecca. *The Sound of Music.* It was another stupid nickname he used to call her. He remembered watching her from the back church office where he often did his homework. This was before they became inseparable. A few times he'd look out the window and see her. She'd take to her backyard, spinning, leaping, and jumping on the plane of her patio and the slope of their field. She was a dancer. His recollection was foggy but he believed she reported having taken lessons at one time or another. If memory served him she was quite good.

Now Will was getting excited. It made sense. That would account for Rebecca's perfect posture and the musicality with which she walked. She had returned with a hyper femininity that made it impossible to deny he was in the presence of a blatantly bodacious woman. He was her preacher and her friend, but even he had to testify that under those short skirts of hers, stockings seemed to be made to silhouette her legs. Will caught himself. He was on a slippery slope with these new thoughts about his good friend, and it had left him with a goofy, wedged smile on his face.

Before he could wonder if Veronica had noticed, she asked, "What are you smiling at, huh?"

"Your ideas." He backpedaled fast. "You're a genius, sweetheart. I'd actually like to see a few of those things happen at Grace."

Chapter 14

Rebecca had gone looking for some aspirin, first in the master bath and then in the hallway medicine cabinet, when she spotted it. A metallic, silver flask was hidden behind a bottle of Robitussin as if it were there to jump kick the medicinal properties of the cough syrup.

This was so unlike the Madame. *In the guest restroom,* she thought. She considered the unlikely event that someone else could have left it there by mistake. Rebecca brought the canister together with the pints of liquor she'd found in the cabinet and on the lazy Susan. She did a sniff test to confirm the same poignant brand of alcohol.

Had her mother become a full-fledged alcoholic? Rebecca had seen the Madame inebriated on occasion, but couldn't recall the frequency or severity of the problem because she was a self-centered teen at the time, concerned only with her own insecurities. Plus, she was almost sure her cousin Gail would have shielded her from a possible addiction if just to protect the Madame's image.

Rebecca decided to leave the evidence right there on the kitchen counter and to ask Gail about it when she returned home from work. She took off for the back bedroom to do her own investigation.

Getting to know the Madame posthumously would mean going beyond her wardrobe and shoe cabinet.

Rebecca had claimed her mother's room instead of her oddly shaped second-floor room. Homes like theirs were pear-shaped, leaving the living spaces and the rare first-floor bedroom with gobs of space. Rebecca kicked past the Madame's mini footlocker full of programs, newspaper clippings, and certificates she had collected over the years. Rebecca had been living out of the two suitcases that she had brought with her, as if her mother would return home to reclaim her space and she would have to leave immediately.

A mixed scent of cedar, mothballs, and a floral potpourri was released into the air as Rebecca went through her mother's bureau drawers. She almost snickered looking through the Madame's unmentionables. Before she closed the top drawer she remembered the context of her mother's death. Gail had called to tell her, and before Rebecca could leave Salisbury for Easton, she had to satisfy her sick curiosity by returning to the scene at a department store in the Salisbury Mall. A slender woman with a tape measure as a necklace had recounted her mother's last conscious moments. In a need to make sense of it all, she had to see what her mother contemplated buying. She had to see the garment. A long-line bustier, a bullet bra for the nearly sixty-six-year-old Madame, now seemed odd in light of the functional foundations Rebecca now expected to find and that the Madame had plenty of in her top drawer.

Rebecca pressed on, more emphatic about finding some answers. She ran her hand through her mother's garments and under them as if trying to find a concealed compartment. When she had gone through all the drawers and had even taken a peep under the bed, she was temporarily at a loss. She leaned against the high bed, looking around. The general aesthetic was immaculate. There were no photos of family reminders displayed, nothing lying about that would indicate the Madame had occupied the room at all.

Rebecca bent at the waist and dangled her body over, hoping the blood would rush to the pulsing site of her headache from earlier. She almost bumped her head on the nightstand when she decided to right herself. She looked in the nightstand drawer as an afterthought. Inside was a humongous house Bible, the kind people left on a coffee table to announce to visitors that they were Christians. Rebecca had to turn it sideways to take it out of the drawer.

A tiny velour envelope-like sack fell from the front of the book. Inside was a lock of curly dark brown hair taped to a small faded card with a hospital insignia, marked with "baby girl" and Rebecca's full birth date. That made her smile, to find a memento of her birth. She palmed the lush material and replaced it in the inside cover. She was confused to find another sack flattened a little farther in the book. It held the same card marked from the same hospital with another lock of hair. This time there was no name, no birth date.

Rebecca felt for her own shoulder-length hair. *How much of my hair did they cut?* she thought. She folded the Bible over and decided to flip the pages of the Good Book from that end. Immediately, she found a letter-sized envelope almost ripped to shreds, as if the Madame was in haste to open it. The contents made Rebecca drop the hefty Bible to the floor.

Ava,
Forgive me for taking awhile to respond to your last letter. I've been a polygamist all this time be-

cause I feel we've always been married. To marry now would make no difference on our love. Don't shut me out. We need to discuss this.
    Our usual place after duty calls . . .

The signature on the love note was a single character, which was indistinguishable, as if it came from a special alphabet. Rebecca looked back at the envelope. There was no way to date the letter or figure out the time of the Madame's rendezvous. Rebecca went back to the letter. At the bottom the Madame scratched out her immediate response in big, red, jagged letters: "Bull." The pen seemed to have run out before the expletive was completely spelled out. Rebecca secretly hoped her mother had delivered that message personally.

The Madame had a lover, and he was married. *Hypocrite,* Rebecca thought. To think her mom beat the sam hill out of her for just being in a parked car, ironically on the same path to the graveyard for which the city now wanted to build an access road. She always wondered how her mother, who didn't drive much herself, had found her. She always secretly blamed Gail for ratting her out. Could the Madame and her mystery beau have been there making out themselves? Was that their secret meeting place? The thought made Rebecca cringe because she had already graduated high school at the time, and when Rebecca did the math, her mother was past fifty years of age. It was all too decadent to ingest by herself. She had to call someone. Once again, she thought it best to wait until her cousin came home to find out what Rebecca had just discovered and find out what Gail might already have known.

Now she understood her mother's sudden and unexpected rages. She understood her rants and warnings. Guilt must have been driving her to drink. Every harsh tone could be attributed to this man. The letter said "all these years." This wasn't a onetime affair. *She must have been horribly heartbroken.* Will came to Rebecca's mind as she picked up her mother's Bible and replaced it in the drawer. He would be perfect to help her process what she had just discovered. She took a chance by calling the church office number she had memorized. She was thrilled when he picked up on the third ring.

"Hey, you got a minute?" she asked almost breathlessly.

There was a hesitation on his end. "Sure, for you. I got to run to Salisbury for a meeting, but I'll be good if I leave in the next fifteen minutes or so. What's up?"

Rebecca looked at her watch and suddenly felt silly for taking up his time on her family drama. She thought of taking the trip to Salisbury with him and filling him in on the way, but remembered she didn't want to darken the city limits, especially since she was MIA from her job.

"I tell you there is never a dull day at the Lucas household," Rebecca said, making it at least sound worth his while. "Boy, if I didn't think I'd get clawed up in the trees, I would walk over there to show you something. Forget driving."

"You'll get more than snagged. There are a few trucks out back doing some work or something. Contee and I have been trying to figure out what they're doing."

"Oh my gosh, the access road! They couldn't have started this already," Rebecca said, clasping her hand over her mouth. "Apparently they meant business. Gail and I both forgot to mention that to my mother's lawyer. I may need your help securing some contractors, or volunteers, or something for a job out back."

"Sure," he said, as uncertain as her request, "and I may need your help for a little project I'm working on for the church anniversary, but I can talk to you about that later. What's up?"

"I don't know how else to say it, but I found out today that the Madame had a lover, and that he was married."

"What?" Will questioned as if he hadn't heard correctly. "So what is it you want to show me?"

"A letter the man wrote my momma, justifying why he had strung her along all this time. I found it in her Bible of all places. He must have had her sprung because I have a feeling that the letter was recent. Man! You believe that?" Rebecca said, grabbing her forehead, although speaking with him seemed to have alleviated her headache.

"No, I don't. I don't even think I want to see the letter, to be honest," he said after expelling a long breath of air.

"Why?" she questioned.

"'Cause that's the Madame's business, that's why, and I just find it really sad. You sound almost excited about it."

"Excited is not an accurate description of my feelings, Will. I don't know how I'm supposed to feel. My initial reaction was to be thoroughly pissed."

"Why?" He chuckled uncomfortably.

"'Cause she wasn't perfect," she almost screamed at the obviousness, "but the expectation was for me to be."

"Will you listen to yourself? I hoped you had learned that no one is perfect. That's a hard ideal to live up to. The beautiful thing is we can use the experience of our little *indiscretions* to be better. That's all I'm really saying when I preach."

"Well, I haven't been reformed yet," she stated dryly. "It's transformed."

"I know," Rebecca said. "I was there Sunday. I was listening. Beyond this latest development, I've had a setback or two of my own this week. I need to reform and then work on the transforming thing."

She immediately regretted that admission and her encounter with Randall all over again until she heard him laugh. She loved that he was not more probing and not the least bit judgmental.

"Leave it to Rebi to remix my message," Will commented, "but it's refreshing that you're making an effort. Preachers love when people take what they say to heart."

"And I love that you *just* listen," she complimented him.

"Well, I'd be a fool to change then. Wait, there is this song—gosh, how does that song go?" he started. "You know the one by Luther."

"Oh, yup, and that's my song too." Rebecca pondered. He was right up her alley with classic slow jams. "Yeah, 'Forever, For Always, For Love.'"

"'If she says she loves the way I am,'" he serenaded her. "Yeah, I'm a fool, all right." He took in a deep breath of air. "Let me stop."

Rebecca sucked in a breath as well and held it. He was too sweet, and a bit of a flirt as well, she thought. She heard the smile linger in his voice after he sang, and imagined that dimple. "What time are you coming back from Salisbury?" she inquired. "We should catch a bite again."

There was a longer hesitation than she expected from a man who was just singing to her. She wondered what he was struggling with.

"Ummmmmmmmmmmmmm," he finally said.

"Hey, you can just tell me if it's not a good time. I know I caught you off guard, maybe another time."

"Here's the thing. Veronica is kind of uncomfortable with us hanging out like we did the other day. It's like she's going through this phase. I'm just trying to keep the peace, that's all. It's a long story. I don't know." His voice dropped off.

This time she remained silent. That was it. There was no long story, the girlfriend was jealous of their friend-ship, therefore the friendship was through. Where were they supposed to meet, talk, and carry on like they did—church? She knew that would not be possible either.

"Look, I got to run, but I'll call you, or you can call me about that work you need to get done. I've got to get you and Veronica together real soon. Just try not to be too judgmental toward the Madame. Even in death, we should honor our parents. She had her own life to live and salvation to work out. I just wished she was closer to the church to have buried those burdens and not the other way around. Try not to dwell on it," Will said, try-ing to summarize a lot of things, perhaps figuring like she had that this would be the last time for a while they would speak in a personal and candid way.

Rebecca felt numb. She was judgmental all right, but it wasn't the Madame she was judging right now.

Chapter 15

She had been denied access. It was the same cycle all over again. First it was Randall. Now, Will couldn't be seen in public with her. Why did they need to be on the down low? She hadn't even slept with Will. She wasn't too happy to find out their friendship was expendable.

So the new rumor was that Rebecca Lucas was back and going after the pastor, she thought. She didn't want to brag about her previous prowess, but she would wreck Will if given the chance. He'd be entranced by her touch. According to Rebecca, as long as she had known Will, she would have already been Miss-First-Lady-in-training at Grace Apostle if she wanted Will. *Wanted Will?* Something tingled within her at the thought. Sure, she wanted him exactly like before, unfettered and not watered down to appease his girlfriend.

She'd show Miss Perfect who wanted Will, all right. A couple of counseling sessions, a few closed-door prayer meetings, and there'd be a substitution on the front pew. She already had him singing to her. *Not Will,* she told herself after replaying her previous thoughts. She couldn't go after him in that manipulative and disin-genuous way. As crazy as it sounded, she cared for him too much to seduce him. What got Rebecca was the fact that Veronica didn't even know her. Where would she get the idea that Rebecca couldn't be trusted around her man? Rebecca took one good guess.

Rebecca realized she still held on to the Madame's love note. She refolded the letter and put it inside her bra. With a tap to her chest she got up to leave the room. Rebecca grabbed a shot glass out of the showcase curio cabinet in the great room on her way to the kitchen. She opened the flask and poured herself a shot once there. It was scorching on the way down. Rebecca convinced herself that a high time was what she needed. She knew where the alcohol was flowing, and she wouldn't have to pay for it. She made plans right then for the next evening to go out in search of a new friend.

Wishing Well Liquors had a seedy bar in the back of its establishment frequented by bar hoppers and truckers from up and down Route 50. No ladies and gentleman in this establishment. In fact, if you considered yourself a lady you waited for a radio-sponsored or invitation-only event at one of the hotel ballrooms to party. The Wishing Well was a place a group of girlfriends went on a dare, for a bachelorette party or a *Girls Gone Wild* type of experience. It was a place where Rebecca would debut her weight loss makeover every couple of weeks after graduation and let the men weigh in by the round of drinks and attention they would pay her. It was also a place where she could dance uninhibited, since the Madame fancied early on that formal dance training was a hobby she would no longer continue to support or pay for on behalf of her only daughter.

Rebecca had pulled out her secret weapon from her suitcase for this occasion. It was a black dress with gathered ruching throughout the bodice that, once on, appeared as if the dress had been snatched tightly from both sides and wrapped around her body like a lopsided glove. She was met at the door of the club by a tall, burly guy who looked her up and down suspiciously as if she were a suspected terrorist. He snickered something to the bartender about her being an open threat and needing to see what she was concealing. Meanwhile, several men walked right into the club while she was being detained.

"What about them?" Rebecca asked, ignoring the feeling in her gut that she should just go home.

"They're regulars. You're definitely not. You are new, or I am blind." His fingers wiggled their way between her arm and the side of her breast for a tighter hold on her upper arm and a quick feel.

Right then she wished she had carried her bat-slinging cousin who had no idea where she was, but she realized she had her own defense. She pulled out her business card and threatened like Randall to pull everyone related to the establishment in court if he didn't back down.

"Here comes trouble," the burly man tried to announce to the general assembly over the thump of the music after letting her go.

She looked around to see who had noticed the scene, but most of the patrons seemed to be lost in the music or in their own pint of beer. She noticed Shelby Gray, waitress and resident eye candy, by the deejay booth. Shelby lent to the *Cheers* TV show vibe. Everyone probably knew one another. It was Shelby who had schooled Rebecca long ago that a strong entrance lined up your prospects for the rest of the night. She suddenly felt silly. She waved at Shelby as if she had come to catch up with the bar kitten, and squelched her crazy notion that being there was a good idea. Then she spotted him.

The first time Rebecca set eyes on Nina Pritchett's husband at the Chosen Twenty-Three reception for her and Gail, she knew he was a regular at the Wishing Well. He sat at the bend of the bar opposite the front door. Rebecca surmised the well-worn baseball cap must be a permanent fixture with him. He still had on his surprisingly new and sporty-looking leather bomber jacket over a button-up shirt, like he had just come in or didn't plan on staying long. She walked across his field of vision while taking off her jacket, as if she were on a runway and her job was to highlight each piece of her ensemble. She took a table just outside of the service bar's dim lighting and proceeded to powder her nose and tousle her hair. She waited until she could feel his attention, as well as the attention of a few other patrons, lock on her.

It was quiet for a bar scene, but Rebecca reminded herself it was in the middle of the week. She wasted no time making her way to the almost deserted dance floor. Her intent was not to be overtly sexual toward him. She wanted to entice him enough that thoughts of her would follow him home when he was with his wife. Rebecca knew it was the music that was her lover tonight, and it would dictate her movements. As if seeing her approaching, the deejay mixed in one of those female anthems by Beyoncé where the men cleared the floor, pulled up their seats, and got their peep show on.

The groove had enough percussion to spark a fire from the friction she planned to strike with her hips and thighs, she thought. She swayed, ground, and even dropped it low as the beat and lyrics spoke to her. Shelby and a mismatched couple who had already hooked up for the night joined her on the dance floor. Shelby raised her tray toward Rebecca as if toasting womanhood, and Rebecca waved her arm in return.

The men were slow to approach. After two cuts, a man in a plaid shirt attempted to keep up with her rhythm. Rebecca turned her full attention to him. The man had brought his drink with him to the dance floor. After the third icy droplet fell on her and soaked through her dress, she left him on the dance floor.

Rebecca noticed two drinks waiting for her when she returned to her table. One she suspected was from a snaggletoothed man in the corner who had been eerily gawking at her. She vaguely remembered him from long ago. He always sat in that corner. Like the dent in the wall right over his head, Rebecca imagined that he was there when they cut the lights off in the wee hours of the morning and when they cut them back on the next afternoon. She grabbed Shelby as she went by to confirm that the other one had come from Nina's husband. Being the invitation she needed, she took the salt-rimmed glass in hand and approached the bar. He smirked when he saw her coming.

Rebecca placed the glass down and slid it toward him slightly. "I don't know who is going to drink this girly drink, but I prefer something stronger."

"Top shelf?" Nina's husband inquired. He signaled to the bartender like he was bidding in a silent auction.

"Scotch on the rocks." Rebecca looked for Madame's brand as she pulled the margarita back in front of her and sipped, boosting her inhibition while she waited. The bartender easily found the decorative bottle on the shelf, poured, and iced the drink with ease. "I hope you don't plan to just watch me drink and dance."

Nina's husband didn't even speak, but signaled that he wanted a duplicate when the bartender placed Rebecca's new drink in front of her. She didn't know what she was thinking, ordering the Scotch. Just like playing dress-up, she was trying to walk in the Madame's shoes. She didn't drink alcohol on the regular. In fact, she gave up intoxicating drinks after leaving Easton. She stomached a shot and knew she'd be nursing her drink all night.

"How ya doing, Randy? Doing all right?" Shelby asked, gaining access to the bar area from the raised hatch next to the cash register.

Rebecca noticed that Nina's husband appeared agitated with Shelby's greeting, and turned away from her slightly to face the dance floor. He had been outed. Maybe he wanted to remain anonymous in their exchange. She decided to level the playing field.

"I'm an old classmate of your wife's," Rebecca said, swiveling on her own stool toward him.

Randy gulped the rest of his Scotch. "I know who you are."

"Well then you know I am Nina's least favorite person," Rebecca admitted.

"I think you have to get in line for that title," he said, thumbing over his shoulder.

Rebecca noticed Randy's eyes held such coldness that she wanted to back off. She couldn't imagine being married to someone who couldn't stand her. It was almost worse than her mother's case. She began to look at him differently.

"Why don't we agree not to speak about Nina tonight," she whispered in his ear.

Two Scotches and two beers later, Randy broke that agreement. They spent the better part of twenty minutes on the dance floor, where Rebecca kept the beat with her hips while Randy awkwardly bumped up against her. They took dirty dancing to a new level as she sank into him like a second skin.

When they returned to Rebecca's table Randy spoke candidly about his relationship with his wife. He told her about meeting Nina as he scouted for a house and how he was persistent in courting her and eventually winning her over. The good times faded fast after that. Then he spoke of the not-so-good times when he and Nina would fight. It seemed Nina was never satisfied with the life he had provided for them being a trucker. He was thankful for those times he'd be away on an overnight or forty-eight-hour run to offer himself a reprieve from their sometimes violent spats, where Nina would demean him and often hit him out of frustration. He began to suspect that Nina enjoyed the breaks as well because he could never catch her at home when he called. Randy spoke of the unborn child that Nina was carrying only once, as if he wasn't certain it was his.

"Yep, we're in a countdown. We'll see when the baby is born if they will have a room at our house or the mayor's mansion," Randy said.

Rebecca contemplated the implications of what he had just revealed. She sympathized with what Randy was going through. He obviously was torn up about it and was trying to find a way to handle it all. Rebecca had no room for that knowledge either with the Madame's baggage cluttering her mind. Nina Pritchett was a home wrecker. That would have been a tasty morsel to devour if she could swallow the fact that her own mother was guilty of the same. What was she doing there tonight? Apparently everyone had a scarlet letter or a scathing one like the Madame's actual letter waiting to be found in the back of a Bible. There was a price to be paid for being indiscriminate and those closest in our lives helped pay it.

Rebecca had to leave. Randy was clinging to her like she was his savior. He even appeared ready to accompany her to the bathroom. He could barely stand at this point. This man needed a friend, not what she had offered him, someone to devour with his eyes and have his way with in his thoughts. When Rebecca returned from the bathroom she gathered her coat to leave. Randy was on her heels, clumsily groping for her. Suddenly Rebecca was worried about appearances. She hoped no one thought they were departing together, especially not him. She would have taken off running if she thought she could outrun her conscience. Rebecca turned to look at him one last time as he fumbled in his jacket pocket for money to settle their bill. He apparently had done more than cry his tears in a solitary pint of beer before she had gotten there.

Rebecca made haste to the door as Randy called out for her to wait for him. In her last act of sympathy, she once again extracted her business card and tapped it so the burly bodyguard could see it.

"What do you want, Trouble?" he asked, exposing her for the Decepticon she was.

"I don't know what your policy is regarding drinking limits, but under no circumstances are you to let my friend over there drive himself home. Call him a cab, so he can make it home safely to his wife," Rebecca demanded.

Chapter 16

"Well, well, well, hello, Pastor Donovan. Fancy meeting you here, and on your vacation no less," Rebecca said, shocked to see the elderly statesman sitting beside her cousin at the conference-style table in Mr. Tremaine's office.

"Well that vacation will be coming to a close soon anyway," Pastor Donovan said, resigned.

"You know, Rebecca rejoined the church last Sunday. We all were so excited," Gail shared.

Pastor Donovan beamed like a proud father. "Great, great, I hope you won't be disappointed when I start preaching again rather than your good friend."

"Didn't you teach your students that the Word is the Word?" Rebecca bent over his shoulder to kiss the man's temple. "You couldn't get that lazy son of yours to fill in for you today?" She wondered if Will was slated to come but was avoiding her to keep his promise to his girlfriend.

"Of course you know Will loves to run himself ragged. He probably would have come with me since he wants to shadow me everywhere these days, but he had to work," he shared. He leaned in and began to whisper. "Plus, I was told I had to be here. So, I had to hang up my leisure clothes and clean myself up so I'd be presentable for you girls."

She noticed the pastor's three-piece pinstriped suit. He looked ready for Sunday morning. Their two o'clock estate hearing had left her cousin classically dressed straight from work. Rebecca looked down at her own dowdy dress that she had covered up with a cardigan. She had come from the local newspaper office, where she took out an ad to promote herself as a local notary, a side hustle she had in Salisbury. She thought the extra money from certifying documents would come in handy per her cousin's warnings. *Not quite the heiress role,* she thought.

"How are you doing, Rebi?" Pastor Donovan asked.

How many times had she heard him ask her just that in high school? Pastor Donovan always allowed her to take refuge in his office when the gossip or peer pressure got to be too much for her to bear. Many times it was after being sent out for reacting in what the teachers called a violent outburst, which could be anything from refusing to sit up to throwing something across the room in their staunch Christian school. He always heard her side before debating whether to call the Madame.

Rebecca just nodded her head slowly to his inquiry now, the universal sign that she was holding on. Rebecca ignored Gail's gestures for her to take a seat on the other side of her, preferring to stand while she analyzed the scene. She had never seen or heard of a pastor serving in an official role during an estate hearing. That could leave only one reason why he was there.

Rebecca decided then to take her place as she counted how many more seats there were to fill. How many more slices of the Madame's pie could be divvied up?

Tremaine and his assistant held a sidebar conversation at the head of the wide table before they began. The woman with him was like Rebecca, barely listening to her boss as she organized the documents needed for the meeting on the table, along with her iPad, complete with keyboard, for recording notes. Rebecca thought about her own job, or possible lack thereof. She wondered if the woman was a paralegal or his administrative assistant, and if the small firm needed another one.

Ralph Tremaine, an ultra-thin Caucasian man who was attractive despite the sagging, wrinkled skin at his neck and jaw line looked around, puzzled in his expression, as if taking attendance and finding his star pupil absent. Just then Clayton Green, the Madame's accountant who Rebecca had been trying to get on the phone for a personal account of her mother's finances, breezed through the door. The Madame was broke, but he was still on the payroll. Everything had been hush-hush up until now. She was eager to find out why.

They all took their places. As the facilitator, Mr. Tremaine initiated introductions. It didn't fare well with Rebecca that everyone had a title except her. Even Gail was tagged the family administrator. Rebecca was just the daughter. He thanked Rebecca and Gail in the Madame's stead for the bond he shared with the Madame and their lasting business relationship. Rebecca wondered for a moment if he could be her mother's mystery lover, but quickly dismissed it. Tremaine shared his hope that he would continue to represent the Lucas women. He continued with an explanation of the occasion and the legal and binding confines of the last will and testament on the estate of Ava Marie Lucas.

Rebecca's focus was drawn away by Pastor Donovan's sudden coughing spell. She noticed the slight tremor in his hands as he poured himself a glass of water from the offering in the center of the table. The room quieted as everyone became concerned. Gail seemed to particularly dote over Pastor Donovan. Quick to grab a paper towel and square it, she mopped up all the water that spilled during his episode, shy of the dribble on his top lip and shirt front. He waved to assure them all that he would be all right.

Tremaine announced the settlement of the Madame's minor debts. Rebecca was relieved she was up to date on her taxes. She had seen huge estates stripped like locusts can clear a field due to back taxes.

"At the eleventh hour we received an odd settlement agreement from the county and a Mr. Earl Clipp, representing what looks like the Women's Historical Society, as it relates to a strip of land they want to shave off for a road of some sort. They told me the family was informed," Tremaine said, looking around the table for clarity. "They issued it as a claim against the account, but they want to make an offer for a sizable chunk of land. It looks like a half acre."

Rebecca looked to Gail, the family administrator, to explain. When she shrugged off any knowledge or insight, Rebecca spoke. "We did get a call. They want to build a road to the rear of the property between our home and the rear of the church. In fact, I need to clear the land out there because Mr.Clip threatened eminent domain, as if he would take the land by force. Maybe you can help us, because I haven't checked to see if any of this is legal."

"Ralph brought it to my attention the other day, and I wanted to check into the fair market value on land for you. A half acre is quite a bit of land, and it seems that they are trying to offer you peanuts for it. Plus, when you get a chance to survey out back there, check to see how close this cuts toward your well. There are Chesapeake Watershed regulations to the runoff that is likely to occur due to construction being so close to a water supply," Clayton Green expressed over another brief spell from Pastor Donovan.

Rebecca was also at a loss. Her to-do list just got longer. When she last spoke to Will it appeared as if they had already started the project. She wondered if there was some type of cease and desist order that could be served to the construction crew until she could deal with some of this stuff. Before she could voice her concerns, Tremaine interrupted.

"Apparently the parties involved presented this now and in this fashion so the direct heir would be forced to act on it. Mr. Clip and his party must know that not all property is covered by a last will, and state laws could change the wishes of the deceased expressed in her last will and testament. So before we get too far off topic let's deal with the matter at hand. I will be happy to advise you all after the estate is settled and closed."

Rebecca swirled the Madame's bracelet around her wrist several times. That meant Tremaine was willing to be put on retainer, Rebecca thought. *More money, more expenses.* The house may have proven to be a real headache, but she was relieved in the knowledge that wills did not change who was to receive benefits from a life insurance policy.

The official reading of the will commenced. There was repetition of the phrase "in the event of my death." Madame left Rebecca her collection of antique jewelry, which didn't even seem like a gift because Rebecca had helped herself to it since taking over her room. Rebecca was touched nonetheless. It pained her to know her mother had planned for an event that Rebecca herself couldn't even fathom. It was still hard to imagine she wasn't here. Rebecca poked through her purse for the handkerchief that Gail had given her at the reception. When she came up empty, Gail tossed a tissue her way and was dabbing her own eye with another. *Good ol' Gail.*

"In the event of my death, I want the house and property at 5920 Zion Hill Road to go to Gail Lorraine Lucas, unless she is married at the time of my death. In that event, I want the aforementioned property to pass to Rebecca Ann Lucas," Mr. Tremaine read.

Good Gail, my foot! She felt like the classic line from the comedy show *The Smothers Brothers:* "Mom always liked you best." Except Gail wasn't her sister. Rebecca felt that she was the sole heir and therefore should get first dibs. She was thankful her cousin didn't try to give her a reassuring pat right now, or Rebecca would be inclined to sink her nails into Gail's knuckles.

Mr. Tremaine continued as if he were previously recorded. "Both Gail Lorraine and Rebecca Ann will split the units of water sold on the well, minus the maintenance and meter tax unless the well is sold, with and in addition to price of the house at 5920 Zion Hill Road."

Oh, and she'd be diligent about checking the units, Rebecca thought, even though she was essentially homeless.

The will continued to show the Madame's biases as her accounts and holdings rolled over to Gail, as well with the same strange stipulation of marriage. Rebecca wondered if the balances were as meager as her cousin led her to believe. Only Gail had the right to know now.

The will was read and certified. It was Gail's job to see to it that it would be executed. Why wouldn't she? They had one more matter to handle, which was the life insurance policy the Madame had tucked away. The fact that she left it with her lawyer to hand out during these proceedings, and not left at home where her family could find it, left Rebecca with less than an ounce of hope that she would benefit there either.

Thinking his part was over, Tremaine held the envelope as if it was a tossup as to who he wanted to give it to.

"Could you just summarize it for us?" Gail asked. "I know everyone is anxious to get on with their day."

Tremaine unfolded the documents from the unsealed envelope and scanned them. They remained quiet as he flipped through the multiple pages as if just seeing them for the first time. They learned that the Madame had taken a $100,000 policy and split it among Gail, Rebecca, Grace Apostle Methodist Church, and the same organization that was trying to siphon off her land, the Women's Historical Society.

Rebecca's blood was boiling. It should have been a consolation to her that they at least split the policy evenly. It wasn't the value of the dollar amount that mattered to her, which was way less than a year's wages for Rebecca if she kept her job in Salisbury. It was the value the Madame put on her life by not putting her first. She was ready to spit fire as everyone assembled got their own copy of the insurance policy as a record of their claim.

"You've got to be kidding me. The same group that is threatening to steal our land gets $25,000? What is so darn sacred back there that those weasels need access to it all of a sudden?" Rebecca said, bringing up old business as if it were up for discussion now. "Why didn't they settle with their good *colored* member before she died, huh? We all know the Historical Society is nothing but a bunch of white biddies who have nothing better to do than to dig stuff up. No offense, Mr. Tremaine, Mr. Green. I'm not even going to blame this on a racist plot of the white folks. This has got Nancy Pritchett's StepinFetchit name all over it. I mean what has the Madame ever done to her?"

Gail was trying to stop her now. The look of embarrassment in her eyes was palpable. She struggled with whether she wanted to muzzle Rebecca's mouth with her hands or restrain her from rising up from her chair.

Pastor Donovan came to her rescue, stepping over Gail, and taking Rebecca by the forearm. "Let me take her out and speak to her."

"No, I won't be quiet, Pastor," Rebecca protested. They were standing now. Her increased tone halted him and caused him to take a step back. "The official reading is over. Isn't this the part where you entertain anyone who wants to contest the will? This doesn't make any sense—you know darn well my mother left Grace Apostle and never returned as a member. Now she is leaving a quarter of the insurance policy to the church. When was this drafted? Because I have a definite problem with this. To think I rejoined the church. As you can see we're not rich, before you ask me to contribute to the next church project. I won't be sponsoring the next senior class—anything. We have no more to give! Tell the whole county, the Lucas girls are not as rich as everyone believes."

Gail stepped between Rebecca and Pastor Donovan as if to shield him from her. Gail was still trying to figure out how to remove Rebecca from the room, but Rebecca stood her ground. She wasn't budging from that spot.

"The Madame wasn't the biggest saint, in fact far from it, but you all over at Grace must have had her brainwashed into thinking she could get salvation through giving instead of actually winning her soul."

"That's enough," Pastor Donovan said, matching her tone, but intensifying his voice with his bass.

Rebecca softened, fearing she was severing a long-standing relationship with the man in front of her, while the others stood around gawking. It didn't matter to her at this point; his son had already written her off, she reminded herself. "With all due respect, Reverend, you're not my father. You don't know my mom. She was troubled, an alcoholic—a drunk. I contest the validity of the will based on that fact alone."

Rebecca heard Gail gasp but didn't bother to look her way.

"I have to tell you . . . And you're a smart woman, you'll understand," Mr. Tremaine started as if he was uncertain about his first statement. "Proving your mother incompetent and the will invalid is an expensive and difficult task. This isn't a fraud. I assure you she wasn't coerced. Unless you have explicit medical evidence that at the time the will was signed she was demented or in a coma, it's nearly impossible. Think about it."

Rebecca looked around. Everyone had the same pleading eyes as those of Mr. Tremaine. She looked to her cousin, who had shifted her weight away from her. Gail's arms were crossed across her chest as if Rebecca was on her own now. It temporarily frightened Rebecca to know her cousin didn't have her back right now. Rebecca was resigned to the fact that she had been here before. She'd been out there alone for the last fifteen years. It was time to institute plan C.

Chapter 17

Will welcomed the opportunity to make a house call to Rebecca. He had heard from his father how grief consumed her at the estate hearing, causing her to act out in an aggressive and irrational manner. According to Gail at church the day before, her cousin was on a destructive path that would leave her dead before her time. That thought left Will's stomach in knots. Like the Madame, Gail felt Rebecca was disconnecting spiritually at a time she need God the most.

Will couldn't quite fight the feeling that he was on his own destructive path. Around the same time they were at the hearing, he had gone to the Salisbury Mall after work and purchased a diamond solitaire ring that resembled the one his mother wore with her wedding band. Guilt followed him in the mall's door and helped him pick out the ring. Then Guilt's buddies, Doubt and Dread, met him at the food court, where he sat for an hour with the bag clutched in his hands before the threesome dragged him to his car.

Will needed to talk to Rebecca more than Rebecca needed to hear from him. He had been fighting new feelings for her that he wanted to figure out. Was this more than excitement that she was back in the area, excitement that they were back in one another's lives? The question he dared not ask a soul was how he could be preparing to propose to one woman when he was quickly falling in love with another. He knew he had to figure that one out on his own. Despite his growing feelings, Will had to be a friend right now. Will knocked on the same door he used to as a kid when he came to hang out with Rebecca or to study, which was a side entrance door under the carport. He smiled when Rebecca's curious face popped from behind the window shade to see who it was. Her eyes shone bright with the mixture of surprise and what he hoped was excitement. She opened the door and gestured with a finger over her lips to keep quiet. In an instant they were sixteen again on a covert mission. She grabbed his hand, and they tiptoed through the mud room and up the back stairs. They stopped halfway up, where they could hear voices above them.

"Ugh, are you going to help me or not?" they heard Gail say.

Then a male voice said, "I'm not going to keep letting you avoid the conversation. You put me off, then you want to use me for manual labor. I'm only good when I'm chauffeur Milo or fix-it Milo."

Will didn't know what he was listening for, but he sat with Rebecca anyway on the stairwell. Although he didn't like the idea of eavesdropping, he took comfort being crouched up in the narrow space with her. She whispered that Gail and Milo had been arguing since they unexpectedly came in midday. Will could see the entrance was blocked by several large boxes and figured they'd be concealed in their hiding place if they kept quiet.

"Oh gosh, Milo, not now. I got less than one hour before I go back to work," Gail said, letting out an exasperated cry. "I got my cousin going crazy, rearranging things. She moved out the Madame's room as if I'm going to take her mother's things or kick her out. I don't know what she is thinking. Look at this, she's got boxes galore up here blocking the way as if even a quarter of these things can fit into her old room. I threatened to throw it all out. You know how I am. This is not working for me. So if we hide them she'll think I kept my word."

Rebecca stood up with her hand over her mouth as if to stop herself from hollering. Will pulled her back down by her arm, buffering her fall with his body. They both concealed their laughter like kids. They were so close he felt a sensation of every part of her body that now touched his.

"How about I make all this easier and move your stuff out—say to my house?" Milo said.

The force of Gail's sigh could be heard in the stairwell. "This was a total waste of time. I don't need this right now. How would we look living together?"

"Have you been ignoring all these years I've been trying to make you an honest woman? At this point I'll take you anyway I can get you. First it was I'm too new to town. Then it was you needed time to get over the fact that I had been married before. Either you want me or not. Then when I say I'm putting my foot down on an expiration date, you're appealing for more time. I just, I just don't know anymore. I'd be a fool to get tangled up more than I already am with you." His dismay was palpable.

"This is a conversation we need to have when I can wrap my head around it. I got my hands full now with my cousin—with, with this house. Later, Milo, now wrap your hands around some of these boxes."

"You do have time to acknowledge me. Acknowledge what I'm saying, Gail," Milo said, apparently letting go of a box, startling everyone.

"I hear you, okay? I hear you, *I hear you,*" she shouted.

"I'm not trying to make you upset, but you take for granted that I will always be there. Your aunt's will only confirmed the fact that we should have been married way before now. Leave the house and this mess to your cousin. She seems to love drama."

There was a period of silence before either of them spoke. Then, as if whispering, Gail said, "You don't get married because a will tells you to do so."

"You're certainly right," Milo said, resigned. "I'm going back to work because I don't have time or energy to give you any more reasons."

Will and Rebecca both stood, thinking they were going to have to beat a hasty retreat down the back stairs with Milo's curt exit. They breathed a sigh of relief when they heard his footsteps go in the other direction toward the front steps with Gail following close on his heels, calling out for him to wait.

They slowly descended the stairs when the sparring couple vacated the first floor through the front entrance.

"I'm sorry, I couldn't resist," Rebecca said, leading the way through the kitchen to the great room. "Wow, what was that about?"

He watched her curl up on the end of the leather sectional, so he took to the other end. "The man is tired of waiting. He wants all of her, plain and simple." He couldn't help feeling he lacked that same intensity with the woman he was contemplating marrying.

"You mean sex," Rebecca said boldly.

"All, Rebi," Will replied, massaging his right earlobe. Being friends for so long, he couldn't recall one conversation they had ever had about sex. They had talked about school crushes and even love. He figured the taboo topic was made even more taboo because they were taught talking led to doing. "I said it all, didn't I?"

"I guess you would know, being in a long-lasting relationship yourself." Rebecca hesitated, questioning with her eyes before her words escaped her lips. "How . . . how do you . . . refrain? Do you?"

Will exhaled, realizing they were going there. He had heard rumors about Rebecca's sexuality. A few guys around town, who happened to work out at the same local gym as he did, boasted of having been with her. One guy in particular went to school with them. Will strayed away from those distasteful conversations for obvious reasons. She had never mentioned any of those guys and if memory served him correctly, the one in particular hadn't given her a second look in high school, so he refused to believe it all. He often wondered if all that talk was true, why was she spreading herself around?

Will had learned in his training that transparency leads to future testimonies, so he figured disclosure would be best. "Veronica and I met in college. Need I say more?"

"At least, I guess, you now know what you're getting," Rebecca said.

"Fornicating is fornicating, Weary. The crazy thing was that we were intimate before we even really knew each other. Then, bam, ready-made relationship."

He heard her murmuring and deciphered the tail end as, "At least your wham bam led to a relationship."

He took a pause as if to insert a "but" into the conversation. "I exercised and exorcised those demons. I couldn't be out there like that anymore. Veronica and I have since made a pact, especially when I started my Biblical studies. I am the gentleman my mom raised me to be, so I will not take what has not been offered to me."

"So if she's a good girl and doesn't come on to you or entice you, then you will control yourself? That's great, Will, put the burden of your celibacy all on her," Rebecca said smugly.

Will took the accent pillow from behind him and tossed it at her. "It works. That's one of the ways I check myself. You got to stay faithful, focused, and mad busy to remain celibate. I now know God invented true intimacy, which goes way beyond any physical act. I also tell myself I got a lot to learn before I shower my bride with it all. I don't know if you struggled in that area, but many people don't realize that they are the gift. Then the question becomes who are we ordained to present it to?"

Rebecca sat silent with a wondrous expression, as if imagining how powerful preserving herself would be. He looked to her for a comment or reply. She had her hair pulled back into a ponytail that highlighted her laid-back essence. He was thankful she wore her hair this way as opposed to down toward her face and distractedly sexy, especially for this conversation. He was starting to lose focus just looking at her.

As if to redirect him, she finally spoke. "I'm surprised you're here. Does your girlfriend know?"

Will could do nothing more than look at her after that jab. He hated to think that she also thought Veronica told him what he could and could not do. He had resigned to either play the role and marry Veronica on her terms or fess up to his foreboding feelings and run the risk of losing her. Thoughts of the ring he had purchased gave him an instant headache.

"You got it wrong if you think Veronica dictates everything I do. I was just trying to be considerate of her feelings. I mean she's been with me since college, change of majors, long hours of study, long hours at the plant, long hours at church. To top it off she moved here," Will said, hammering out all the reasons why he ought to seal the deal with Veronica. She had proven faithful. Rebecca was a friend who fifteen years ago left with not so much as a forwarding address or a good-bye. All this time later, her plans to stay in Easton were equally uncertain.

"I guess I understand her point of view. Here comes this phantom friend all of a sudden trying to suck up all her man's time. Like I said, I understand. I just don't like it," Rebecca said as she ran her hand along the piping on the accent pillow now balanced in her lap. "I just wonder, where does that leave us?"

"It leaves us here," Will said, stretching his arms out to indicate the relative space and time they found themselves in. He pulled out a folder and extracted some bills for her to see. "I'm here checking up on you, aren't I? I guess I have to do a better job communicating to Veronica how important your friendship is to me."

"What's this?" she asked, leaning in.

"It's the complete record of our water and sewage bill for the church, paid to Ms. Ava M. Lucas," Will said, watching Rebecca close her eyes and lower her head. He slid over quickly to catch it. They caught a tender moment as his hand caressed her shoulders and then her arms. "The Madame was a giving person, but we weren't just on the receiving end at the church. Grace was a faithful patron to your family well in return. When everyone else turned to Easton Utilities or other private companies, we stuck with you guys. We have no plans to change that relationship."

"I am so embarrassed by the way I acted," Rebecca moaned, cupping her forehead in her hand. "The whole

hearing just highlighted some insecurities I guess I've
felt my whole life. I owe your dad an apology."

"Well you can give it to him in person. He'll be back
in the office tomorrow, in fact. Count your blessings
though, Weary. The Madame provided for you. You're
a business owner and didn't even realize it, especially
with the units of water that are about to kick in when I
start the horticulture project with the kids of the school
in the spring."

Will smiled when he saw her brighten up at the mention of his plans.

"What you will not do is build a supersized terrarium
out back." Rebecca pointed her finger at him in a sassy
manner. "That's what you will not do."

"What you cannot do is withdraw like your mother
did. God hasn't turned His back on you, so don't turn
your back on Him. I want to see you at church."

"I just missed one week—because I was sort of going
ballistic around the house. Poor Gail, I've got to figure
out my place in the universe before I drive her crazy. I
don't know. . . ." She sighed.

"You don't have to stay faithful to Grace Apostle,
although I hear they have a really handsome assistant
pastor," Will said in his best Groucho Marx impression. "How are you trying to find your place without
God? Stay faithful to Him. That's all I ask. He'll bring
about your heart's desire."

"Whatever that is," Rebecca said, taking liberties by
resting her head on his shoulder. "I don't doubt anything you're saying. It's just hard for me right now. I've
personally been trying to get back to this time in my
life when things were consistent. There was a time in
childhood I really felt connected, and like I belonged.
Then I found contentment in Salisbury also for a time.
That is when things rung true for me, you know like

spiritually. Something always comes up though, or I do something to offset that. I got this knack for knocking everything out of whack. Then I've got this guilt that I, literally, try to get away from—in search of that consistency again, that contentment. Crazy, right?"

Will relished the feeling of both her physical and emotional weight on him. He resisted the urge to bend over and kiss her forehead or nestle back farther in the couch as a permanent fixture like a back massager meant for her soothing. He had to remember he was working now. She was giving him an opportunity for true ministry. He couldn't help but think that she encouraged his passion, whereas Veronica would be offended if he, as she put it, "preached to her all the time." Rebecca genuinely wanted to know what God wanted out of her life. She also wanted to know what he thought.

"You just summed up half of the struggles the characters went through and recorded in the Bible. You're being Weary," Will offered. Then sat up abruptly when a revelation hit, causing her to struggle for balance. "How long have I been calling you Weary?"

"Longer than I care to remember. Why, what's wrong?" she asked.

"Let me tell you how God works." Will was getting more excited with each word. More than when talking with her, he was really attentive to the Holy Spirit, and the Spirit was revealing itself in that moment. "There is a scripture in the Bible that tells us, 'Be not weary in well doing for in due season you shall reap if you faint not.'"

He watched her wrinkle up her face in the most adorable expression. "That's me," she said.

"Ms. Welldoing. You told me yourself you've met an obstacle and think you can't go on anymore. Then you decide to change directions instead of stay the course."

"Goodness, that proves I am a big, fat quitter," she said, resting her head onto her hand propped now up on the edge of the couch.

"That proves your nickname and spiritual identity to this point. You might as well have been named Weary N. Welldoing." He lifted her head off the perch with the palm of his hand. He didn't want her to be ashamed with him. "It is those times when you are following Christ that you have to take heart and not faint. You're moving toward the consistency and contentment of Christ."

They stared at one another for a while as pastor and parishioner, as friends and a hint of something else.

She lowered her gaze first. "I almost don't know what to say when you do that fortune teller thing. You are an amazing theologian, and clairvoyant, too, to top it off."

Will didn't bother to tell her it wasn't clairvoyance but rather his gifting. If he were clairvoyant he would not be feeling blindsided by his attraction to her like he was feeling now.

Chapter 18

Rebecca saw Will the very next day as she was coming out of the back office area at the church. She had come from apologizing to Pastor Donovan in person. She decided to cut through the sanctuary instead of taking the long trek around through the side hallway. Will was perched at the piano stool with his head down, plucking out a tune. She smiled as she thought that they had seen more of each other than before their friendship ban imposed by his girlfriend.

Rebecca approached him slowly, trying to decipher if he was playing a tune or playing around, "What are you doing?" she asked as a way to announce herself.

"Hey." His shocked expression quickly subsided. "I am actually working on a sermon, and you?"

Rebecca stood at the curve of the piano as if she were the soloist to his accompaniment. "Just saw your father, I apologized, we talked."

"Oh, yeah, how did that go?" he asked, temporarily halting his tune.

Pastor Donovan was quick to put her guilt-ridden mind at ease by accepting her apology. She still couldn't believe she all but accused him of extorting her mother for money. Pastor Donovan admitted that he would miss the Madame. She could tell by the stories he told of Madame's relentlessness and stubborn nature in the community that their camaraderie was genuine. She was glad she wasted no time coming over to share her regrets.

"Your dad was as gracious as ever and looks quite happy to be back to work," Rebecca shared.

"The kids have a big field trip to the County Seat tomorrow. You remember that? Of course he's going to rally them together for a conduct assembly at noon. Can't have some knuckleheads ruining the Grace Apostle reputation." Will looked at his watch then back at her with a slight tug of his ear. "He told me this morning that I'm still flying solo in the pulpit though for at least the next two Sundays. That will take us into the anniversary season here at the church."

As Rebecca stood there, she inhaled the warm mixture of scents that reminded her of tobacco and incense, which had impregnated the wooden benches and drapes of fabric. All she had planned for the day was to update her resume. Neither of them appeared to be in a rush to get back to their tasks. She looked about, suddenly intrigued by something he had said, and decided to inquire. "You said you were writing a sermon, here at the piano. I'd be interested to know how that process goes."

That brought out that dimple of his that she loved so much as he smiled. "I have sort of a weird ritual before I write a sermon. It always involves music. It's like I drown out noise, mainly my own, with noise. I become my own DJ: jazz, hip hop, and gospel, lots of gospel. Cuckoo, right?"

"You've said stranger things, Will Donovan, but go on and finish telling me how this helps you hear from God. G-o-d because I am trusting that the Word I hear at Grace Apostle comes from Him not Sir Mix-a-Lot," she teased.

"Just don't tell anyone when I start quoting Eminem " Will said, placing a finger of secrecy over his lip. "Naw, seriously, I empty my mind, so I can hear from the Lord, not all the time, but a good eighty-five percent of the time. Just like I never know what I will play next, especially when I have my MP3 player on me, I don't know what scripture or sermon topic He'll give me. Then I'm seeking solitude for at least a couple hours. Now you know my secret." He winked.

Rebecca repositioned her purse on her shoulder. "Well, don't let me bother you. I don't think I'd be able to look at you the same way if you start banging out 'Jesus Walks' by Kanye West on that thing."

She couldn't resist a chuckle at his expense as she slowly began to walk away. She had to admit she never met a man quite as layered. There was no end to his interests and apparent talents. He joined in on the laughter good-naturedly while catching her by the arm.

"Don't go just yet, I need you to do me a favor," Will said.

His touch tingled her and she gave herself a little room by sitting on the nearest pew after he released her.

He cleared his throat. "You're a dancer, right?"

It was an odd inquiry coming from him, especially with the way he returned to the piano and began playing a simple tune. Had he heard something about her recent visit to the Wishing Well?

"I haven't 'dance' danced in a long time. Why?"

"That's my question to you. Why did you stop, Sound of Music?" he threw over his shoulder while continuing to play.

Rebecca threw her head back in remembrance of yet another nickname dredged up from the past. "Oh my

God, you're killing me with all these nicknames. How many nicknames do you have for your girlfriend, may I ask?"

Will halted the tune again as if contemplating whether he was going to answer. "One—Veronica. I tried to call her Vee once, and she practically ripped my head off. Somehow, I offended her. So I do it from time to time to get on her nerves." He shrugged.

They both chuckled. Will picked up the tune just as quickly as he dropped it. "Dancing didn't seem like just a pastime with you."

He was right. Dancing brought about that consistency in her childhood that she spoke of in their previous conversation. That was another thing her mother robbed her of. She immediately crossed her arms across her chest. "Tell that to my mother."

"I want you to do me a favor." Will turned in her direction, maintaining his connection to the keys. "I want you to dance here during the church anniversary, two weeks after Thanksgiving."

His request caught her completely off guard. She'd have loved to have a reason to dance again. Then she imagined herself dancing solo at the Wishing Well with an addition of a choir robe and tambourine. He was not talking about her sin-churning interpretation of a Bar-Kays, Bobby Brown, or Beyoncé tune. She immediately began threading her arms through her purse straps again. She stood. She contemplated taking to the aisle but knew Will would chase her down for an answer just for the fun of it.

"Wait, hear me out," he said with his seemingly sixth sense for what she was thinking. He stopped tinkering with the keys again, and turned to face her. "We thought of adding a dance ministry. I know some of the saints are not ready for that. I figured we could show better than tell. I know it can be a powerful expression of praise."

"Why me, Will?" she asked, finding his earnest expression hard to turn down. She fanned her sweater behind her to put her hands on her hips. "You know my track record. I'm just reconnecting with the church, for goodness' sake. I can't imagine I have more to offer than someone who has been here longer. I tell you, I would swear you and your father both planned to gang up on me today, as if you knew I'd be coming or something."

Pastor Donovan shared a similar desire for her to become involved in the life of the church. She wasn't totally against that idea, but felt she needed more time. Dancing for the Lord? She remembered the spectrum of her dance experience starting with the intro to ballet with the Teacup Toddler's Dance Camp to training at Julie Queen's Dance Academy, where some had gone on to tour with ballet companies up and down the East Coast. When the Madame made her quit in favor of more study time, she ate for recreation, increasing her waist by at least three dress sizes.

Rebecca would enroll in an adult class in a heartbeat, but she needed to get settled somewhere first. She'd even dance as Will wanted her to if it could cancel out that night at the Wishing Well.

"God casts us in a new light when we use our gifts. He's highlighted through us. I've seen dance ministries where some merely pantomime the words of a song, which is powerful in itself, but you know movement. I think you can embody the words of the song that I plan to minister that day."

She thought about the misconceptions about her and her family in the community, then of those she thought

Veronica and her cronies held about her. She didn't know if dancing along to Will's singing would help or hinder those notions.

"I'm not sure. Can I think on it?" she asked.

"If you help me out with this idea then I'll clear my calendar and find help to clear your grounds out back."

She smirked at the prospect of occupying his whole week. "Your dad told me not to worry about it, that he'd handle it."

"Please, him and what army? He just returned from being ill. I doubt he'll have the time to break away once he gets back into the swing of things," Will said smugly. He swung his legs back under the piano. "I'm the man for the job. I'm on it this week. I promise. Now back to my idea. Let's say you're helping me organize a group of dancers, if you don't want to do it alone. Let's just try some moves out."

"Wait, now?"

"You don't need a special time or place to worship. Just like I told you when I need to write a sermon, praise opens the door," he said.

"Yeah, but you're usually alone."

"Eventually I bring it before the congregation. C'mon, *Weary,* you can do this. I know this is new to you. For me, please?" He plucked the keys as he pleaded.

Rebecca plopped on the pew near him and rocked her feet back and forth to loosen the cement that was keeping her in place. She slung her purse beside her, resigned to nothing and everything at the same time.

He was like a coach on the sideline, giving a pep talk. "You know I haven't had piano lessons since the age of thirteen. It all comes back to you."

"Yeah, but you have a photographic memory," she reminded him.

"You've got an answer for everything, don't you? Get off that pew. Save all that talking for Him through your dance."

Rebecca stood, not knowing where she was going or what she would be doing. She watched him disappear into an unknown melody. His smooth face was a blank slate at first as he closed his eyes temporarily. Then came the colors of expression. The intense arch in his eyebrows and the passionate pucker of his lips seemed to be painted on as she watched. He was like a work of art.

She was privy now to his process and wanted to share hers in return. Then she thought about all the times she'd come before the Lord. Usually she was in duress, raw from her circumstances, knowing God was the only one that could get her out of her mess. Rebecca knew she would have to draw from some of that to give the full expression Will was looking for. She wanted to shield him from the ugliness of being chafed, for he would surely watch her. She wanted to shield herself.

Rebecca was about to take a seat again, content to be an observer, until Will began singing. A simple one-liner, "God is able, and He never fails," fit comfortably in his voice's register. The repetitive nature of his soul's song spoke to her, demanded presence and movement.

She swayed. She thought of doing an arabesque or a *demi-plié* as if the metronome were ticking and counting down a sixteen count. She stopped as her ideas stunted her fluidity. She blew a puff of air upward to disrupt her bangs. She realized her problem as she looked over at her maestro on the piano. She was all thinking, and he was all feeling.

Rebecca appealed to her competitive nature. She vowed not to be weary in this moment. She noticed her awkward first steps had brought her in front of the altar as Will changed into a new song. He was their deejay.

"What dance would you do for this?" he asked before finding his singing voice again and declaring, "'I give myself away so you can use me.'"

Similarly simple and spiritually charged, Rebecca waited until Will went into his own dance with the keys before contemplating the words. She stared at the altar and imagined giving herself over. She had given herself away, if only temporarily, to various men, but never to God, never totally. What did that feel like? Instead of shaming her, it challenged her. She knew that was the key to her getting lost like Will was.

Rebecca stepped outside of herself as she listened to the vulnerable lilt in her best friend's voice. She grabbed the tail of her full skirt by two points and tied them to hang loosely between her legs. She forgot positioning and previous training. Her body resisted the obvious urge to splay her arms wide open at the thought of giving herself away to God. Instead she clasped her hands tightly and thrust them forward toward the cross on the back wall. She tilted herself backward and around on the axis of her spine. The phrase "use me" became an arc, a kick, and even a leap with each refrain.

Her breathing became ragged as she was drawn deeper into what she could only imagine was God's presence. She pushed herself to show Him through each movement that she was open to explore all that He wanted to show her. Her training came back to her, yet she moved in styles she had never been trained in. She gave and gave and gave some more, reverencing the altar and all it represented.

Rebecca did not hear Will stop playing, nor did she hear him approaching. This time when he modulated his voice she became a human arc, bending backward as far as she could and still stand. With a wide sweep of her arms toward the sky as if in a sun salutation, she pulled herself up slowly by pure adrenaline and God's grace.

She spun out of that move and was met with the solidness of Will's chest. The shock, not necessarily the impact, thrust her out of the moment. His arms were wide and stretched on either side of her, almost encasing her.

"What," she said breathlessly, "exactly, are you doing?"

"I am consecrating you—in prayer. It's like asking God to preserve you and your gift for His purpose," Will said, just as winded as she was. A smile parted his lips. "Not everyone can do what you have just done, Rebi. You ministered—to me, and I know you can do the same for the entire congregation."

Maybe her head was still spinning from the dance, but Will had three heads, three personas. There was the pastor, the friend, and another. She closed and reopened her eyes to find him still staring down at her. God was allowing her to see his three shades, but it was the last, newer, and deeper shade that scared her.

"Stop it," she demanded. She walked past him to the pew that held her things, and this time, slinging her purse alongside her, she made her way toward the entrance.

"What?" he asked incredulously.

"Just stop it, okay?" She looked back at him at the base of the altar one last time, shaking her head at the memory of being touched like she had never been before.

Chapter 19

Will could tell something was different about Rebecca when she met him on her back porch early that next week. He had kept his promise to her by clearing his calendar to help her. He needed the time off. Taking time off from his relationship was a little trickier. It was the week of Thanksgiving and he knew Veronica was itching to see her family and friends in Wye Mills. He encouraged her to go, vowing to be a good boyfriend and spend Christmastime with her there in her hometown like she had wanted.

Rebecca had on a blue jacket with coordinating gray jogging pants that highlighted her toned figure. They were secluded in her backyard, enclosed by nature, so he took every opportunity to ogle her. She offered him a bottled water as if he were her workout partner, as she gulped the rest of her half-empty bottle. He placed his in the front pocket of his hoodie.

"I don't think I've ever seen you in pants," Will said, turning his baseball cap around, bearing his college alma mater's emblem backward on his head.

"Are you serious?" she said, looking back at him while shielding her eyes from the brightness of the sun. "Well, I guess that's about right because Madame wouldn't allow Gail or me to wear pants out in public. I always feel funny in them now except when I am working out."

"Well, I hope you haven't planned a workout for me down here. I just planned to take a look right now. I got a few guys who could be here this afternoon if need be," he told her.

"You got some nerve, Will," she said, planting the flat of her palms on her hips. "Like I *planned* on dancing around the front of the church like I did the other day, which, by the way, I'm never doing again. So, don't ask me."

He thought she was guarded about something. She was like others in the congregation who weren't comfortable with the change that they claimed they wanted. Watching her dance confirmed the transforming power of God to him. He just hoped he didn't scare her off or push her too far the other day in the sanctuary, because what he witnessed was beyond beautiful; but, then again, he knew he was biased.

Rebecca took off across the clearing, leaving Will to catch up. He didn't press the issue. They walked the next fifty yards in silence. At the slope in her field he trained his eyes on the thicket of trees that lined her land to the right and acted as a border between the Lucas property and an old graveyard.

As if taking in the exact same spot, Rebecca said, "I found out why they're building that road. The Historical Society thinks it is one of the oldest integrated graveyards around here. They think some descendants of Harriet Tubman might be buried up there. Tell me, how are they going to prove that one?"

"Remember history class with Mr. Watkins? I swore that man wanted to preach. Said there's no state like the Old Line State, remember that?" Will said, holding out a steadying arm just at Rebecca's elbow when her foot faltered as they continued their gradual descent. He noticed she resisted his help, but he held it there nonetheless. "I can never travel up and down Route 50 without thinking about runaway slaves."

Rebecca reached down now in the calf-high brush to grab a stalk of dried grass to fiddle with. They could see the rusted top of the carriage house in the distance and lumber from old stables piled equally as high. "We sat in those classes and boasted that we are halfway between Harriet Tubman's and Frederick Douglass's birthplaces, like we should be proud. It just proved to me that we were never meant to stay here. That's why I vowed to leave Maryland all together."

"Huh?" Will said.

She stopped, causing him to stop as well. He didn't know where any of this was coming from. Was she talking about then or now? He wondered for a second time why he was wasting his time developing feelings for someone who had a problem with her roots and clearly planned to continue to run from them.

"We talked about it in undergrad philosophy class. Self-hatred runs rampant among blacks here more than anyplace else," she declared as fact.

He resented the implications, but more than that, he wanted to understand why she was getting mad all of a sudden. "First of all, it's not like philosophy is an exact science. It's a nutcase debate. But for the sake of argument why, pray tell, are we plagued with self-hatred?"

"We're on the Mason-Dixon Line," she practically shouted, as if he were an imbecile. "Who stops short of the border and doesn't cross over? We even had the black Moses making return trips to lead folks to freedom. There should be no blacks in this area. They all should have run. Then I wouldn't be where I am right now."

"Exactly," Will said, wondering if there was any logic behind what she was saying.

"My parents' parents and your parents' parents were here because someone in our lineage was either a punk or gave up."

He wanted to ask her which one accurately described her since she had run and come back home. "There were runaways and those who stayed, endured, saw an end to slavery and set down roots so we can be here today to live in big houses with acres of land." He began to walk, stretching his arms to the extent of his wingspan for illustration.

She held her physical and philosophical positions, unimpressed.

Their whole conversation had him thinking of the biblical Moses and the children of Israel on the verge of the Promised Land. Because of disobedience and a lack of faith only a small portion of a whole generation reached God's promise. This was not about runaway slaves. It was about a lack of faith. He asked the Lord to help him figure out what had her bound. He wondered if freeing her would make her just flee again.

"What is it?" Will asked. "I feel like you have been trying to tell me something since we left your house . . . since the other day . . . since you got back here."

"I've been telling you a whole lot of something, obviously, you haven't been listening. I think maybe it's you who has something to tell me."

They stared at one another, fuming for no reason. He contemplated spilling it all, about the ring he bought Veronica, about his serious doubts, and of course, about the mutating madness that now raged inside him whenever he was with her.

"You're an intellectual snob. You know that, right?" Rebecca said after the appropriate wait time revealed that they weren't ready to give up their secrets just yet.

He fired off the first thing that came to mind. "And sometimes you wear your dresses entirely too short to be considered a lady."

Rebecca covered her mouth. "What does that make you for looking?" she asked after her initial embarrassment.

"A man," he said, equally as snappy.

She was about to reply to his trivial jab when they heard something in the distance.

"Wait, did you hear that?" she asked.

They continued in the direction of the sound, letting the momentum of the slope carry them through the now waist-high shafts of weeds and dead grass. At the base of the carriage house they could make out a figure of a man, hammering away at the side of the house as if he had a death wish for the structure.

Upon further inspection the man who was disrobed to his undershirt and suspenders with his shirt flying free from a nearby post became recognizable. "Dad? Are you completely crazy? What are you doing here? Come away from there before this whole thing collapses on you. I told you I'd handle it."

Will's worst fear was being realized. His dad looked around with such a look of bewilderment that Will knew he must be going senile. He looked like he had been to war and made no apology for the agony of shell shock that could be seen in his eyes. Will was almost embarrassed for Rebecca to see him in this state.

"Why don't you kids go home," his dad said.

"No, Dad, you forget I'm an adult, which makes you, as my father, way too old to attempt this on your own. I've got buddies who I'm going to call to help us with this project. Now, come down from there," Will shouted.

As if straight out of a hostage negotiation, his dad brought his hammer down to his side, but remained in his place.

Rebecca had to hoist herself up on the foundation level, not trusting the four wooden steps that were starting to erode and cave in through the middle. Will did the same. She idled for a minute before she went right to access the front of the house. Will watched her as far as his periphery would allow. She stepped around what appeared like a mattress in the doorway before disappearing inside.

"Don't go in there," Pastor Donovan yelled after her. "Son, tell her not to go inside."

Will was in a quandary as to whether he should supervise his dad or accompany her inside to make sure she was safe. He looked at his dad again and noticed slightly over the old man's shoulder that somehow he'd gotten his old station wagon off-road and through the brush. Where was his army? How and why was he doing this?

He heard Rebecca call to him, "Will, come here. I think you should see this."

Will gave his father a look one would give a dog when commanding it to stay. He quickly pushed past the twin mattress himself to gain entrance, to find Rebecca bent beside the foldable bed frame of a cot, staring into a bag.

He approached cautiously, taking in the place. It was a modest, open space that was apparently set up cozily for a single occupant, maybe two.

"I thought this place was abandoned. All this time she warned us not to go near here," Rebecca announced, fishing through a plastic bag of things haphazardly tossed together. She came out first with a silk scarf and burnt remnants of old candles.

Will was by her side, also taking his chance in the grab bag. He came up with an empty matchbook, with his thumb and pointer finger pinching a piece of paper that was also held by Rebecca. He gave it over to her but became interested when she gasped at what it said.

All color seemed to drain from Rebecca's face. "Oh my God, it's from him. It's the same mark, initials or something, on the letter I found from the Madame's lover that I told you about."

Will had a hard time putting two and two together. All the pieces seemed so odd and isolated. Then, like the snap of a puzzle piece put into place, it clicked, and he snatched the letter from her.

"Is it like a W and H wrapped into one?" he asked as he witnessed for himself the signature he tried hard to emulate ever since he realized he was a junior and had the same initials as his dad.

Will went after him with no further explanation. With angry hands and feet he backtracked, jumped off the porch, and caught his father by the suspenders as Pastor Donovan retreated toward the grove created by the city to carve a road separating this land from the church property line. The mattress his father was now dragging from the premises fell to the ground in their struggle.

"Will," Rebecca squealed as Will spun his father around to face him.

"You and the Madame! You were going to Salisbury the day we got the call that she had passed. You had Contee take you home instead of me. I wanted to take you, to make sure you were okay, but . . ."

He tried to suppress it, but bile rose in his throat at a feverish pace and anointed a pile of plywood as he diverted his body away from his dad. As the first wave washed over him, he could hear Rebecca wailing as she stepped down to see if she could be of some assistance.

"Will?" she called.

In light of what he just found out, he was relieved he hadn't expressed his feelings for her earlier. He couldn't face her now. "*Go home, Rebi,*" he rumbled, hoping not to set off another internal tidal wave.

Will seethed and writhed with the aftertaste of recollection and regurgitation. He grabbed for his father again as if he were going to drag him home. This time his father had the gumption to fight him off. He could feel Rebecca's presence closing in on him. This time it was he who didn't want her stabilizing hand. He stomped off, leaving her and her mother's lover in the grove of land between sin and salvation.

Chapter 20

Will sounded like an asthmatic by the time he reached the top of the hill. He did not stop. He did not turn back. He was on a collision course that wouldn't stop until he interfaced with his dad again. He preferred that the confrontation not take place in church, so he decided to drive to the outskirts of town where his dad lived.

He caught a glimpse of himself in his rearview mirror once he reached his car in Rebecca's driveway. Somewhere along the line he had lost his baseball cap. His face was pale. He wiped the spittle away from the corner of his mouth with the sleeve of his sweatshirt and swallowed hard. It felt like a thousand tiny granules of sand clogging his throat.

Will put his car in reverse and sped away. He replayed the scene of the last hour over and over as he drove. He had never put his hands on his dad before in such an aggressive manner. Part of him felt extremely guilty for his actions. Yet, he had never been more disappointed in his dad than he felt today. His dad had been called to preach and serve. He wasn't exceptional like he had preached to others. He had fallen into repetitive sin and caused Madame Ava to fall as well.

Will entered his parents' house without fear this time. The overwhelming sense of his mom's presence once he came through the door almost dropped him to his knees. The family portrait, the furniture she had picked out, and the memories now flooded his soul with sorrow. Was it all a lie?

Unable to get comfortable on the couch and wait for his dad, he crept to the back hallway. He felt as if he had been transported back in time to the night his mom died. He had packed his stuff to stay with yet another buddy from church as nurses and volunteers came and went. His dad was on an ice cream run that could last from ten minutes to a couple of hours depending on the kind of mental break he needed. Will remembered wanting to say good-bye to his mom, so he approached his parents' bedroom door like he was doing now to see if this was one of the rare times she was awake.

One look at her lying so still under a ton of sheets and blankets, with her eyes fully open and vacant, let him know something was wrong. He called to her, alerting the hospice nurse and others. They pushed past him, scrambling to find vital signs to prove she was all right, but they never did. Just like tonight in the field, he brought up his grief on the corner of carpet near his mother's deathbed.

Will covered his face with his hands at the thought of his mother's role in his father's sordid affair. His desire to know the gory details not only led him back to the front room, but almost led him to his car to track his dad's whereabouts. Where was the overlap? When did his dad's real life and secret life intersect? He wondered if his mother could have known, and if his dad could have been so callous and cruel to have had an affair when his mom was sick and dying.

He paced and pounded his fist like a prize fighter up for the title match. He did everything except pray. By the time his father came in, over thirty minutes later, he knew he was not fit to have a rational conversation. His dad came in tentatively with his Bible and Will's baseball cap. The sight of both infuriated Will anew, and he stood abruptly to remove himself before he charged the man standing before him.

"Look, son, I know you're upset," said his dad, daring to come into his son's space. He sat gingerly on the arm of the sofa. "You don't know what it was like as a young man straight out the Navy, forced to take jobs way outside to the city limits to make a living."

"What in the world does this have to do with you being in a covenant relationship with my mother and you disregarding that?" Will asked.

"I was with Ava first. I loved her, son. We were so young. We got pregnant, and I convinced her to get an abortion. I'm not happy with myself, but it was a decision my maturity, at the time, dictated I make. I was new to the ministry after my discharge from the Navy, and didn't know the congregation at Grace would have put enough faith in me as to elect me to be pastor at twenty-four."

Will took it all in, seeing if it registered with the questions he had rattling inside his head. "You're right. I don't understand how you could be so careless to your commitment to either of these women, so casual with your calling."

Will's dad extended Will's cap to him, and rested his arm on his hefty Bible balanced now on his leg. "We were on again, off again, Ava and I. Then I met your mother. Everything changed. I fell in love again. This time I did the right thing. We married, we had you," he started.

"Did you cheat on my mother? Did she know about you and Ms. Ava? Did you add to her misery?" Will demanded, taking his dad on.

Pastor Donovan stood as well, causing Will to shift backward. "I've repented for all this awhile ago. I think

I've told you all that you need to know, son. It's not going to help either us going through all that now."

Sure, my mother knew, Will thought. As close as Madame Ava remained to the church and surrounding community before finally leaving Grace must have been her way of asserting herself. She taught at their school, for goodness' sake. He tried to refrain from judgment when it came to her. All blame was reserved for his father.

"You epitomized manhood for me. Now, I find out you weren't half the things you taught me a man should be. Decent, honest, respectful," he listed out with his fingers.

"Wait, now you're being self-righteous almost to the point of disrespect," his father cut him off. "I'm still your father. There are still some things I don't have to take from you."

"You cheat on my mom and call me disrespectful? And to find out the way I did. You ripped my heart out, man." The tears didn't ask permission to fall from Will's eyes. He didn't wipe them. He needed his hands free to gesture and illustrate like he did in the pulpit. "Mom was so devoted to you. She didn't deserve what you did to her. You didn't deserve her at all."

His father held his hands out in an exasperated gesture before letting his hands fall loudly at his side. "Those without sin should cast the first stone, son."

"Then your name should be Barney Rubble. You're an imposter in the pulpit each and every week, tossing stones at everyone else. You're the disrespectful one, to me, my mother, and the gospel you claim to hold up. But, no more," Will declared.

Pastor Donovan wrinkled his face. "What does that mean?"

"That means I am sitting you down. I don't think you're fit to preach the gospel." Will shook his head.

"Oh, boy, now you have this burst of confidence." Pastor Donovan turned his back and walked into the adjoining dining room to set down his Bible. He roved around with his hand up to his forehead for a minute as if in thought, then came back. "I recognize I have hurt you, and it will take awhile to mend our relationship, but you cannot stop me from returning to *my* church. In light of all this, it is the place I need to be. We both need to be there to heal."

His father made it all sound so easy, and it wasn't, not to him.

"Why don't we see what Contee thinks, the board, the whole congregation? You can consider yourself officially retired. You can attend, but you won't run a thing," Will declared.

Will noticed his father wasn't fast to answer with the threat of exposing him to his beloved congregation. That was just what it was: a threat. A secret like this would rip their church apart.

"You're gonna take responsibility for the flock? You're ready for the sacrifice that entails, and are willing to quit your job to be there all the time? Who is going to run the school, Will?"

He had to admit he hadn't given it much thought. "I guess the same people who ran it when you were off mourning your lover."

Chapter 21

Something told Will she'd be up when he called. It was one A.M. Thanksgiving Day and their lack of communication since they both discovered their parents had been lovers added to his despair.

At first he was at a loss for words when she answered. Her voice was weathered with her greeting, different. Then he regrouped. "Are you having a hard time finding something to be thankful for?"

"You ain't never lied. I can imagine things got a lot worse for you though." Rebecca yawned then sniffed. "What did you find out from your dad?"

"I don't want to talk about your mom or my dad, or your mom with my dad," he pleaded. "My Aunt Rose and her people are coming down for the Thanksgiving dinner, so I am forced to do the family thing. I just don't want to think about it."

"What are you calling me for then? 'Cause that's where we are right now," she said with a considerable amount of bite in her voice. "Don't brush me off. I'm a big girl; I know things are messy, and I can take it."

Didn't she understand he didn't want to get into the shame and guilt of it all? He spent the last couple of days imagining Rebecca somehow blaming him in association with his father. After the shock of finding out her mother was in an adulterous relationship, to her quirking out at the estate hearing, now knowing that her mother's lover got an equal share of the inheritance, Will just wanted to know their friendship could be salvaged.

Will sat up in his bed, finding no way to leisurely impart what he was thinking and feeling. "I had a hard time facing my dad. Really, I don't think he really has looked himself in the mirror for the past forty-nine years. That's a long time to hide. He told me he dated your mother before he got married, even before he became pastor. Their relationship was pretty much makeup to break up after then. The facts get blurred after that, and to tell the truth, I'm not fast to grab the Windex to see beyond the smudge."

Will knew he was leaving a lot of things out. He didn't want to be disrespectful. He couldn't bring himself to call either guilty party by name. Dad and Madame Ava had different connotations to him than the sinful, secretive characters they'd become.

Rebecca remained eerily silent on the other end of the line between her apparent sniffles.

He sighed heavily. "I'm sorry, Rebi."

Her voice was hoarse, like a squeak of a rusty pipe that hadn't been used in a while. "What could you possibly be apologizing for?"

"For leaving you down there, just the whole scene of me and my father," Will said, trying to pinpoint one thing. "And to think, I was the one who got on you about judging your mother when you found out, but you had to witness me being a hypocrite and practically fighting my own father."

"You were being human," she said. "I don't know what I would have said or done to the Madame if she were alive."

"I'm trying to take us out of it, you know? Remove our friendship from the mess, 'cause you're all I got right now." He found it hurt less to speak in hushed tones. "God, I'm so mad right now, Rebi. Things have never been this tense between me and my father. I just thank God Veronica is out of town. There is no way she would be supportive right now, you know?"

Will knew she didn't know. There was so much he hadn't told Rebecca. He wondered if he'd ever get the chance now.

Rebecca brought her voice down as well. "I don't want to tell you what to do in your relationships, but nothing says you have to tell Veronica. I'm mad I confided in Gail. Really, it was more like I confronted her. By her being older, I just assume she knew a little of what went on in the Madame's life. She's such a goody two-shoes, always in her place. She was terribly upset when I told her. She came down on me like we were a pair of silly kids meddling in grown folks' business. I tried to explain to her that the truth up and smacked us both in the face as well."

Something in Will's stomach began to bubble at Gail's reaction. As wrong as his dad had been, he didn't want his dad's indiscretion to shade others' opinion of him. Would Gail's reaction be the reaction of the entire congregation once the word got out?

Will wore out his left earlobe with a pinch hold of his thumb and pointer finger. "I told my father he couldn't return to the pulpit, not yet. What am I going to do? The church anniversary is coming up."

"I don't know," Rebecca said, "but let me tell you what a friend told me."

She proceeded to summarize exactly what he had said to her after she found the first note his dad had written her mom. Rebecca was also able to synthesize text and applications from his sermons. She reminded him of God and how He has a divine plan behind every circumstance. He closed his eyes and let her words wash over him.

"So, should we just keep this a secret?" Will asked.

"Who else am I going to tell it to?" she asked. "You and your dad need time to sort things out without other people weighing in."

Her encouragement gave him a breather from the stench of what he and his father still had to deal with. She alleviated one of his fears, but he still had a dilemma on his hands. The church anniversary was always a special occasion at Grace Apostle, with a lot of pageantry and fanfare. How could he hold up the foundation of the church as the spiritual leader without letting everyone see it was all crumbling?

"You know what, friend?" Will said. The wheels inside his head were churning. "Since you always see the grand scheme of things, I know you will find it in your heart to reconsider your position about dancing for the church anniversary."

Chapter 22

Rebecca was chasing a sensation, the highest expression of herself. It was the feeling she felt when she danced. In that way she was an exhibitionist. One dance that day in the sanctuary gave her far more of a payoff than the many nights she spent dancing at the Wishing Well for the accolades of men.

When Will told her that he'd made the call for whosoever would be willing to dance for the anniversary, she didn't imagine it would include Nina and Veronica. She didn't bother to scope out the six or seven others. She heard them from the vestibule. Rebecca, before being seen, dipped inside the bathroom in the hallway leading to the side entrance of the sanctuary.

She might as well have been transported fifteen years back and 150 yards away in the lower level of the actual school. She instantly began crying angry tears. This was her thing. Why didn't she just tell Will that she would dance alone like she had done before? Why had he brought his girlfriend?

She figured the turmoil of finding out her mother's secrets was still making her too emotional to be productive. Some of that inner insanity she wanted to release within her dance. She didn't exactly buy into the fact that she was a minister to anyone while she was dancing, but she knew the medicinal powers it had for her. She needed this.

That fact alone helped her wipe her tears and regroup.

"Where is this choreographer?" someone asked before Rebecca could get to the threshold of the door to see.

Then she heard Will's voice. "I don't know what's holding Rebi. We said seven o'clock when I talked to her."

Rebecca craned her neck to gauge the reactions. The resistance was almost immediate.

"Uh-uh, we're dancing with her? This is not going to work," Nina said, shaking her head and smirking at the same time. She shot a knowing look at Veronica. "Rebecca Lucas? I told you, did I not? I told you something was up."

Everyone's eyes were on Nina, including Rebecca's, who looked through the thin gap between the hinges in the door. Nina sat on the second pew with everyone surrounding her. Rebecca wondered how much dancing someone in her sixth, or more, month of pregnancy planned to do.

"What?" said a fresh-faced woman sitting next to a man Rebecca did not know.

"Rebecca Lucas is a friend of Will's. He's felt the need to help her since she lost her mother and relocated back here," Veronica said, practically stepping in front of Will as if in defense.

Rebecca's eyebrow arched north upon hearing that statement. Could it be that Veronica knew, and in her own way was in support of her dancing?

"Since starting a dance troupe was my idea, I just assumed I would lead the group. There are tons of dance videos on YouTube," Veronica continued.

"Rebecca is an amazing dancer," Will said, kneeling one leg in the pew to address them all. "You'll see."

"Yeah, we'll see all right," Nina said. "I hope your girlfriend can see."

Rebecca could tell by Will's expression that Nina had stretched his capacity to love everybody as the Bible instructed.

"I don't know what you're talking about," Will said.

"I'm sure you don't," Nina replied.

They were in a stare-off now. There was no amount of goodwill toward men that could shield their disdain.

Will cleared his throat loudly. "Yes, Rebecca has been my friend for over twenty years, and one thing I remembered was that she was a dancer."

"If you're talking about Madame Ava's daughter, word is she dances down at the Wishing Well bar." The fresh-faced woman's male companion spoke up.

Rebecca's heart sank as she flattened herself against the wall, no longer able to take in the scene. How could this be happening?

"I'm sorry, Brother Lymon. I can't speak with authority on a partial understanding. How do you know so much about the Wishing Well?" Will asked sarcastically. "Look, this is not Salem and there will be no witch hunt in this church."

"Let's face it, Rebecca is a second-generation skank. Don't let the fancy house and handbags fool you. Look at how she dresses. She went after my high school boyfriend. Then Sheila down at Starbucks told me Rebecca had even been with her boyfriend, and we all know he was the mortician who handled her mother's funeral. This is a joke," Nina said.

Does Nina have a case file open on me? Besides being a part-time real estate agent, she must spend the rest of her time as a detective. Then she remembered whose daughter she was. Nina was a second-generation snoop who didn't have her history correct. Jerry West came after her and not the other way around. Rebecca looked down at her modest yet form-fitting liturgical gown she had just purchased from her old dance school and wanted to cry all over again.

"How are you even considering having her dance here?" Nina asked.

"Because I am the pastor," Will snapped.

"Oh, boy, you are just a placeholder for your father," Nina said, standing as if she was about to leave. No doubt her posse would follow. Rebecca wondered what side Veronica would be left on.

"Thanks, thanks for that Nina," Will said. "Just like Jesus was a placeholder for you and me both on the cross, or, or how about this one, shortly thereafter when Jesus sent the Holy Spirit as a placeholder for Him in our lives. So, I am happy to be a placeholder. You just don't get it."

Rebecca almost cheered as she snuck a peek. Nina had this incredulous look as if what he had said was absurd. She didn't get it. Everyone was standing now.

Veronica held up both her arms as if to hold both sides at bay. "Guys, c'mon now. Y'all know Will has a big heart. Let me help you out, honey," Veronica said to Will. "Obviously having your little friend dance here sends the wrong message."

"I didn't ask for help, *honey*. I am a grown man," Will said, putting enough space between his last two words for them to fill in the blanks. "I don't know what Christianity has taught you all, but I don't have the luxury to discount anyone, to hate this one or that one. I was told to love all people."

"Got to love the whoremongers," Veronica said, taking a final dig at Rebecca by shrugging her shoulders with that last comment.

Will leaned away from his girlfriend as if seeing her for the first time. "You are way out of line, and just like anyone else who has a problem with the way I run this church, you can leave."

"Oops," her best buddy, Nina, said.

Veronica was left flushed and batting her eyelids a mile a minute. Apparently she had crossed the thin line between challenging him to be better and simply challenging him.

"Will," Veronica started.

"Don't speak," he commanded with the caution in his voice and rigidity of his pointer finger.

She didn't say another word. Everyone else was set to bail on him, possibly causing a chain reaction once the whole church found out.

Rebecca didn't know what to do, but she wasn't going to let Will take the fall for her. How could they think Will, of all people, was carrying on a love affair and using this ministry as a cover-up? Then Pastor Donovan and her mother came to mind. They had set into motion the bomb that was ready to implode the church.

She realized she wanted to dance so badly. She wanted desperately to be seen in a different light. She was tired of fighting the same battle of recognition and respect with her animosity. It seemed no matter how much she tried she would always be a second-generation skank.

Rebecca came out of hiding and entered the sanctuary. She stole the spotlight. "They are right. I am drenched in sin. I've danced at the Wishing Well and have been in the company of more than a couple guys on occasion. I shouldn't even be trying to praise the Lord."

"See, right from the horse's mouth," Nina gloated.

Nina's laughter was magnified in Rebecca's ears. It was a chorus of all her laughter through the years. "Before you get right comfortable in your self-righteousness, Nina Pritchett, tell me, how is it that you can rest with one man's last name and another man's baby in your womb? Skank knows skank. Make sure you give my best to Randy and Mayor West for me while you're out there juggling, will you?"

Gasps could be heard all around. No one expected the sucker punch. Veronica came to the aid of Nina, who was clutching her belly as if she was sent into premature labor. Tears were forcing their way out of Nina's eyes as she shouted names at Rebecca that further proved she had no respect for the church.

"Wait, for the love of God, will you all stop? Stop!" Will shouted, aiming a pointed look of disgust at Rebecca. The bass of his voice silenced her rebel spirit now looking for a way out of her rebellion. "You think God is this petty? You think He doesn't know what Rebi has done, and Nina has done, or me, for that matter—all of us," Will said, pointing around the circle. "None of this takes Him by surprise, but it sure as heck does me. I didn't know Grace Apostle was such a mean-spirited church. No one can claim to be any better than the other by this little display today."

Will took an unsteady step backward. Rebecca could tell he had taken about as much as he could bear. He placed both hands on his hips, and stared around the circle at each of them. "I might as well quit today if you won't repent and allow God to transform your hearts. Falling out with each other is not worth losing favor over. I know what God spoke to me and maybe I need another group of individuals to perform it. I pray God shakes each of you to the core, wakes you up, because life is not a big soap opera. I suggest you not leave here tonight until you check yourself at this altar because I fear my prayers for you all alone won't be enough."

Rebecca watched as Nina was escorted out by her support team. She assured her followers that all Rebecca had said was untrue. Rebecca feared they would go straight into excavation mode until they dug up every one of her skeletons, which included those of her recently deceased mother. Will had asked them to pray. She squeezed her eyes together, trying to shut out the pain and irritation of being chafed before those who remained and, once again, bringing her madness before the Lord. She asked for forgiveness, and she asked for grace to walk out of the church with her head held high. When she opened her eyes only she and Veronica remained, making her wonder if Veronica had come back from helping Nina to confront her. Rebecca's eyes took a lap around the sanctuary, looking for Will, before resting on Veronica.

"Just for the record, I'm not after Will," Rebecca shared.

Veronica raised a suspicious eyebrow that slid back in place with a cleansing breathe. "Oh, sweetie, I'm hardly worried about you."

That left them both to worry about Will.

Chapter 23

How long would he sit there and watch her disrobe, enticing him? Would it be until she came to her senses or until he lost his own? He figured this was her way of apologizing for not standing with him in support in the sanctuary the previous evening. This was for showing her true colors. This was as much about psychology as it was physiology. This was an all-out offer.

Veronica wanted Will to cross an imaginary line they had inked with faith to recommit and keep themselves pure until marriage. She was just a few eyelet hooks and swatches of satin away from full nudity. She had worn her good stuff, but soon that would not matter. If she had been closer he might have helped her undress. Just a few feet separated him from using her body to smother the flames of desire that engulfed him. He couldn't take his eyes off of her. He became all at once parched.

Will struggled to keep his eyes on her face as he sat on the microfiber couch in his own modest home. Still sorting his feelings from the other night, he had little to say to Veronica when he let her in. Now her striptease had rendered him speechless. He quite enjoyed being desired as more than a prop but a proposition. Indulging himself would make a perfect end to an insanely difficult week. His body was willing; he was just waiting for his mind to weigh in.

She had done all that she could do alone. He took in all of her; stripped of any pretense she strutted over and sat across his lap, draping her arms and clasping her fingers around Will's neck. He ran his right hand through her hair, trying to ease his way into her abyss through the shallow end. He'd convinced himself that he had to take a dip. He allowed her to kiss him slowly and seductively. His body ached so for skin-to-skin contact, he wouldn't have been surprised if his clothes went up in flames.

He barely found his voice. "Veronica—"

"Something has been missing in our relationship lately, and I think I know what," she said, cutting him off. She leaned as if to blow into his ear and whispered, "Rebecca may have a wealth of experience when it comes to pleasing other men. She may have a better body—fuller in places and probably store bought, but remember I know exactly what you like."

The floodlights came on in his mind at the mention of Rebecca's name. He pushed Veronica up and off of him. With his back to her, he began tossing her discarded clothing at her.

"Put your clothes on," he commanded. With his hands on his hips, he kept his eyes away from her and on the front door.

"Don't," Veronica started, using the fistful of garments as a shield for her nakedness. "Don't you dare let her come between us."

"This is not about her," he rattled off easily to the back of the door between glances.

"Liar," Veronica said.

Will looked over his shoulder with that accusation, enough to see her hobble over to the couch on which they both sat and begin to put her clothes on. When she was back in her coordinating undergarments, she was brazen enough to approach him again, dress in hand.

"Look me in my eyes and tell me this is not about Rebecca," she demanded, pushing him in the forearm.

"This is not about Rebecca," he said, using the play on words and his hands to point out the space between them. "This is about us wanting two different things. We're going in two different directions, Veronica."

She brought her hand up to her mouth, feeling the full impact of his words. "What are you saying?"

Will swallowed hard, knowing the time had come to air it all out. "I'm saying, this evening and yesterday at the church is all evidence that we're not connecting like we used to. You said it yourself. I don't think you respect where I'm at right now. You don't respect my ministry. I don't feel like I can even come to you with what's been going on with me for fear it would get lost in how it will impact you."

She started swinging, catching him in the corner of his eye. He wondered if the guttural sounds of her trying to hurt him could be heard outside of his door, and he was glad his neighbor's house was a considerable distance from his house. He had to shield himself to even grab her arms.

"So, I'm the selfish one. How dare you? I moved here to be with you. Who's the one who sat idly by while you figured out what it is you wanted to do with your life? I put in too much time with you for you to do me like this." She spat at him, trying to tussle out of his hold.

"We are not Nina and Randy. I don't want to fight, and I am not about to let you fight up on me. I never asked you to sacrifice yourself. I think it has only made you resentful, made me resentful for feeling guilty all the time. I still care for you. We need to take a break and—"

"Let me go, Will," she said, and he obliged when he could see reason resonate in her eyes. She thrust her arms into her dress and closed it with the wraparound belt so tight she might have cut off her circulation.

Will knew she didn't have the presence of mind to hear him out. Would she rather he not say anything and let them roll into old age together, miserable? He waited for that familiar pain in the pit of his stomach to warn him he was making a grave mistake, but all he was feeling was relief.

"There will be no breaking up and getting back together. I can tell you that now. I'm going back to Wye Mills. If you let me leave, I'm going to get on with the life you robbed me of. And we'll see who comes creeping at the other's doorstep."

She paused to pull on her shoes and then hesitated again at the door before slamming it shut behind her. Will did not have the presence of mind to stop her.

Chapter 24

He was back on her doorstep. *Did he knock or did I just know?* Rebecca thought. Although she hadn't been back to church and hadn't called, she'd prayed she'd get an opportunity to apologize to him for turning his world upside down. She watched him through the curtain as he sat on her front stoop, intermittently pulling at his earlobe.

Rebecca unlatched the screen door and joined him.

"I wasn't going to leave this stoop or even knock on your door until I was certain what I was here for," Will said. His jeans and long-sleeved shirt were slightly soiled as if he'd just come in from planting something, his face a new shade of melancholy as he looked at her beside him now. "I strong-armed this church from my dad, and now, I feel as though I'm a joke. I want to beg you to dance a solo at church even though my members tried to assassinate your character. I'm not sure there will be an audience, though, when tongues get to wagging. I really need this anniversary to be a revival."

Her heart went out to him as she listened. She noticed other imperfections about him, like the lint in his hair and a bruise that looked like a remnant of a black eye, which made her want to nurture him.

"But then, I had an even more burning desire to ask you why," Will continued. "As if it is my business, what's with all the guys, Weary, why *those* guys? Randall? Jerry? Randy?"

Rebecca rose up to smooth her skirt that was bunched under her, as she was suddenly conscious of its length. Like a suntan, the surface of her skin felt painful to cover and equally painful in full exposure. "I'm not even going to separate the past from the present, real or fiction. You obviously already got your mind made up about me like all the others. I hooked up with some guys the same reason other people hook up. Some I got with out of pure lust, I wanted to be touched, and some to show that I existed, and still others out of revenge on their wives or girlfriends. There. Are those that the deadly sins you wanted to hear?"

"And where are those guys now?" Will asked through a gritty expression. Then, answering his own question, he murmured, "Nowhere to be found."

"A few, if not all, would come running if I called," she asserted.

"Oh, so you're *that* girl?" Will shook his head vigorously. Rebecca couldn't tell if he was refuting what she had said, was in full agreement, or signifying the shame of it all.

"I guess you really don't know me like you thought," Rebecca replied.

He stood as if he was going to leave. Then he faced her so she could see his melancholy replaced with anger. "You are the one who doesn't know yourself. You're so caught up in carnality. Don't you see, God loves you, I love you?"

She suddenly wanted to set the record straight, knowing full well now that the image he had of her in his mind, next to God's, was her best likeness. She stood also.

"I didn't sleep with Nina's husband, just danced with him down at the Wishing Well, and Jerry West attacked me in the backseat of his car that one and only summer I came home from college. Apparently Jerry and Nina had gotten into a fight, and I was so thrilled and *ignorant* just to go out with him." Rebecca reached for Will's arm, which she clung to as she talked, and tears fell freely from her eyes. "Mostly, I turned to guys on a whim and a prayer that the sex could actually turn out to be something else. No one was telling me I had better things to do with my body. No one was telling me I was worth more than the price I put on myself but you."

Before she knew it Will had his strong hands clenched around her neck, pulling her forward into a kiss that left them so emotionally charged and spent at the same time that they leaned into each other for stability. They remained forehead to forehead, like molten hot lava that has to cool completely before falling apart. Her neck tingled beneath his touch.

"That did not help. In fact, that probably set my sanity back," Rebecca uttered, waiting for her senses to realign. That kiss left her smelling sandalwood and thinking of sweet plums as firm and as juicy as those lips of his, which spoke sacred words both from the pulpit and just now with their first kiss.

"Yeah." He laughed, reaching for her hand, obviously impressed with himself.

"I guess we'll just pretend that didn't happen," she said.

"Are you crazy?" Will asked.

"Are you crazy? I didn't ask you to kiss me. Men don't ask anymore. They just take what they want and take and take." She took a peek at the door, half expecting the Madame to be standing there. She wiped at the trail of tears left by her mixed emotions. She was suddenly infuriated with the notion that she was put into the same position as her mother. *Why'd he have to kiss me?*

"I don't need another uber-confusing, friends-with-benefits relationship," Rebecca said.

He released her hand. His countenance registered that he'd been hurt to his core. "This friend begs you for the benefit of the doubt. I had no business kissing you like that if you have no idea of my intentions, but I can assure you, this wasn't a whim. I knew I was fallin' for you about the same time we went to lunch that day. Ever since then I've considered you in every way a man considers a woman. That's enough to tell me that this goes beyond our friendship. I want to be with you, Rebi. I want to pour into your life. Eventually, I want it *all.*"

His words set a thousand butterflies to flight inside her stomach. "Shut up! This is all news to me. Might I remind you that you're a minister, a minister who has a girlfriend?"

"Who is no longer my girlfriend and has gone back to Wye Mills. It's over between us. It has been for a while. I realize now she was just a placeholder—for you, you know? As much as we are friends, you've got to know I am feelin' you, Rebi. Tell me it isn't reciprocal."

Rebecca was wondering where all this swagger was coming from. This dork was actually hot. She must have been squirming and swaying so much that Will grabbed her by both arms to hold her in place. Her mind was a flurry of activity.

"Uh-uh, you can't do this to me," Rebecca said, shaking her head. "Everyone will think just like Nina and Veronica that the harlot seduced the preacher."

"Personally, I don't care what people think. All that matters to me, right now, is how we feel," Will said.

"I don't think it even matters what I feel." Rebecca bit down on her lip.

"Sure it does, Weary," Will said incredulously.

There was an elongated period of silence where Will tried to get her eye, but she avoided his. She looked up tentatively to see his piercing eyes, that dimple, and those lips she longed to feel on hers again.

"What's up?" he asked.

"It's Newton's Law." She shrugged. "I'm thinking you and me, and I think Newton's Law."

He let his arms fall to the side and tilted his head back as if in contemplation. "A riddle, really? I'm pouring my heart out right now, and you want to talk about laws of motion. What about Newton's Law?"

Something within her didn't want him to want her, not like the other men. What would happen to their friendship then?

"An equal and opposite reaction," Rebecca tried to explain. She turned away at her feeble attempt. They were too intense right now for her to think, let alone talk straight. She needed time to process all that had taken place in such a short period of time.

"So what, when I pull you just have to push? Is that what this is all about?" He bucked, getting in her face, not allowing her to avoid him.

Rebecca stopped and tried to focus. "I just have an opposite gut reaction to us being together."

"Opposite as in hate? Opposite as in disgust? Opposite as in indifference? Tell me, what it is?" Will would not let it go. Rebecca could hear the desperation in his voice. He held on to her arm again and got a hold around her waist with the other. His touch threatened her clarity.

"I don't hate you. I hate this situation. They shouldn't have been together," Rebecca said, pointing at her own house while prying herself out of his grip. "We can't ignore that. We haven't even really addressed it. Your mom was terminally ill and your dad cheated on her—for all those years—with my mother. Don't you see they are the force that stops us from moving forward?"

That landed a blow that made him step back. With his head held low, he wiped at his own eyes. "Just because they shouldn't have been together doesn't mean we shouldn't be together."

"That's exactly what it means," she said.

"Who says we have to pay for their sins?" he reasoned.

Their eyes were on each other, communicating their own regrets. Her emotions overtook her and she began to sob. She hid her face in the crook of her arm in an effort to buffer and conceal her pain. As Will started to approach her again, she held out a stiff arm to halt him.

"So, that's it, we're not going to talk about us?" Will said with his arms extended as if he was owed a better explanation.

"I can't," she peeped. She made haste to the door before she suffered any more abrasions, before she dropped any more tears.

Rebecca had an overwhelming feeling that she needed to stay far away from Will for a while. She was starting to wonder if Easton was even big enough for the both of them.

Chapter 25

Rebecca tried to ignore the sounds of the crew in the distance taking down the last of her mother's love den. Will had brought by a group of coworkers, who worked in waste management down at the Perdue plant, to assess the job and the possible runoff into the family well. Since she vowed to limit her personal contact with Will, she was done with the project, deferring it to the rightful heir of the estate, Gail. Rebecca was almost jealous at how chummy Gail and Will had become during the three-day process.

Gail was with her in the kitchen now, slicing a banana into her morning cornflakes. They were close-quarter roommates, both sharing the top floor like they did growing up, but might as well have been two strangers passing in the night.

"Tell me about your mom," Rebecca asked. She knew her inquiry came from left field but she was scrambling for a connection beyond the one she shared with Will.

Gail inhaled deeply and sighed with a smile. "Cynthia Cinnamon Lucas was the prettiest thing this side of the Choptank. That's what she always used to say. She was so funny. She was an extraordinary seamstress and so, so bubby, just joyful all the time. You would have loved her. My momma used to tell me all the time I was smart as a whip. Told me I know things way beyond my years but am gracious enough to let the grown folks keep being the fools." She chuckled with fondness.

"You must miss her," Rebecca said.

Gail paused with the knife in one hand and half a banana in the other. "She died young, you know? I was so young when I came to stay with the Madame, barely a teen. It's like memories of her are wispy, like catching a cool breeze. In the dry heat you really miss the feeling."

Rebecca reached for the quart of milk Gail brought to the table, and poured herself a glass to drink after taking a cup from the drying rack. "Coming here must have been like culture shock."

They shared a knowing look and Rebecca shrugged her shoulders as if to give Gail permission to be honest. Rebecca wanted her to know it wasn't blasphemous to badmouth her momma, to be real about being stuffed in the Madame's baggage.

"I hate to say it," Gail said, barely audible, "sometimes she was sooooooooo mean, the exact opposite of my momma. She would say stuff like, 'It's frustrating as heck to live with you. You ran your father off.' Who says that to a child? You think my Cinnamon momma would have told me that even if it were true?"

Gail was tearing up now, and Rebecca squared her paper towel and walked over to dab her cousin's eyes.

"I clung to her though because she was all I had," Gail admitted.

"Were you there the night she nearly beat me to death? Found me with Jerry West back there between the Perkins place and the graveyard," Rebecca asked.

"Someone should have beat your tail. You were foul and throwing your life away. I never understood it. You are so smart and have so much going for you, Rebi."

"Well, if I thought the Madame didn't like me before it was all but confirmed that she hated me then."

"The Madame did not hate you. We both know that was inner rage turned outward. I said she was mean as the devil, but I never thought she hated me." Gail was quick to defend her.

"Regardless, I had to leave after that. I had to admit to Will the other day how Jerry had practically raped me, and then to come home and have your mother beat you like she had some personal vendetta against you leaves you with scars. No amount of hugs or kisses from him can take that pain away."

Gail could not hold back her incredulous look. "Oh God, the two of you? Mother, father, now son and daughter?"

Rebecca wiped her face with her hand. "God, that sounds so much more horrible when you put it that way. He thinks he's in love with me all of a sudden, and I . . . I know, he hasn't thought this completely through. He just broke it off with Veronica, and everyone is gonna think I'm trying to fill her shoes, or worse yet, I stole those bad boys. But I swear I didn't do anything sleazy or wrong. I scaled sexy way back when I was with him. I didn't make a pass at him or seduce him or anything."

"No one said anything about you doing something wrong. It's love. That's when you know it is genuine, when it comes naturally. You two have been friends forever. It happens," Gail said, removing Rebecca's hand that she used to shield her own face.

"I didn't want this to happen. Not necessarily the feelings I have for him, but the context. Just like in high school I would have fixed him up with anyone other than me, thinking all along that I wasn't good enough, but hoping all the same that he would choose me. I've even tried to push him away recently." Rebecca questioned her own sanity as she spoke.

"Why?" Gail asked.

"What do you mean why? I imagine it's just like you and Mr. Milo. Everyone knows he wants to marry you. I even know for a fact you've turned him down repeatedly. What's up with that? I mean are you waiting for someone else to come along?"

Before Rebecca could plant her hands on her hips Gail shoved her, slightly throwing her off kilter.

"Honestly, I couldn't cleave. The Bible says that's what a man and a woman should do, leave their mother and father and cleave to their spouse. I couldn't leave while the Madame was alive," Gail said.

"And now?" Rebecca said, eventually getting her right hand to her hip to make a statement.

Gail was thoughtful. "And now, I've stayed and taken care of *your momma* so long, I have become resentful about it. Milo was my only bright spot. That's too much to expect of him. I started to resent him because I had nothing else I could really call my own. I have a void and I don't know if Milo can fill it. If I am incomplete what service am I to him?"

"You've just got to have faith it will work, Auntie," Rebecca pleaded. She needed one love story to reach happily ever after. "That's one of the things you pray about and go to church for."

"Well, what do you know? Older doesn't mean wiser. It means more screwed up, so I suggest you take your own advice. Reach for your happiness while you're young. If I had to do it over again, I'd err on the side of love."

"So, if you were me, and Milo was Will, knowing what we know about our parents' past relationship, you're telling me you'd go for it?"

"I'm telling you we shouldn't let the Madame take any more of our happiness to the grave with her," Gail said adamantly.

Chapter 26

Will became will.i.am when he programmed a playlist on his iPod docking station set in his entertainment console. It was go time. He had a sermon to prepare for the church anniversary. Here in his personal sanctuary and in the pulpit of the actual sanctuary were the places he felt closest to being an actual rock star. He started off his session with a few techno tunes by The Black Eyed Peas, which he bopped and swayed to, scanning his song list for more songs to bring into the mix. He clicked songs with no respect to genre or tempo, before settling in the middle of his couch with a pad and his favorite Bible.

The music did little to drown out his thoughts of Rebecca. He brought his finger up to the middle of his lip as if in thought and could still feel the imprint of her lips on his. Intellectual snob aside, there was a lot he didn't understand about her, the situation they found themselves in, or the force that had yet to reveal whether it would drive them apart or back together. He thought she was the Promised Land that he could just march in and possess, but her reaction to their kiss and the notion of them being together was unexpected. He needed her and she was pulling away even from their friendship. It was like he was forced to be alone at the most difficult time in his life.

At that moment God gave him words he didn't want to hear, let alone preach: words about mercy and forgiveness that should be extended to each other. It was a recurring theme with classic reciprocal implications: forgive and you shall be forgiven.

He knew this stuff. He knew he needed to forgive. He had kissed Rebecca, but a small part of him wanted to hold her accountable for giving herself away so freely. He was also preparing to preach to the members of his congregation who he felt didn't support him when he took over for his father. They were coming up on their seventy-third church anniversary, and the main reason he was reluctant to deliver a sermon with such a deeply personal reference was because there was one more person he had yet to forgive: his dad. It would require too much of him and possibly take too much out of him. Time supposedly heals all things, so why was he forced to deal with this now?

Will felt a prompting and decided to call his dad to broach the topic the both of them had been avoiding. He felt a twinge of anxiety as the call rolled into the fourth ring. Then he heard his dad's voice, and instead of concern all the pain of finding out his dad's secrets came back to the surface.

"Uh yeah," Will said, trying to remember why he had called. "Are you planning to come out for the church anniversary?"

"Hello to you too, son," his dad said. "Are you calling me 'cause you need me at church or want me there?"

"It's the anniversary. Everyone in town comes out of the woodwork if for no other reason than the food and fellowship. It would be kind of noticeable if one weekend you're back in the pulpit alongside me and the next you're back on sabbatical." Will realized his dad wasn't going to make this easy for him, and he regretted initiating this call.

"That doesn't necessarily answer my question, but to answer yours, I'll be there."

Will sighed with relief. It was a start for them. "You want to dust off one of your sermons and preach?"

Pastor Donovan chuckled. "I'll have you know I'm still receiving fresh revelations. No, I think I'll leave dividing the Word to you this year. You wanted it, right?"

They were far from a truce, but it was good for Will to hear his old man chuckle. Will found his good-naturedness to be the perfect segue. "Speaking of revelations, are there any you want to share with me, you know, about you and the Madame. Help me understand, Dad."

"Will," his dad moaned. "I'm not letting anyone touch the who, what, when, and where details of that relationship like a reporter in a newspaper. I loved Ava and your mother both, but I didn't do a good job loving and protecting either of them when they were alive. I can only honor them now by not rehashing everything."

"What about the truth?" he wanted to shout but managed to keep his voice even.

"I'm not denying it—not anymore. I'm just not explaining it, or justifying it. I hope you understand and forgive me, but my reconciliation is with the Lord," his dad said firmly.

"Funny thing, that forgiveness." Will chuckled to himself at the irony. They had a game they played where they tossed around ideas like teacher and student. Some of their best topical sermons were cowritten that way. "Be the teacher, I'm the student, what is forgiveness? 'Cause you can imagine I can't even get a handle on that concept right now."

Pastor Donovan wasted no time. "It's broad, cleansing, all encompassing. It's what we have to do, no matter how hard. The Word says you ought to forgive people to the excess of seven times seventy. You never reach your quota, never truly reach your capacity to forgive." It was as if Pastor Donovan was preaching.

"In other words, it's the law, a mandate," Will added, reaching for his pen and notepad.

"A necessity," Pastor Donovan confirmed. "There is a story where Jesus was invited to dinner. A certain group of Pharisees who knew the law and even his own disciples admonished Jesus because he allowed a sinful woman to wash his feet. In their eyes all they could see were her transgressions, not her service."

"The woman with the alabaster box?" Will questioned. "Jesus set them all straight, noting that using the expensive oil wasn't a waste when anointing the feet of the Master," Will answered like a show-off in school who lived to say the answer first. He knew the moral of the story. "Probably left them all speechless."

"Wait, this is similar. The story is recorded four times in all the gospels. Luke in particular qualifies her deed rather than quantifies it," Pastor Donovan cautioned. "Look it up, the host admonished Jesus because the woman was a sinner in this version, not because she used oil that she could have sold for profit, but Jesus said her sins, which are many, are forgiven, for she loved much."

His dad was in fact the teacher, and he had much to learn. "What do you make of that?"

"I'm still studying it. I guess you can say I need its revelations right now too. God rewards faith, and He shines the light on extraordinary examples, knowing none of us are perfect. I do know forgiveness takes a measure of love and a handsome amount of faith. I do know it takes time."

Although Will found his dad to be unfair to be so guarded with the details of his affair, his father was gracious with his lesson. Will was grateful to him for not hammering the implications to their situation. Although Pastor Donovan had cracked the verse out of the nutshell there were many nutrients to be found inside. Will had found his starting point. His dad would not be the only one studying the story.

Will toyed with the ink pen he was holding. "I don't want to hold you, Dad. I guess I'll see you on Sunday."

Pastor Donovan lingered on the phone. "Like you said before, forgiveness is a funny thing, especially when you need to apply it to yourself." His dad let out a breath. "You know, there was something Rebi said to me at the estate hearing that really hit home. She implied that I didn't do all I could to fortify her mother's salvation and faith in God. Ava and I had a lot of great times, and now I have to forgive myself for encouraging her to live a lie. We were laughing and living it up when we both should have been praying."

This time Will didn't ask for any further details. He thought about the undeniable impression Rebecca had left on them all as he brought his finger back to the center of his lips.

Chapter 27

Will was sitting in his parked car out in front of Julie Queen's Dance Academy, where he was told they held a Zumba fitness class every Thursday night. He was looking for the woman with the alabaster box, and when Rebecca appeared carrying a hand towel and water bottle he wondered if she knew how expensive her gift was.

He had parked two cars down from her car and had to honk to get her attention. She recognized him immediately and sauntered slowly over to the passenger side window.

"Hey," Will greeted her.

"I've learned my lesson about getting into parked cars with men, thank you, Pastor," she said.

"Will you get in, please?" he said, "I want to talk to you."

Will watched her give his request much thought before folding herself into the passenger seat and backing up against the door as if it were necessary to keep her eyes on him at all times. "Let me guess, Gail told you where to find me," she said.

Will shrugged as if he wasn't giving up his sources. Part of him was at a loss for what to say that would make a difference in how they departed the last time.

"You all talk quite a bit now," Rebecca continued.

"We do." He perked up. "That's Bit. I call her that sometimes because she's an itty-bitty thing, but bossy like, you know, your mother. It's funny, I called one day, hoping to talk to you, and ended up staying on the phone about an hour with her. Gail is cool. We're peoples."

"How cute, how about you get your own confidant," Rebecca urged.

He looked up into her chestnut-brown eyes. "I had one, but she went ghost on me."

"Yeah, well, sometimes you run out of storage for other people's secrets." Rebecca tousled her bangs.

"C'mon, Weary." Will pleaded for her not to give him a hard time.

"It might be the endorphins talking, but if this is about Sunday, I've already decided I'd come back to church and dance for the anniversary if you want me to. What else have I got to lose?"

Will pumped his two hands up toward the roof of the car in his own expression of hallelujah. He leaned over in an attempt to unlatch the glove compartment on Rebecca's side of the car. The sudden movement toward her caused Rebecca to press back even farther in her seat. "Don't put your lips on me, Will," she warned. "I'm not playing. It doesn't give either of us enough space to be objective."

Will chose to take that as a compliment. He definitely wasn't in control of his emotions when he was close to her. *Who said we need to be objective?* Quickly and without a word, Will extracted the disc that he had been after, extending it toward her. "I made you a playlist for Sunday, plus a few extras at the end. Stay in prayer because, right now, I'm not exactly sure where I'm headed this Sunday."

They both smiled sheepishly at the memory of their kiss and the fact that she had just jumped to conclusions. "Really, I feel I owe you that much, to dance and

212 Sherryle Kiser Jackson

not leave you hanging for the anniversary. I remember those times around Grace Apostle. I know how big it is. I can't turn you down."

You already have, Will thought as he backed up against his door too so they were positioned eye to eye. "I'm glad you agreed to dance, but that's not the only reason why I wanted to catch you, obviously." He paused. "Tell me, when did I become the bogeyman? You're scared to even talk to me now. How does one kiss undo a lifetime of friendship? In my mind it should be a building block. Honestly, I don't think my feelings can get any stronger for you."

Rebecca looked out the front windshield for a long while, and he didn't stop her apparent introspection. "I remember our senior year—cotillion ball time. The Madame was in her element. She was the advisor, coordinator, and sponsor, but her daughter couldn't buy a date, not even from her best friend, who was toting around a list, as only a dork would do, of potential dates. My name was nowhere to be found on your stupid list, oh, but Nina's was. You didn't see me as a date or mate then. My mother had to appoint an escort for me who split before the stupid dance could begin."

Will watched her expression change as she bit down on her bottom lip and took deep breaths. He remembered that list dwindling to Leslie Franklin, who spent the whole evening towering over him because she was at least four inches taller and looking down on him because she was a snob. "You know what that was about? That was about the mothers in our congregation approaching me or my dad after church and asking if I could escort their daughters. They figured their girls would be safe with the preacher's son. I wasn't the bad boy. I didn't appear sex crazed. I had good breeding. It might have had my head gassed up until I had girls turning me down left and right when I called them up. None of them really wanted to go out with me."

"I was the dork who did." Rebecca pointed into her chest. "I was the one always trying to keep up with you, pushing myself academically to make sure I would be in your classes—paired with you. Those mothers were right. You were safe, and I craved that security from you. I loved you first."

Will released a lungful of air as he turned to nestle into the backrest of his bucket seat. He wondered if that love was in past tense. This time he pointed to himself. "Valedictorian, but not the sharpest knife in the drawer. I wish I had known, Rebi. Gosh, I hope that is not the reason you left and never kept in touch."

Rebecca rolled her eyes and followed his lead by allowing herself to rest in the passenger seat. "I guess I've been confused about my feelings toward you for fifteen years. If that ain't weary, I don't know what is."

To Will, that only fueled his argument that they should be together now. He leaned over the middle armrest and dared to grab her hand, which was soft and slightly cold to the touch. Her fingers easily intertwined with his. "I'm glad you told me though. I say, let's get it all out, remove all the obstacles, your mom, my dad, whatever it takes to clear the way for us to happen, because just like the past fifteen years, I'm missing you."

She held their hands up as a unit and rotated hers at the wrist as if to examine their union. He leaned forward to kiss the curve of her hand. He was in violation, but she appeared to be giving him a pass. "How are we even friends knowing what we know? Could it be possible we've even known about our parents all along?" Rebecca questioned.

"Not unless you're clairvoyant." Will shook his head, content to stay there with her as long as it took.

"I wonder, if we pricked our fingers, would we bleed the same blood? How do we know your dad is not my dad also?"

This time Will pulled away from her touch. Hadn't his dad said that he and Madame Ava had conceived a child? He stared at Rebecca, knowing he should tell her, but kept his mouth shut. He tried to reassure her, tried to reassure himself. "My dad would have told me."

"Did he tell you about his decades-long affair with my mother? This is a reality show if there ever was one." She emphasized with her hand as if it were written on a marquee. "A man's wife and mistress pregnant at the same time. And you think he would have told you? C'mon now." Rebecca pulled the lever to open her door. "There is no getting over or around that. I have to know for sure. Until then I can't get comfortable in your space, feeling the way I feel."

Will was relieved to see her go this time. He didn't want her lips anywhere near him either at this point, sprouting the unfathomable. He would give her all the space she needed. Then when they got through the anniversary, he'd give her all the proof she needed.

Chapter 28

"God's sovereignty reminds us we're not in charge. I'm good at math among other things, but I didn't fully understand the full formula for forgiveness," Will said from the pulpit. He looked very much like a professor from Rebecca's vantage point as she snuck to a seat in the back row. "Don't leave His sovereignty out of the equation. So take yourself away: subtraction. Add God in: addition."

Rebecca wondered how much she had missed being late. Murphy's Law almost prevented her from coming to church all together, but she sent Gail and Milo along without her and pulled it together. She had to. She couldn't let Will down. The couple next to her, who had been staring no doubt at her odd attire, pointed at a passage of scripture pre-printed in the bulletin. Rebecca grabbed a Bible out of the slot in the back of the pew, turned to the passage, Isaiah 45: 5–7, and began to read to herself.

> *I am the LORD, and there is no other; There is no God besides Me. I will gird you, though you have not known Me, That they may know from the rising of the sun to its setting That there is none besides Me. I am the LORD, and there is no other; I form the light and create darkness, I make peace and create calamity; I, the LORD, do all these things.*

Rebecca got caught up on the word "calamity." She certainly knew something about that, but wondered why God would allow unfortunate things to happen to His believers. She looked at Will, proud and prominent, and it was as if her blood coursed with the new sensation of a drug. He had been her lover without the shame. Why was it that when she had finally found the perfect guy, the perfect love, God would allow it to be marred with such controversy?

"I remember when I was younger my parents stood as a unit. There was no playing one against the other. What my dad said was generally the rule. He was a man of God, and he was the true head of his household. There was no challenging him." Will dropped his head as if he had lost his train of thought.

Rebecca looked between Will and Pastor Donovan sitting behind and off to the right of where his son was preaching. This was the first time seeing him since she and Will found his desperate alter ego single-handedly trying to take down their old carriage house. Pastor Donovan was clean and classically suited as expected, tapping out time on the armrest of his chair, but Rebecca noticed new lines around his mouth and eyes. She wondered where Will was going with this story, knowing that the recollection of his parents must be grating him. She wondered what both Donovan men were thinking.

Will had not lifted his eyes from the Bible set before him. "I'm sure there were some times my mom may have had a better idea. She was so kind, y'all, so sweet. I'll admit I was a big momma's boy, and I miss her terribly." His voice broke. "But she believed in her husband's ability to care and make decisions for us, to stand before God on our behalf. She believed in his judgment. She believed in order."

Rebecca tried to will him to lift his head. Will stepped back and appeared to kick lightly at the podium stand with his foot. Rebecca and the rest of the congregation waited for his rush of emotions to subside and for him to make the correlation to the text as only he could make.

Finally, Will lifted his head and took a glance over his shoulder at his dad, who was on the edge of his seat now. "What if we were like that with our Heavenly Father's sovereign rule? Accept what God allows in our life. Take the burdens of what hurts us to Him and leave them there. Trust that He has your best interest at heart and can use every situation for your personal growth. And forgive." Will counted down with the fingers on his right hand.

Rebecca could see a rainbow spring from the tearstain on his cheeks. There were people on their feet at his simple checklist. He was triumphant and much more evolved than she was. She instantly thought of the Madame.

"Forgive as freely as you would to hold on to that pain, that disappointment, that grudge. Addition and subtraction, separate yourself from it—subtraction, and add in God's mercy." Will dared to smile.

Rebecca looked around to see if those in the congregation she felt really needed to hear this conversation were present. First she saw Gail and Milo huddled up, and knew their forgiveness was eventual after the conversation they had shared the other day. The man who was fast to rat her out about dancing at the Wishing Well was sitting next to the same woman he had brought to the dance ministry meeting. Then she noticed Candice and Elizabeth Hughes, Randall's sisters, and wondered if big brother ever made a spiritual pit stop. Of course, Veronica and Nina weren't there, but she did see Nancy Pritchett, Nina's mom. Rebecca wondered if Mrs. Pritchett knew that Rebecca and her daughter had played hot potato with the grudge that she and the Madame had baked up. After Will's sermon today she was ready to hand it right back to the originator.

Rebecca stood as Will urged those crippled by unwillingness to forgive to come to the altar. She delighted in the fact that he reached out for his father to help him close out the sermon in prayer while he made his way through the crowd, laying hands and whispering words of encouragement.

Rebecca was full with the contentment of God's Word, and she almost forgot her role until Will approached the piano instead of returning to the pulpit. When he was positioned behind the piano he played the chord progression for track two on the CD he had given her: "I Give Myself Away." He said, "I promise you I got prior authorization from the choir. I have sanctioned this with the soloist. I need you all to back me up."

Had he spotted her on the back row? Because she had not seen him scan the crowd for her. Did he know that she was there?

"I was so nervous about this anniversary. A lot of times I feel like a little boy in my dad's oversized shoes, until I realize it's not about me. Is it all right if we worship the one that's gonna take us from one degree of grace to another this anniversary? It may happen today. I pray that it will," Will said. "This is my invitation to you."

Will sang, and Rebecca could see his separation from his past. He sang, and she could get a handle on forgiveness for herself. He sang and people started to respond. The message was so powerful and palpable in his voice. When his voice began to thin and give out, she knew pure passion was holding the notes.

Then she realized Will had started without her. Apparently he didn't need her after all, but then, she realized almost immediately, God didn't need her either. He wanted her. She was God's choice.

Rebecca heard a voice over Will's and decided to move, or she knew she would surely miss the move of God. People were swaying and singing along and she took to the aisle. She remembered Will told her to be in prayer. It was not about her or him, but all about the conversation she needed to have with Christ and He with her. She glided gracefully toward the cross on the back wall, pulling the train of her royal blue and white liturgical gown behind her. Will seemed to modulate his voice as she hit the mark previously mapped out in her head. Then he started the simple refrain over again, with most people catching on and carrying the tune with him. She took her cue from him and danced the way he sang: unabashed and unashamed.

Chapter 29

Rebecca was told she was being booked for a repeat performance to dance. The announcement of the occasion was kept secret by Gail until Milo and Will assembled over at their house the following Saturday.

"We're getting married." Gail beamed once they were settled in the great room with leftover croissants and coffee.

Will and Rebecca were forced to share the larger leather sectional to reserve the loveseat for the happy couple, so Rebecca had to step over his legs to examine her cousin's modest ring, which was a delicate solitaire, perfect for her hand.

"When did this happen?" Rebecca asked, kissing Gail on her right cheek.

Will was also on his feet, congratulating them, starting first with Milo, with whom he shared a handshake and grip. "So you sealed the deal."

"Well," Milo started.

Once they were all back in their seats, Rebecca realized they had no further details. "Well?" she asked.

"I asked him this time," Gail admitted with a sassy hand on her hip.

They all shared a laugh at how ironic, yet ideal, the circumstances turned out for the two of them. Will and Rebecca stole another glance at one another like they had been doing all morning. Once again she was the first to look away, not wanting to communicate what either one was considering.

"Let me understand this, you proposed to him, and got a ring?" Rebecca asked.

"What's up, Milo? Where is your bling?" Will teased. "She is supposed to light your finger up."

The usually reserved Gail gave herself permission to gloat. "He'll get his, it's momma's time now. Yes, indeedy." She wiggled her fingers.

"That's right, Aunty, make him put a ring on it," Rebecca said, imitating Beyoncé as she stood to slap the awaiting hand of kin. She had to stop herself one hip rotation short of a full Wishing Well rendition. She felt Will's hand on the back of her tunic dress, tugging her back into her seat, apparently taking over Gail's role as the modesty police. They shared serious-turned-playful taps once she was firmly planted in her seat.

"Save all of that for the ceremony, 'cause, girl, I need a repeat of what you all did last Sunday. It was absolutely beautiful. What we couldn't figure out was whether it was planned, and when the two of you found the time to pull it all together," Gail shared.

"Let's say it was orchestrated by the Spirit," Will said.

Rebecca smiled, still not completely comfortable with the accolades she received after their anniversary performance. People who had never spoken to her in church came up to testify on how they were moved by the way the song was ministered. Praise rained over the place like confetti. She didn't remember the benediction or anything. Will's dad met her at the base of the altar with tears streaming down his face. She felt his admission of regret and request for forgiveness in his hug, and she actively gave back the salve of forgiveness that she hoped would heal their once viable rela-

tionship. She could have floated home she was so high
after that. Will was right, the flight was chartered by
Christ, and the two of them were just flying by the seat
of their pants.

The four of them kept the conversation as cozy as the
fire Milo was now stoking in the fireplace, which was
large enough to warm a ski lodge. Maybe it was their
engagement, but Mr. Milo took a new look of confidence as he tended to the fire as if he was completely at
home. That gave Rebecca a thought as she continued to
watch her adorable in-law-to-be. The scene was a Nor-
man Rockwell painting , albeit a little twisted . Rebecca
was glad someone was certain about their romantic
relationship. The betrothed pair stared at Will and Rebecca as if it was their turn in the show and tell.

Rebecca scrambled in the awkward silence. "We
should go out and celebrate."

"Actually, I kinda wanted to steal Rebi away for a
while," Will announced, squelching to a low grade the
growing excitement of actually having an occasion to
celebrate. He turned to Rebecca and thumbed toward
the door. "I made a reservation, uh, an appointment,
really, at one P.M. if it is okay with you. I was going to
talk to you about it."

Gail was gracious. "Go ahead, handle your business.
We'll wait for your father. I invited him here too. We
wanted to get everyone together because Milo and I
want to have a small ceremony before Christmas if possible."

Rebecca looked around, not knowing whether to
be more bewildered about a wedding that would take
place in less than three weeks or an appointment that
would occur in less than two hours. Both she found out
about in the last two minutes. Both she was expected to
participate in.

"I'm sorry, Bit. I'm spoiling things all the way around," Will said, standing now. "I sent Dad ahead of us to our . . . appointment. Gosh." Will sighed as he shook his head at what he had to know was ambiguous gibberish to everyone else.

Rebecca crossed her arms and refused to move. That gave Will one alternative: fess up or miss his one o'clock appointment. "What's this all about?"

Will proceeded with caution in explaining that his father had agreed to do a paternity test or anything else that would put their minds at ease about his affair with the Madame. Her appointment at the local health department would ultimately prove or disprove whether William Henry Donovan Sr. could also be her father. Will had appointed himself her escort and would have his father's sample number to tell the lab to compare to hers. *This is my doing,* Rebecca thought. The compulsion of knowing and requisite to provide the proof washed the remaining celebratory spirit out of the room.

Chapter 30

"You know this is ridiculous and unnecessary, right?" Will asked as he drove down the auxiliary road back to the main road that opened up to two lanes of traffic each way. "It's about as crazy as me going in there and taking the test myself, as if I am all of a sudden uncertain the man is my dad." *Why am I trying to convince her when an exact science awaits us?* he thought.

"I don't know my dad. The military vet story the Madame always told me doesn't pan out with me, or Gail either, and your dad is her only confirmed partner," Rebecca rationalized. "I guess I never figured he agreed to an actual test. What else is he saying about all this?"

"He's not saying much, but he categorically denies this," Will said, bearing down on the gas once he reached Route 50, as if she were pregnant and it were necessary to get her to the hospital before she delivered. The whole thing was grating his already unsettled stomach. "Could it be, I don't know, since I am almost ten months older than you are, that maybe your mom knew that my mom was pregnant and . . ."

As if thinking the same thought, she was ready with a reply. "Got pregnant by someone else to, what, get back at him or prove she didn't need him?" Her head dropped like a lead ball. "It is entirely possible because it sounds like something I would do in the same situation. Oh God, to think I was getting comfortable thinking I was loved and looked after all this time by your dad because we had a deeper bond. I'm not some love child. I'm the exact opposite."

Will's indigestion was made worse when he heard Rebecca begin to sob beside him. He cursed the fact that he had even said anything. To know that he thought the whole ordeal was of greater agony to him— because his parents were married and his mom was sick, more than likely, while the infidelity continued— made him see how selfish he truly was. When he veered over in an attempt to pull to the side and console her, she waved him on. Part of him would rather she be his sister than the illegitimate and unloved child she had always internalized she was.

They were both questioning the point of going through with the test by the time they reached the lobby of the health department. They had to consult the receptionist to find out if they were in the right place. A huge room with rows of chairs served as a waiting room for those who were there for a plethora of other services. That provided a sigh of relief at the anonymity it provided. After all, he had sent his dad there, and he also had to worry about being seen and scrutinized by a member who was getting a flu shot while they got swabbed for a paternity test.

After checking in, taking care of the service fee for her, and ensuring that her results would be matched with his father's sample, they were told to listen for Rebecca's name. He took a seat along the far wall and when she sat two chairs down from him, he slid over one, closing the gap.

She looked at him as if to challenge him. "This is ridiculous, isn't it?"

He stretched his arm along the back rest of the empty seat between them and offered his hand, and she grabbed on like a lifeline until their grasp rested comfortably in the seat between them. "It won't change a thing," he said.

Although he was unsure if what he had said was true, it seemed to calm her trepidation. She grabbed a magazine nearby and began to flip it with her left hand while she held on to his hand with her right. She was called to the back, and he scrounged through an abandoned newspaper for a Sudoku puzzle. He welcomed the added challenge of figuring out the rows and memorizing each 3x3 box as he went along because he didn't have a pencil to write all the figures down.

When she returned it took no coaxing this time to get her hand or interlock her fingers with his. "How was it?" he asked.

She waved it off as nothing. "Just a mouth swab. I don't know why I thought it involved more bodily fluids. They said it would take three days to get you the results. I can call or log in to this Web site."

Before Will could respond he felt a shadow of someone's presence standing over them. He was surprised to see Gail minus Milo. Her complexion was pale, and he wondered what could have happened between the time they left her and Milo that had her looking as if she had contracted a contagious disease. Rebecca was the first to stand as if to come to her aid.

"Gail, what's the matter?" Rebecca asked.

"Where's Milo?" Will asked, fearing it was a bad idea for her to have driven on her own. "What happened?"

"He's fine, he dropped me off. I didn't want him to come inside with me."

Will noticed that they were causing a stir in the community waiting room, so he signaled for them to take the conversation to the hallway. They led her to the solid security of the wall as they looked on. She had not stopped shaking her head.

"What's going on, Bit?" Will asked.

"I had a feeling I should be down here with you," Gail shared, more concerned with smoothing her clothes than being clear.

"Well that's cool. You should have said something, then you could have ridden with us," Rebecca said, appearing aggravated at the uncharacteristic dramatics of her cousin.

Gail grabbed at the lapels of Rebecca's sweater. "Remember I told you that my momma always told me I was gracious enough to let the grown-ups be the fools?"

"Yeah," Rebecca said, forced to give her cousin's inquiry serious thought.

"I think I need to take the test," Gail said to Rebecca with a wide-eyed expression. "I need to take the same test you've just taken."

Will had to interject now, although he wasn't privy to their earlier conversations. "Wait, what now?"

"When I went to stay with the Madame I knew I had been there before," Gail mumbled. "I get motion sickness to this day, so I know when I've been tossed to and fro. I always knew I started life on Zion Hill. Then I moved to Vienna with my Cinnamon momma. I know what I've been told, but I have been left to fill in my own blanks. Now, I've been to the desk and paid my fee. All I need is the sample number."

Will bent as if to sit, then realized they were in the hall and he wasn't hovering above their seats in the waiting room. He lengthened himself and clasped both hands on top of his head to stop his head from spinning.

"Okay, okay, okay," Rebecca chanted with wide, distant eyes.

His logic went into overtime. This didn't make sense to him, but lined up with his reality of late. Gail was significantly older than he and Rebecca, which would put her conception around the time his dad said he met and dated Madame Ava. That would account for the fact that she had the exact frame and body type as the Madame. She was the Madame's daughter and more than likely his dad's as well. Will wanted to punch the wall with this revelation. *Why not test everyone here with my dad's DNA,* he thought.

He looked at Gail and Rebecca and felt he owed them the service of not buggin' totally out. He didn't mind having Gail as a sister; he just didn't want her to also be Rebecca's sister. What would that mean? He walked in between Gail and Rebecca, who, by appearances, had not quite figured out their next steps and hooked their arms. Like a unit they approached the receptionist's desk just inside the door and told the lady that Gail's sample would also be added to the lot that would be compared with his dad's sample number.

Individually, they each found their way to the back row where Will's and Rebecca's coats marked their place. They allowed their likely sister to now sit between them, and settled in for the wait to prove the inevitable. He passed over his newspaper to Gail, preferring to contemplate in what world this predicament wouldn't pose a problem. He stretched his arm over the back of Gail's chair to graze Rebecca's arm. This time Rebecca's hand wasn't there and it wasn't forthcoming.

Chapter 31

"What do you want to do?" Will asked Gail in the kitchen of their home, but Rebecca felt his inquiry held double meaning for her as well.

Will and Rebecca exchanged uncertain glances before allowing their eyes to land back on their focal point—their sister.

True to their word, the paternity test results were made available by an automated phone-in service. The twosome who tested together checked their results together as well earlier that morning. It turned out to prove positive that Gail was Pastor Donovan's daughter to the exactitude of 99.99 percent, but disproved paternity for Rebecca. Positive and negative, as Rebecca was coming to understand, were relative terms. She felt as if Gail had once again won a prize and she wasn't offered a consolation. They called Will, and he got over to their house in less than twenty minutes.

"I want to go see my father," Gail finally said.

There was no way to know how Gail was digesting the news from her outward appearance, but it was eating Rebecca alive. She had to remind herself what it all meant. At least she wasn't blood related to Will. Maybe they could move forward into a romantic relationship, or at least salvage the relationship they already had. Oddly, that didn't make her feel any better.

"I'll go with you since Milo is at work," Rebecca volunteered. She didn't want to be alone with Will's probing eyes and even more challenging demeanor. They had an argument over the phone the day after she and Gail were swabbed for the test. It came down to whether there were circumstances where even love couldn't survive. Leading the conversation away from their particular situation, they talked about hypotheticals like cheating spouses and accidents that would result in the death of an offspring. It ended in a name-calling session where she called him naïve and out of touch with reality. He accurately described her as gutless and indecisive. Ever the optimist, Will chose to believe the Bible, which says love never fails. He hung up before Rebecca, as he put it, had a chance to nullify what it was she felt for him. She was the pessimist. She wasn't a fan of love right now.

This morning they had nothing much to say to one another, which was both a relief and a concern to Rebecca.

"I'll take you both over," Will said, establishing his role. "He should be home."

They were all emotional wrecks, and Pastor Donovan was at the center of their collision. No one bothered to call and alert him of their arrival. It would be a surprise, just as finding out their family ties had been to them. Rebecca and Gail didn't know that Will didn't intend to come inside until he dropped them off with a promise to come back and get them when they called. Rebecca studied Will's determined face over her shoulder as he shifted gears and pulled off. Where was her support system going? She was preoccupied with imagining what Will must be thinking while Gail rang the doorbell. She forgot she was supposed to be there as an emotional support for Gail.

"Can we come in?" Gail asked an understandably surprised Pastor Donovan when he answered the door.

"Sure," Pastor Donovan said, doing a double take at the door. "Was that my son who dropped you off?"

They both nodded and stepped inside. Like her, Rebecca suspected Gail was hesitant to speak as to why Will refused to come inside or how they had come to be together in the first place. There was no prolonging the inevitable, however, once the three of them were settled in the living room.

"To what do I owe this pleasure, two of my favorite gals?" Pastor Donovan said.

Both he and Gail cleared their throats in tandem, making Rebecca wonder if it was a hereditary trait they shared as a result of nervousness. She thought of his coughing spells during the estate hearing and wondered if he knew what was coming.

"I don't know what Will has told you, but I, too, went to the health department the other day to be tested with Rebecca," Gail said, reaching her hand out for Rebecca, who was beside her. Rebecca clasped her sister's hand in hers and could felt Gail's anxiety in her sweaty and trembling palm. "It was a hunch really. After all this time, forty-seven years, I discover my true identity. My father, no more than a hundred yards away from me at any given time—the most respected man in town, the pastor of the flock."

Pastor Donovan looked between them both with sad and sympathetic eyes. He brought himself down on one knee before them, centered in front of Gail as if he just discovered he was in the presence of the queen and not just his daughter. "I . . . I . . . I don't know what to say," he said.

"Tell me, did you know?" Gail asked, her last word caving under the weight of her emotions. A single tear fell from her eye and none of them sought a purse or pocket handkerchief to wipe away the result of what was way past due.

He shook his head as an initial reaction. Then he closed his eyes as if recalling the accuracy. "I've always lived with the guilt that Ava had terminated her pregnancy because of me. I suspected . . . suspected something, but she was very convincing—very calculating."

He opened his eyes and gave his pupils a chance to get readjusted before they made their own appeal for compassion as he continued. "Our whole relationship was risky. We broke it off, but, obviously, we were never too far from each other, from the temptation. I knew your . . . I knew Cinnamon, and to see you two together, no one could convince me you weren't hers. So, I stopped thinking of the possibility. I couldn't fault Ava's decision, seeing how loved you were."

The mention of her Cinnamon momma made Gail smile, and she graciously took her hand from Rebecca and extended it to her father. He said no more, but palmed her hand in his and kissed the back of her delicate palm. She stood, and helped him into a standing position before falling into a bear hug. Rebecca might as well have been a fly on the wall. She hadn't realized she was crying multiple streams until father and daughter broke their embrace and looked back on her.

"Rebi?" Pastor Donovan said. "Are you all right?"

Gail sat on the edge of the couch beside her, using the pads of her thumbs to mop up the trail of her siser's tears. Pastor Donovan made haste to get a napkin from his dining room table to hand to Gail to use on her. He looked on, not knowing what to do or what spawned this outbreak of emotions.

"The reason my *sister* here is crying uncontrollably, and my *brother* dropped us off without looking back, is because our little revelation has proposed a particular dilemma to them."

"Gail, no!" Rebecca shouted, standing in her own defense. She was her big sister, but could not possibly know what was going on inside Rebecca's heart and mind right now.

Gail stood and shrugged her shoulders as if she were left with no choice. "They're in love with one another and temporarily lost in all this."

Where is Gail's allegiance? Rebecca thought. The truth of Gail's words ripped at Rebecca like a sword. Gail leaned in to continue to wipe at Rebecca's tears. This time Rebecca didn't let her, thinking her portable pain had just as much of a right to fall like hers did. She looked into Pastor Donovan's wide eyes. She needed to deny what Gail had just shared. *Lord knows what he must think of me now.* "That's not it at all. What about me? Everyone else is finding themselves. What do you know about my father? Who had my mom been with in between dating you?"

She knew even before she saw Pastor Donovan's lip curl or Gail bring her hand up to cover her face that her inquiries were inappropriate.

"I can't help you there," Pastor Donovan said, turning his back on them temporarily.

Rebecca dropped to the couch below her. "I'm sorry," she said, shaking her head.

"It's perfectly okay," Pastor Donovan said quickly to pacify her. He turned. "You know, I have always had a special place in my heart for you girls. I tried to care for you as much as Ava allowed me. It's not a time to try to make sense of it all. Let's not lean to our own understanding, but trust in God. I just wish there was something I could do to make it all up to you girls."

"There is one thing you can do for me," Gail said, turning to face her father now. "I guess in all this I always wanted to feel loved, uniquely special, and important to the people I cared most about in my life. The funny thing is that I couldn't see that I had that in Milo all along. I've had a man by my side who wants to stake claim to me now—he wants to marry me, and I don't want to keep him waiting anymore. I want to do it before Christmas, and I'd appreciate it if you would walk me down the aisle at my wedding."

Gail and Pastor Donovan shared another hug as an acceptance to her request. They then looked to Rebecca to see if their affection would have possibly caused her to have another meltdown. She couldn't be mad that at least Gail had closure. She had no more words, no more tears. *It is what it is, the past and the future, both positive and negative,* she thought. Rebecca was ready to call Will to come claim them both and take them home.

Chapter 32

The wedding of Gail and Milo served as a distraction to everyone. Finding out she was Pastor Donovan's daughter seemed to make Gail more determined to wed right away. After the crying and consoling about the past, whirlwind planning went into paving the way for her future. In the end, Rebecca served as an attendant, Will officiated, and the father of the bride, as printed in the program, walked her down the aisle.

It was not until the reception that Rebecca danced to an amazing harpist's rendition of the twenty-third Psalm, then made her getaway. The gift she left in an envelope on the kitchen table was a letter expressing her desire that the couple live out their days on the family estate. *No more motion sickness for my sister-aunty-cousin,* Rebecca thought. Zion Hill was where Gail belonged; Rebecca no longer felt the same about her destiny.

She left the party of thirty under the guise of changing out of her dance ensemble. Now she only had twenty minutes to make her getaway without being noticed. She slipped out of the gown and into a dress, and found her awaiting bags on the back stairwell. No longer wanting to play dress-up, she was taking only select items of the Madame's, including the jewelry her mother had willed her, and her suitcase.

Rebecca heard a car approaching on the gravel drive once she reached the carport. She hastened to get her bags inside and shut the door in an attempt to conceal her plans. She didn't have to look to know it was Will. She tried to appear natural in her stance halfway between the car and the back steps. The slamming of his car door rattled her, and she wanted to take off running.

Will's eyes bounced between her and the packed car neither one wanted to admit existed. She had a plan for this, she thought. She would tell him that she was going to pack more of her things, but decided once back in Salisbury that she had to resume her life. Rebecca knew when she looked into his forlorn expression that she wouldn't lie to him. She couldn't.

"Tell me you are just going to Goodwill or some other donation center," Will said. He didn't give her the option to lie nor the chance to speak. "You know how I feel about us, but I've got a home here, responsibilities. My dad is here. If you roll out like this I won't chase you."

Rebecca swallowed hard. "I don't expect you to."

He had his hand jammed in his suit jacket. "Why are you doing this, Weary?"

"It's Rebecca." She closed some of the space between them so he could focus on her and not the car or whatever was in his pocket that was distracting him. She needed him to get this. "I'm not Weary anymore, I'm not confused on this issue. I am very certain. I'm going back to my unfinished mess at home in Salisbury. Like you said, try to leave the place a little better than I left it."

She couldn't explain that she didn't want to be trapped by love like her mother. There was a thin line between love and hate, and she didn't want them to teeter on that line.

"Why?" Will asked. "Is it me or someone else in Salisbury? Do you not think you could be faithful to me—happy with me?"

Rebecca was prepared at this point to let him think whatever he liked. "I just know that on a good day I wouldn't be able to fulfill your expectations. What do you think will happen if I stay? What fairy tale have you concocted? We'll marry and I become the eventual first lady of Grace? A first lady is called, I assume, in much the same way a pastor is called. I can tell you now, I wasn't called. It would just kill me if it didn't work."

"You are my best friend." He smirked. "You have my heart."

Rebecca covered her face with her hands and shook her head at the same time. "And I'm saying that's too much pressure."

"God, what do I have to do to convince you?" He flapped his arms like a desperate bird trying to take flight. "Why do I have to convince you?"

"You're right. You shouldn't have to." She tried the sincere approach again, wondering when they had switched roles. He was always the rational one, and she was flighty.

She watched him struggle with whatever it was in his pocket. It was bulky, and he was having a hard time getting it out. She panicked at the thought of what it might be.

"Don't," she yelped, pulling his hand into hers. Her heart was being torn apart and it was self-inflicted. "Go find Veronica. She was called. Tell her our truth, that we found out that we have a common sister and we are trying to heal from that revelation. Don't you see, with time and space both our backs can heal from the darts and daggers people have started and are sure to continue throwing at us, first with Gail and your dad's informal announcement, then us dating? We can't risk what we mean to each other, our . . . *kinship*."

He closed his eyes and stiffened his entire body at her touch as if she were a needle being injected into his veins. "My dad isn't hiding anymore, isn't forfeiting happiness, and neither am I. You must certainly be crazy if you think I could even approach Veronica again. I put everything on the line for you."

"Tell Veronica you've been a fool. Then tell her that you want to marry her. This time pick a date for the spring. I'll be there. I'll wear sky blue or sunny yellow." She was speaking without thinking.

"Stop playing with me, Rebi," Will warned.

"I intend to." Rebecca realized how going to law school might have benefited her right now; she had put up her best arguments. The case was closed. She removed his left hand from his ear, palmed his smooth cocoa face, and kissed him with all the passion she had stored up for the last fifteen years before walking away.

Epilogue

Rebecca was on Route 50 headed due east, back to the life that she had left. She could not relax in the driver's seat of her car until she could smell saltwater and hear the sensual sounds of shorebirds in the open space. Until then she felt eerie, like old souls were watching her, scrutinizing her through the smattering of the trees. She drove, but they were on foot. Runaways. As soon as she thought she had out-driven one group, she came upon another.

It made no sense to try to not think of Will and what she left behind. She pulled out the CD with the playlist he had made for her and popped it into her car's disc player. There were three gospel songs with which she was familiar, one of which they ministered together. She sang along, knowing that she would surely have to give herself away to God to get over her heartache.

Just when she thought she had played the entire playlist, she heard a chorus over hard-hitting percussion. It was "Jesus Walks" by Kanye West thrown on there as an inside joke that made Rebecca laugh through her tears. At the tail end of the playlist, Will had left another message for her through a ballad, haunting in its carefully selected words and soulful serenade. She listened, and her heart ripped apart once again: "Did somebody say that a love like that won't last? Didn't I give you all that I've got to give, baby?"

It was "No Ordinary Love" by Sade, and she relished the fact that she had experienced one and the same with Will. Rebecca knew she looked like a schizophrenic to passersby who happened to look into her car as she drove. In essence, she was. She planned to repeat the entire CD and be inspired and made to laugh and cry all over again. To think of Will. It was the perfect riding music.

Readers' Guide Activities and Questions

1. *Land of Promiscuity* highlights the indiscretions and broken promises of its characters. Pick a few characters and discuss how they were indiscriminate throughout the book, and how those indiscretions led to broken promises.

2. Will prided himself in being a gentleman when it came to his relationships and sexual immorality. Discuss the flaws in a plan to remain celibate that is based on the actions of others.

3. Discuss Veronica's character. In what ways was she a good or bad match for Will? In what ways was her friendship with Nina an influence on her? Discuss her position as a long-term girlfriend and the validity of her arguments against Rebecca. What do you think was the real reason why Will broke up with her?

4. Read about the woman with the alabaster box in the Gospels of Matthew, Mark, Luke, and John. How is the story written in Luke different from the others? What implications does her story have on Rebecca?

5. Discuss the Madame's legacy and that of Pastor Donovan on their children. Will and Rebecca craved to know the details of their parents' affair. Is it always necessary to have closure to forgive?

6. Create a playlist of songs mentioned in this novel. What other songs would you add to the LOP playlist that highlight the characters and events in this story?

7. In what ways was Gail always a "big sister" to Will and Rebecca?

8. Which character or storyline would you like to see expanded in a sequel to this novel?

UC HIS GLORY BOOK CLUB!

www.uchisglorybookclub.net

UC His Glory Book Club is the spirit-inspired brain-child of Joylynn Jossel, Author and Acquisitions Editor of Urban Christian, and Kendra Norman-Bellamy, Author for Urban Christian. This is an online book club that hosts authors of Urban Christian. We welcome as members all men and women who have a passion for reading Christian-based fiction.

UC HIS GLORY BOOK CLUB pledges our commitment to provide support, positive feedback, encouragement, and a forum whereby members can openly discuss and review the literary works of Urban Christian authors.

There is no membership fee associated with UC His Glory Book Club; however, we do ask that you support the authors through purchasing, encouraging, providing book reviews, and of course, your prayers. We also ask that you respect our beliefs and follow the guidelines of the book club. We hope to receive your valuable input, opinions, and reviews that build up, rather than tear down our authors.

WHAT WE BELIEVE:
—We believe that Jesus is the Christ, Son of the Living God

Urban Christian His Glory Book Club

—We believe the Bible is the true, living Word of God

—We believe all Urban Christian authors should use their God-given writing abilities to honor God and share the message of the written word God has given to each of them uniquely.

—We believe in supporting Urban Christian authors in their literary endeavors by reading, purchasing and sharing their titles with our online community.

—We believe that in everything we do in our literary arena should be done in a manner that will lead to God being glorified and honored.

We look forward to the online fellowship with you. Please visit us often at *www.uchisglorybookclub.net.*

Many Blessing to You!
Shelia E. Lipsey,
President, UC His Glory Book Club

ORDER FORM
URBAN BOOKS, LLC
78 E. Industry Ct
Deer Park, NY 11729

Name: (please print):_____

Address: _____

City/State: _____

Zip: _____

QTY	TITLES	PRICE
	3:57 A.M Timing Is Everything	$14.95
	A Man's Worth	$14.95
	A Woman's Worth	$14.95
	Abundant Rain	$14.95
	After The Feeling	$14.95
	Amaryllis	$14.95
	An Inconvenient Friend	$14.95
	Battle of Jericho	$14.95
	Be Careful What You Pray For	$14.95
	Beautiful Ugly	$14.95
	Been There Prayed That:	$14.95
	Before Redemption	$14.95

Shipping and handling-add $3.50 for 1st book, then $1.75 for each additional book.

Please send a check payable to:

Urban Books, LLC

Please allow 4-6 weeks for delivery

ORDER FORM
URBAN BOOKS, LLC
78 E. Industry Ct
Deer Park, NY 11729

Name: (please print):_____

Address: _____

City/State: _____

Zip: _____

QTY	TITLES	PRICE
	By the Grace of God	$14.95
	Confessions Of A preachers Wife	$14.95
	Dance Into Destiny	$14.95
	Deliver Me From My Enemies	$14.95
	Desperate Decisions	$14.95
	Divorcing the Devil	$14.95
	Faith	$14.95
	First Comes Love	$14.95
	Flaws and All	$14.95
	Forgiven	$14.95
	Former Rain	$14.95
	Forsaken	$14.95

Shipping and handling-add $3.50 for 1st book, then $1.75 for each additional book.

Please send a check payable to:

Urban Books, LLC

Please allow 4-6 weeks for delivery

ORDER FORM
URBAN BOOKS, LLC
78 E. Industry Ct
Deer Park, NY 11729

Name: (please print):_____

Address: _____

City/State: _____

Zip: _____

QTY	TITLES	PRICE
	From Sinner To Saint	$14.95
	From The Extreme	$14.95
	God Is In Love With You	$14.95
	God Speaks To Me	$14.95
	Grace And Mercy	$14.95
	Guilty Of Love	$14.95
	Happily Ever Now	$14.95
	Heaven Bound	$14.95
	His Grace His Mercy	$14.95
	His Woman His Wife His Widow	$14.95
	Illusions	$14.95
	In Green Pastures	$14.95

Shipping and handling-add $3.50 for 1st book, then $1.75 for each additional book.
Please send a check payable to:
Urban Books, LLC
Please allow 4-6 weeks for delivery

ORDER FORM
URBAN BOOKS, LLC
78 E. Industry Ct
Deer Park, NY 11729

Name: (please print): _____

Address: _____

City/State: _____

Zip: _____

QTY	TITLES	PRICE
	Into Each Life	$14.95
	Keep Your enemies Closer	$14.95
	Keeping Misery Company	$14.95
	Latter Rain	$14.95
	Living Consequences	$14.95
	Living Right On Wrong Street	$14.95
	Losing It	$14.95
	Love Honor Stray	$14.95
	Marriage Mayhem	$14.95
	Me, Myself and Him	$14.95
	Murder Through The Grapevine	$14.95
	My Father's House	$14.95

Shipping and handling-add $3.50 for 1st book, then $1.75 for each additional book.
Please send a check payable to:
Urban Books, LLC
Please allow 4-6 weeks for delivery